D0192816

Nigel McCrery worked as a policeman, until he left the force to become an undergraduate at Cambridge University. He has created and written some of the most successful television series of the last ten years – his credits include *Silent Witness*, *Born & Bred*, *New Tricks*, *All the King's Men* and *Back-Up*. He is also the author of five internationally bestselling Sam Ryan mysteries. Nigel lives in London.

Also by Nigel McCrery

Core of Evil

Tooth and Claw

Scream

The Thirteenth Coffin

NIGEL McCRERY

FLESH AND BLOOD

Quercus

First published in Great Britain in 2017 by

Quercus Editions Ltd
Carmelite House
50 Victoria Embankment
London EC4Y 0DZ

An Hachette UK company

Copyright © 2017 Nigel McCrery

The moral right of Nigel McCrery to be
identified as the author of this work has been
asserted in accordance with the Copyright,
Designs and Patents Act, 1988.

All rights reserved. No part of this publication
may be reproduced or transmitted in any form
or by any means, electronic or mechanical,
including photocopy, recording, or any
information storage and retrieval system,
without permission in writing from the publisher.

A CIP catalogue record for this book is available
from the British Library

PB ISBN 978 0 85738 235 1
EB ISBN 978 1 78648 206 8

This book is a work of fiction. Names, characters,
businesses, organizations, places and events are
either the product of the author's imagination
or used fictitiously. Any resemblance to
actual persons, living or dead, events or
locales is entirely coincidental.

10 9 8 7 6 5 4 3 2 1

Typeset by Jouve (UK), Milton Keynes

Printed and bound in Great Britain by Clays Ltd, St Ives plc

AUTHOR'S NOTE

Flesh and Blood is a work of fiction. Names, characters, places and incidents are either the product of the author's imagination or used entirely fictitiously.

For my much beloved son Luke who has taken life by the neck and shaken it hard, making me very proud, and for the beautiful Tyta his fiancée who has brought the family and myself nothing but joy.

PART ONE

1

Barrister Toby Sinclair moved back and forth in front of the witness box, eyes shifting with his thoughts, for a moment drifting to the public gallery before resting back resolutely on Chief Inspector Lapslie for his next question.

'So you are telling this court, Chief Inspector Lapslie, that it was five full days before you started searching for young Ben Tovey?'

'Yes, that's correct.'

'A lot of time for vital leads to go cold. For the *real* perpetrator to cover his tracks.' Sinclair paused after emphasizing 'real' hopefully to let it hit home with the jury. 'Or indeed try to shift or plant blame on others.'

'Yes, I suppose. But that was the first moment we were informed of his disappearance.'

Sinclair continued as if he hadn't heard the answer, or at least chose to ignore it. 'What is it the police say about a disappearance or suspected murder?'

'In what way?'

Sinclair smiled thinly. He was sure Lapslie knew full well the context he was implying, since his lead-up had mentioned 'five days', but was just playing cute. 'About the first forty-eight hours of any enquiry, Chief Inspector.'

'Oh, I see. Yes. We maintain that the first forty-eight hours of any investigation are crucial. After that, it becomes more difficult to track down clues.' Lapslie returned Sinclair's smile tightly. 'But as I say, it wasn't until after five days that we were informed of Ben Tovey's disappearance.'

Sinclair decided to home in on the comment now. 'And why was that?'

Lapslie saw the trap, *too late*; no way of sidestepping it now without appearing obstructive. 'B-because he'd gone missing before.'

'Oh, I see. And how many times was that?'

'Uh, four or five times before . . . his parents weren't sure.'

'A young boy gone missing, and his parents aren't even

sure how many times it has happened.' Sinclair's eyes narrowed. 'Not exactly the ideal parenting situation, is it?'

Lapslie didn't respond to the mostly rhetorical question, resisted even a perfunctory nod. He doubted most jurors saw travellers as ideal parental role models in any case, so few points would have been scored.

Sinclair continued. 'And on any of those previous occasions when Ben had gone missing – however many that might have been – were the police contacted?'

'No, they weren't.'

'Or social services?'

'No ... not as far as I'm aware.' Lapslie took a fresh breath. 'A lot of these people live outside of the system – the "grid", as they term it – so social services find it hard to keep track of them and intervene, so—'

'I'm quite aware of the politics of just why travellers live outside of the system and what problems social services might have with that,' Sinclair cut in. 'What puzzles me, though, is why on those previous occasions of young Ben's disappearance – a number, indeed, when he was much younger – his parents chose not to contact the police, but on this occasion they did?'

'Because on those past occasions he'd returned quite quickly, within a day or two.'

'I see. A day or two? Is that what you maintain?' Sinclair looked at Lapslie sharply before turning to his files on the bench.

Lapslie's stomach sank because he knew what was coming. 'Except on one occasion,' he added swiftly.

Sinclair appeared to ignore the comment as he leaned over his files. He'd started moving back and forth more agitatedly as his questions gained momentum, and his hands too would move more excitedly against his gown, with a slight flapping motion. He often took on the appearance of a menacing bird circling its prey, and his hook nose and sharp blue eyes had gained him the moniker 'the Falcon' in legal and police circles. Some judges would ask him to calm his movements if they became too distracting, but most let it ride; as today, with judge John Cleveley presiding. Sinclair prodded with one finger as he found the reference in his files.

'Yes, indeed. And on that *one* occasion Ben was, in fact, missing for four full days – and still no contact was made with the police.'

'There was a reason for that.' Lapslie sighed. 'Which also partly led to the delay this time around.'

'Yes?' Sinclair raised one brow, a faint smile evident,

as if he knew already he was going to enjoy this explanation.

'Previously, when Ben was away for four days, they'd heard he might have gone off to see his uncle, but it took them a while to check. This time, at first, they thought the same thing might have happened – that he'd gone off fishing with his uncle in Norfolk.'

'Fishing or poaching?'

'Best you ask the uncle directly. As you can appreciate, with a murder investigation, we had bigger fish to fry.' Lapslie smiled patiently; some points had been scored back against Sinclair.

But Sinclair seemed unfazed. 'And why the delay each time in making contact with the uncle?'

'First time around he didn't have a mobile and they could only leave messages in a local pub. Second time he did have a mobile, but hadn't renewed his credit or recharged it for almost a week.'

Sinclair nodded thoughtfully. 'So the initial stages of the investigation were fraught with problems and irregularities.'

'I suppose you could say that,' Lapslie conceded after a second.

'But those were by no means the only problems and irregularities with the investigation, were they?'

'No, they weren't.'

They'd arrived at dusk at Everdale Farm – a play on words on 'Emmerdale' and the time one of its founders had proclaimed to the press they intended to stay; though now, thirty years on from that date, it wasn't looking like an empty prophecy.

The encampment on the edge of woods and farmland, six miles from Epping Forest, had expanded threefold since then. A motley collection of trailers and more permanent wooden sheds and yurts closer to the woodland edge, it looked like a cross between a trailer park and a Mongolian refugee camp.

Woodsmoke, combined with the more acrid fumes of rubbish burning that obviously included a number of plastic water and milk containers, hung heavy in the air. Lapslie inhaled the stench of it as he stepped from the car. Whatever smells his synaesthesia might engender would no doubt be overlaid by that.

'Seems familiar,' he commented to Detective Emma Bradbury.

'Yes, sir. We came here about three years ago.'

In her late thirties, Emma Bradbury had been Lapslie's assistant and colleague for six years now, but their working relationship went beyond what would normally be forged by such a time-span. Part of that was due to Lapslie's synesthesia, so she'd find herself allowing for that in practical terms – ensuring noise-levels were low in venues – as well as making allowances for his mood swings when he was affected. She also had one foot herself outside of normal police conventions by having an ex-villain as a partner, something which Lapslie had railed against in the past. Many of the extra shades in their relationship had therefore been gained through it being part caring, part combative.

Lapslie looked at her more directly. 'And what occasioned that?'

'That was an enquiry where the circumstances were the other way around: a young boy of nine had gone missing not far away, and some locals suspected the travellers here might have been responsible.'

'Ah, yes. I remember now.' Lapslie had in fact recalled from the outset, but Bradbury might have remembered it from a slightly different perspective, provided an extra slant. Travellers regularly got the blame for any local mishaps, so it had been in part a routine enquiry. 'And, as I recall, we did for a while focus on one possible suspect for the boy's disappearance.'

'Yes. Davey Kimball.'

Lapslie nodded as he watched a burly sergeant accompanied by two constables get out of the car that had pulled up behind them. They'd gone with backup, because a police visit to a traveller camp could turn hostile. But it was quiet today, with no sign of agitation; no doubt word had spread that they were there to help find out what had happened to young Ben Tovey, now missing for five days.

'So Kimball will be one of the first on our list to question.' Lapslie took a fresh breath. 'After we've spoken to Marianne and Donovan Tovey.'

Mrs Tovey had been named after Marianne Faithful and Mr Tovey after sixties star Donovan – so it was a marriage made in heaven or hell, depending on how you viewed that era. In the course of the Toveys sharing that trivia, they'd explained that there was nowhere else they could think Ben might be now that they'd discovered he wasn't fishing with his uncle.

'No other relatives he might be with?' Lapslie pressed.

'No.' Marianne Tovey shook her head. 'The only family member we still have contact with is my mum in Battersea. And I spoke to her two days ago.'

'And apart from the time before, when Ben had gone off with his uncle,' Bradbury asked, 'did he have a habit of drifting off much?'

While Bradbury noted down the details of the four or five times Ben had gone missing for a day or two, Donovan Tovey held one hand out helplessly, half a dozen brightly coloured wristbands jiggling with the motion.

'He's an inquisitive boy, that's all. Not really into mischief or anything. And he only went off at holiday time – he was good with attending school.'

'That hasn't always been the case with all of them,' Marianne offered. 'But with five of them now, it hasn't been easy.'

Lapslie nodded in understanding. Married now for fifteen years, the Toveys had had their children at almost set eighteen-month intervals; Ben was their second eldest, and their youngest was due to attend primary school next year. Unlike many travellers, the Toveys had elected to get their children into state school – although, with five of them, perhaps educating at home hadn't been a practical option.

In many ways, Lapslie felt for them. London property prices had been out of young people's reach for decades, and now that blight had spread to parts of Essex. It seemed as if they'd been forced out of the system as much as opting out, perhaps partly due also to Donovan Tovey's career choice of casual farm and construction work combined with music. Now they'd paid the ultimate price for that freewheeling lifestyle – they'd lost a son.

'So will you be able to find Ben?' Donovan Tovey ran one hand over his long wavy hair, and Lapslie noted that his Aztec Indian headband matched a couple of his wristbands. 'I'm sure he's okay out there somewhere.'

Lapslie noted the present tense and the tone – Donovan Tovey was obviously full of hope that his son was still alive – though from bitter past experience, he knew that after five days the chances were slim.

'I'm sure we will,' Lapslie said, experiencing a bitter almond aftertaste at his own lie. 'To which end, we'd like first of all to question some others here at Everdale. Some of them might well hold clues to where Ben is now.'

Bradbury flipped back a couple of pages in her notepad. 'Amongst them, Davey Kimball – if you can point us to his current trailer?'

Donovan and Marianne exchanged a look.

'Davey was off-site for almost a year,' Donovan said. 'Then he turned up again just a couple of months back. But I haven't seen him around much these past days.'

'How many days?' Lapslie pressed.

'Four or five.'

After almost three hours of questioning around the Everdale site, Lapslie and Bradbury finally got a lead and, two days later, tracked down Davey Kimball to a travelling fairground which had downed pegs that week at Banbury, Oxfordshire.

Kimball looked less than impressed as they explained the reason for their visit. He wiped oil from his hands with a rag after seeing to a linkage joint on a Magic Carpet ride.

'So is this to be the nature of things every time a boy goes missing anywhere near Everdale?'

'No,' Lapslie said on the back of a sigh. 'And why should that be a concern of yours? After all, you were found innocent in that enquiry. No connection to the missing boy – and no harm had come to him, in any case.'

Kimball arched one brow. 'Exactly. So more the wonder of why your visit now?'

Lapslie grimaced patiently. 'Yes, but while you were cleared of any wrongdoing with that particular boy, you weren't exactly innocent on all fronts with young boys, were you?'

In their last questioning of Davey Kimball, they had discovered his almost Dickensian-style habit of procuring boys between twelve and fourteen to assist him on fairgrounds and building jobs.

'And young Ben Tovey is now thirteen.'

'So you think I might have got him here as my helper?' He finished wiping the oil from his palms, but made no move towards a handshake.

'It struck us as a distinct possibility, given your past form.' Lapslie smiled tightly.

Bradbury added, 'And at least if that was the case, it would mean that, thankfully, Ben would be found unharmed.'

Kimball looked from one to the other, as if unsure for a moment how to process the accusation combined so quickly with a back-handed compliment.

Kimball's gaze fixed on Lapslie. 'A couple of things you appear to have forgotten, Chief Inspector, from that past form. First, I never got those helpers without first asking the parents' permission – so if Ben was here with me now, Marianne and Donovan would know about it. Secondly, I only asked boys who were able-bodied and reasonably strong. And at last sight, Ben Tovey was small for his age and slight.'

Lapslie nodded. 'So you maintain that Ben Tovey isn't here with you now and you have no knowledge of his whereabouts?'

'No, I don't.' Kimball looked to one side for a second, as if struck by another thought. 'Though it seems not everyone uses the same rule of thumb when it comes to young children.'

Kimball went on to explain that, the day before heading to Banbury, he'd seen a van similar to his not far from Everdale with its driver leaning out and talking to a young boy by the kerbside.

'How old?'

'Nine or ten. Eleven at most.'

Lapslie nodded thoughtfully. With his slight build, Ben Tovey could easily have passed for a ten- or eleven-year-old. Not old or strong enough to fend off a potential abductor. 'A white van, you say?'

'Yes. But what made me suspicious, like, was that as I approached and slowed down – curious as to what might be going on – the van driver quickly straightened up and sped off again, as soon as he became aware of me.'

'Any idea as to the make of van?' Bradbury enquired.

'Not a Volkswagen like mine. Maybe a Ford or Peugeot.'

Lapslie wasn't hopeful. How many Fords or Peugeots were there in Essex? And it was probably just a ruse to offset blame – make Kimball's habit of procuring young boys for work seem not so bad, given that comparison.

'But I recall part of the registration number, if it might help,' Kimball said. 'HEX 0-something. Its first three letters stuck in my mind.'

Lapslie focused back on Toby Sinclair in the courtroom.

'So let us all get this clear, shall we?' Sinclair took a fresh breath. 'Your only seemingly tangible lead was indeed supplied by a main suspect—'

'But in those few days of tracking down Davey Kimball we had exhausted scores of other possible leads,' Lapslie interjected.

Sinclair rode over the last of it, as if it were of little relevance. 'Then it turns out the main reason for that recall was the suspect's background – part Romany gypsy – and therefore what those three letters from the number plate sparked off in his mind.' Sinclair looked towards the jury with incredulity before staring back at Lapslie. 'You have to admit, Chief Inspector, it all becomes a somewhat difficult story to swallow.'

'It just happens to be the truth. And it's what occurred on this occasion.' Lapslie didn't have the patience to explain to Sinclair the many strange incidences he'd seen in twenty years of policing; how half a policeman's off-duty time was spent swapping just such strange stories. But now wasn't the time or place for it, so all of his experience was boiled down to, 'And I've seen stranger things over the years.'

'I daresay you have, Chief Inspector. But that wasn't the only thing to occur in this catalogue of strange events, was it?'

It took them seventeen hours to whittle down the list of possibles, combining a white van with the start of its registration number HEX O, until they were left with only one strong likelihood: a white Peugeot van registered to Alistair Tulley of Danbury, six miles from Everdale.

Within another hour, they were at Tulley's door. Lapslie purposely left a uniformed officer in front of Tulley's door, while

another waited in a marked car in front. In Lapslie's experience, there was nothing like a visible police presence to get the
neighbours talking, start noticing things which might otherwise have gone unnoticed: 'It's funny that you should have
called to see him, because just last week I saw him do something
that I thought was odd . . .'

A nondescript semi-detached in the better part of Danbury,
away from its council estate, Lapslie noticed the white van in
the driveway as they approached the house, but still one of his
first questions was to confirm with Tulley whether the white
van parked in front was his?

'Yes . . . yes, it is.' Tulley was a second slow in responding, as
if first weighing up the implications of his answer. He had lank
black hair that looked well past its wash-by date. He swept back
a few stray matted strands from his forehead with one hand.
'Why? What's this about?'

Bradbury commenced by mentioning that Tulley had been
seen in his van, stopping to talk to a young boy of a similar age
to one who had recently gone missing in the area. 'So we have
to ask – why were you stopping to talk to that young boy?'

Tulley looked momentarily perplexed, stroked his forehead
again. 'And when was this?'

Bradbury consulted her notes and read out the date recalled
by Davey Kimball.

Tulley nodded after a second. 'Ah, yes. I was asking some directions then.'

'Where to?' Lapslie cut in sharply.

'Uh . . . Fyfield. A small village near Epping Forest.'

'I see.' Noting the hesitation, he was sure Tulley was lying, but had no way of proving it. 'And why didn't you ask directions from grown-ups rather than a young boy?'

'There weren't any grown-ups nearby at the time.'

Lapslie looked down. It was something they should have checked in their questioning of Kimball. But he doubted Tulley would know one way or the other. He decided to run with the bluff.

'I'm afraid that's not true. Adults were seen passing nearby, witnessed by the same person who observed you stopping to talk to the young boy.'

Tulley flushed slightly, pulling a taut grimace. 'I'm sorry. I didn't see them.'

Lapslie kept his gaze steady on Tulley. Difficult to tell whether he'd answered that question honestly, or had read the bluff and simply decided to discard it in short order. But one thing he was certain of: Tulley was lying overall. Not just from his hesitation on certain questions, but the telltale bitter almond aftertaste assaulting Lapslie's palate as soon as Tulley had started answering. But suddenly it was overlaid with another smell; one that he knew only too well from attending countless crime scenes and autopsies. His eyes drifted up to the source of the smell. He stood up sharply.

'We need to check on something.'

'But, sir, we don't—'

'Mr Tulley – if you can lead the way,' Lapslie cut in on Bradbury, his tone that of instruction rather than request. If she mentioned warrants and permission, Tulley might dig his heels in. And by the time they returned with the paperwork, he'd be able to cover up any evidence.

'I . . . I don't know.' Tulley's eyes darted hesitantly between Lapslie and Bradbury. 'Not without first speaking to my solicitor.'

Lapslie contemplated Tully stonily. 'Are you being purposely obstructive? Trying to impede an officer in the execution of his duty?'

'No, it's not that. It's just that—'

'Mr Tulley,' Lapslie cut him off brusquely. 'From information received, we have reason to believe you're holding vital evidence on these premises. And we're duty-bound, in the course of our investigation, to check on that.'

Lapslie headed into the hallway and started up the stairs without waiting for a response. Bradbury dutifully followed, with a now perplexed, red-faced Tulley two steps behind her.

Lapslie opened two doors before finally homing in on the room which he was now sure was the source of the smell. Nothing obvious as he walked in: a single bed, the bedspread slightly ruffled, as if it had been made in a hurry or someone had been sitting on the bed. Drab floral wallpaper, dark beige curtains half-drawn. Looked like a spare bedroom, one of three in this suburban semi.

Lapslie focused on the wardrobe at the side of the room. As his senses became attuned, the smell seemed to be coming from there.

As he went to open the cupboard, he noticed Tulley, now looking on from the doorway, stiffen with apprehension; and for a moment, Lapslie feared being confronted with a full corpse. But at first sight, there was nothing. Just five jumpers, a grey anorak and a sheepskin coat. Perhaps a backup winter wardrobe for Tulley.

Then, sifting through, Lapslie noticed the fifteen-inch-long package wrapped in brown greaseproof paper at the bottom of the wardrobe. Like someone's takeaway fish and chips or kebab.

Lapslie bent down and started unwrapping it. Even if he hadn't been sure what would confront him, he'd have known from Tulley suddenly bolting back down the stairs.

As Lapslie heard the scuffle and the unmistakable sound of Tulley being creamed by the front door – Lapslie always made sure to put his best rugby-trained or unarmed combat men on door duty – he uncovered the package's contents: a young teen's hand and forearm, cut eight inches above the wrist.

2

Stratford, east London
September 2013

Obsessed.

Josie Dallyn wasn't sure whether to take the term as a compliment or a criticism.

Certainly in her profession, journalism, an intense dedication was invariably needed to see a difficult story through to the end, to work it to the point where it was ready to 'break'. And the line between dedication and *obsession* was often thin.

That dedication or obsession had managed to gain her a first-rung journalist spot at a leading London newspaper at the age of only twenty-six – having spent five years with a provincial newspaper in Plymouth – but it had cost her in terms of relationships. She'd had only three semi-serious relationships in those five years. She used the term 'semi-serious' because none of them had lasted more than four months. In her mind a relationship had to go over the six-month mark to be termed serious *sans* semi. So now it was just her and her custard-coloured Persian cat she'd brought with her from Plymouth.

'There you go, Creampie,' she muttered as she bent down with a saucer of salmon and chicken in sauce. 'You're doing better than me. I've just got microwavable lasagne for one.'

She'd felt as if she were doing a reverse Dick Whittington, fleeing from Plymouth to London, except with a Nike compact backpack replacing a knotted hanky. She'd certainly travelled light; there hadn't been much room for extraneous luggage or belongings in her new Stratford bedsit anyway.

The major case where some colleagues felt she'd crossed the line from dedicated to obsessed had involved the death of a man aged ninety-three in Truro who had lived in Plymouth for most of his life. John Farren's was an unexceptional story on the surface, but it had been his deathbed confession which had made the case stand out.

He claimed to have been involved in numerous child abductions and murders over the years, a number of which he had carried out with 'respected citizens' from the local area. 'And I can't go to my grave with a clear conscience, without sharing what I know.'

His claims could have just been the wild ramblings and imaginings of an old man near to death – and not fully lucid due to the drugs he'd been given to alleviate the pain of the cancer consuming him the past two years – but Josie found that many of the details rang true.

Central to these accounts – and, indeed, the main case which had sparked the *Plymouth Gazette* editor's interest, prompting him to then send her out to interview the old man – had been the 'unanswered' death of schoolboy Colin Payton, only eleven years old at the time, in 1944, a year before the end of the Second World War.

There were a number of disappearances during the war – most of them in fact down to bombing raids or the general movement and dislocation of people in wartime – but Farren argued that he and his accomplices had cynically used the cover of war to abduct and kill a number of children, whose deaths would later be put down to 'war casualties'.

The death of eleven-year-old Colin Payton looked no different on the surface: killed in a disused Plymouth warehouse by a bomb dropped from a German Dornier bomber. However, what remained 'unanswered' at the time was what a leading British naval officer, a local Plymouth city councillor and a Westminster MP – all also killed by that bomb – were doing in the same warehouse when the bomb dropped. The first explanation offered was simply that they had been in the area at the time of the bombing raid, so had sought shelter in the nearest warehouse, as had eleven-year-old Colin Payton. But then there was also the question of Colin's missing right forearm, cleanly severed, and not directly attributed to the bomb blast or falling rubble at the autopsy.

John Farren on his deathbed had an explanation for all of it. He said he had been there at the time and part of the murderous ritual taking place when the bomb fell. He gave not only a vivid and gory account of what happened, but also details of who was there and managed to escape the bomb blast and falling rubble, along with himself. He indicated the shrapnel wounds on one shoulder and his stomach.

'There were others more seriously injured than me. But whoever could make it out of there before the police or wardens arrived, did so, for obvious reasons.'

Other prominent citizens were among the names of those who got away, according to Farren. Josie wondered if their families still lived in the area. What could have driven apparently ordinary, law-abiding men to commit such atrocities? She became obsessed with finding a connection – a way to make Farren's shocking story relevant to a modern readership.

But when she'd gone back to her *Plymouth Gazette* editor with the story, he'd bottled it, protesting that the newspaper could get sued from here to hell by the families of the men allegedly involved, especially with so little proof. 'All on the say-so of some old codger on his deathbed who claims that he himself was deeply implicated in these crimes. So he's not exactly going to be seen as a reliable witness or source, is he?'

All her Plymouth editor had agreed to run was Farren relating that he was in the same warehouse building as schoolboy Colin Payton when the bomb dropped: 'Although, along with five others, I managed to escape without serious injury.' It was printed simply as a Plymouth wartime story from a dying veteran who'd survived a local bombing.

When she got to London, she was keen to see whether her editor there, Kevin Lanham, might have the balls to print the full story. She waited almost a year to get her feet fully under her desk, then ran the story by him.

Lanham was intrigued and asked all the right questions to get the story clear in his mind. In the end, though, he felt that it was too old a story to run on its own. 'Farren is now dead, and his account relates to a period almost seventy years ago. We need something else to anchor the story more in the present day. If we can find that, let's look at it again.'

What encouraged Josie was that Lanham wasn't deterred by the prospect of exposing those in high places and possibly getting sued. But after another two years with nothing that could connect current events to these past cases, she started to become despondent. Then, one bright May morning, the police alerted all national newspapers and TV that a twelve-year-old boy, Daniel Clough, had been missing now for three days from the Shrewsbury area. She went to Lanham again with the story.

'Three days ... that pins his disappearance to the sixteenth of May, only four days after Colin Payton's supposed abduction, also in May. And it fits in exactly with the other dates that John Farren gave for his crimes, all of which were carried out within the same time frame.'

'Yes. But we don't even have a body yet, let alone a severed arm to match with the Farren-related case. If and when we have those, let's talk again.'

After more than a year with nothing on the Daniel Clough case, and with no body, motive or suspect in sight, Josie decided to spread the net wide and put out an alert through Reuters and the Associated Press for any murdered boys in the age range eleven to fifteen, in the month of May: 'Particularly with oddities such as any limbs being severed.'

When the call came through, almost three months later, from a journalist in Gdansk, Poland, Josie realized that she hadn't specified the UK only. Perhaps a subliminal error, because as an experienced investigative journalist Josie knew only too well that child murders and abductions crossed all national boundaries.

This time Josie knew she had Lanham on the ropes.

'Gdansk, Poland. Thirteen years old . . . 1977?' Lanham nodded thoughtfully with each point confirmed. He managed a strained smile. 'Still somewhat historic.'

'Yes, but many of these murder investigations from eastern Europe didn't come to light until after the Berlin Wall came down.' She held out a hand. 'And we're coming at them from three sides now. A date match on each, and two with identical limb-severing.'

A final, deliberating nod from Lanham. 'Okay. We're in better shape now. Let's talk more tomorrow.'

Chelmsford Crown Court, Essex
June 2014

'So let us recap,' Toby Sinclair said swiftly, keen not to let the image of Ben Tovey's severed forearm in his client's cupboard linger too long with the jury. 'So, despite fully knowing that you should have had a warrant, you still commenced to search part of the defendant's premises just on a whim.'

'Well, it was more than just a "whim". It was the smell that first alerted me.'

'I see. The "smell". And did your assistant, Detective Bradbury, also notice this smell?'

'No. Not that I'm aware of.'

'So, just you, Chief Inspector?'

'Yes. Just me.' Lapslie saw the doubt rising in Sinclair's face, and added, 'But I have a particularly acute sense of smell.'

'Not just "acute", though, is it, Chief Inspector? You have a condition known as synaesthesia. Would you care to explain to this courtroom what that entails, so that we might better understand it?'

Lapslie's stomach sank as he realized the path Sinclair was leading him down. 'It . . . it translates sounds and some actions into smells and tastes.'

'I see. And forgive me if I've got it wrong, Chief Inspector. But from what you said earlier, it was this very same sense which led you to first suspect the defendant?'

'Yes, it was. I thought he was lying.'

'Lying. I see.' Sinclair looked around at the jury, a faint smile teasing his lips. 'And pray tell us all, Chief Inspector – just what smell or taste does "lying" give rise to with you?'

Lapslie stared at Sinclair levelly for a moment. He knew Sinclair was making a mockery of his condition, but he had little way of avoiding answering without appearing obstructive.

'Bitter almond or sour cream, with an acrid aftertaste.'

'I see. Bitter almond or sour cream.' Sinclair's lopsided smile became cynical as he surveyed the jury. 'But this isn't a wholly recognized condition, is it, Chief Inspector?'

'Yes, it certainly is.' Lapslie leapt quickly on Sinclair's misstep, suddenly surer of his ground. 'Not only is it medically recognized, I receive regular medication for it.'

'My, my ... medication, no less, to keep our police force functioning properly.' Sinclair's cynical smile quickly faded, his expression stern. 'Let me make myself a bit clearer, Chief Inspector. It isn't a recognized condition relative to the rigours of police investigative work, such as might be accepted by the law and the courts.'

Lapslie was suddenly tongue-tied, realizing that Sinclair had backed him into yet another corner.

'If it is recognized,' Sinclair continued, 'then I must have somehow missed the swathe of crimes solved due to the synaesthesia of police officers.'

Lapslie held Sinclair's gaze for a moment before a final blink of submission. 'No, it's not recognized in that regard.'

'I thought as much.' Sinclair resumed pacing; a predator's final circling of its prey to ensure it had been fully subdued. 'So, we return again to my first suggestion that you searched the defendant's home on just a "whim". And with total foreknowledge of – and disregard for – the fact that you should have had a warrant to do so.'

'The suspect would likely have moved any damning

evidence by then,' Lapslie said sharply. 'There were reasonable grounds for an immediate search.'

'Were there now?' Sinclair arched one eyebrow sharply. 'I think, as we've already established, Chief Inspector, hunches or whims inspired by oddball ailments are not considered "reasonable" cause. At least not in the eyes of the law.'

Prosecuting barrister Giles Crawford was quickly on his feet. 'Objection, Your Honour. Defence Counsel is making light of Chief Inspector Lapslie's ailment. Which while to him and some others might seem "odd", is very real and personal to Chief Inspector Lapslie.'

Judge John Cleveley nodded. 'Objection sustained. Please rephrase, Mr Sinclair.'

'Yes, Your Honour. In light of my learned counsel's prompt, perhaps "personal" ailments would be more apt with regard to not being considered "reasonable" cause.'

Lapslie said nothing, sensing that any extra comment might be turned against him. In any case, Crawford's objection – one of the few so far – had halted Sinclair's flow, if only temporarily.

Sinclair contemplated him a moment longer, as if ensuring that his submission on the topic was total. 'And having "chanced" upon this discovery at the defendant's home, how long was it before you discovered Ben Tovey's body?'

'Only two days later.'

When Lapslie had arrived at the scene with Bradbury, it had been late morning. The body was barely concealed by branches and leaves, next to a woodland path. It might, indeed, have been discovered by ramblers or dog-walkers rather than his search team – if it hadn't been for inclement weather the previous four or five days. Even before the autopsy, Lapslie knew it was Ben Tovey's body due to the missing right forearm – though they later discovered that wasn't the only body part missing.

A large chunk of flesh from the abdomen, pathologist Jim Thompson had commented. *Almost Merchant of Venice-style. And the liver is also missing.*

'And how far from the defendant's home was the body discovered?'

'Just over two miles away.'

Sinclair nodded thoughtfully. 'Doesn't that strike you as odd, Chief Inspector?'

'Not really. Many murder victims are found within only a few miles of a suspect's home.'

'So why wasn't the body discovered beforehand?'

Lapslie's stomach dipped again. At first he wasn't

sure why Sinclair would wish to make an issue of the body being found near Tulley's home; now he realized where he was heading.

'Because at first our search efforts were concentrated close to Everdale Farm where Ben Tovey was last seen.'

'Close to? What sort of distance are we talking about?'

'Within a three- or four-mile radius.'

'Oh, I see. And what distance is the defendant's home from Everdale Farm?'

'Six or seven miles.'

Sinclair nodded slowly. 'So in fact you changed your search-pattern criteria based on your suspicion of the defendant.'

'Yes, we did. It was the obvious thing to do.'

'So you say, Chief Inspector.' Sinclair took a fresh breath. 'But are you aware that the defendant has claimed he has no knowledge of the body parcel in his cupboard. That, in fact, it was planted there.'

'Yes. He has claimed that when interviewed.'

'Likewise that he's been falsely implicated. No doubt by the same person who told you where to look for Ben Tovey's body.'

'That's not the case. We found young Ben through our own devices. Standard procedure.'

'Oh, come now, Chief Inspector. You can see how bad it looks. Days searching with nothing to show for it, and suddenly you get a lead to the defendant from a past suspect in a previous case, no less. Also, I might add, known to young Ben and his family; where, as you well know, amongst family and those close, 95 per cent of suspects are successfully found. And, *hey presto!*' Sinclair waved one hand dramatically. 'Suddenly you've not only found your suspect but, unaided, go straight to a damning item of evidence. Then, only two days later, you magically find the body. You can see how this all fits in perfectly with the defendant's claim.'

Lapslie's stomach was in knots. Sinclair was giving him a comprehensive mauling. He was sure Tulley was guilty, and the thought that his testimony now might be complicit in getting Tulley freed made his skin crawl. He could sense Donovan and Marianne Tovey's eyes on him from the public gallery, desperate for justice for young Ben. And he noticed Bradbury look increasingly agitated as Sinclair's mauling gained intensity, at times chewing worriedly at her lip.

'That's not how it was,' Lapslie said, an edge now to his voice. 'I've told you what happened.'

'You certainly have, Chief Inspector. And I've also

made it patently clear where that might fall foul of the law.' Sinclair held out one palm. 'So you maintain, Chief Inspector, that at no time did you get inside information on the defendant?'

Lapslie noticed Bradbury look down at that moment, her expression pained. Perhaps Sinclair's questioning was suddenly too much for her to take. But she kept looking down, as if she'd suddenly got a worrying message on her mobile.

'Apart from Davey Kimball's initial sighting, no.'

Sinclair left a moment's pause for the comment to sink home with the jury, then briefly consulted his file on the bench.

'So if I may at this point, Chief Inspector, remind you of a comment you made to the defendant on first visiting his home. "From information received, we have reason to believe you're holding vital evidence on these premises."' Sinclair looked up. 'Do you recall making that comment, Chief Inspector?'

Lapslie flushed, and with the second's pause Sinclair had his answer, plain for the jury to see. Lapslie saw Bradbury get up at that moment, and caught a glimpse of the mobile in her grip as she left the courtroom gallery, her expression heavy. Whatever message she'd received must have been important for her to leave at such a vital juncture.

'Yes, but . . . but that was more a combination of what we'd received from Kimball and what I suspected in that moment.'

'Ah, you mean the "smell" that conveniently assaulted you at that moment.' Sinclair smiled drolly. 'Combined, of course, with the taste of bitter-almond-flavoured lies.'

Lapslie swallowed hard, said nothing. It seemed that every comment was being used as extra rope to hang him with by Sinclair; and with the bile suddenly rising from the butterfly contortions in his stomach, keeping his mouth shut seemed the safer option.

'You have to admit, Chief Inspector, that isn't how the comment came across to the defendant. Indeed, it seems to entirely support his claim that the evidence was planted and he's been falsely implicated. Thank you, Chief Inspector.'

Stratford, east London
September 2013

Josie's cat Creampie watched with mild disinterest as she did her morning yoga exercise, as if to say: *Why do humans put themselves through such agony? You'd never catch me contorting myself like that.*

Gymnastics had been one of Josie's best subjects at school, and being supple and almost double-jointed also helped her do the more challenging yoga movements now.

She recalled one past boyfriend commenting in the middle of a bedroom session, 'Wow, you're flexible.' But it still hadn't been enough to keep him around for long. The constant pursuit of the next big story, being put before pub or dinner dates he'd arranged, quickly began to tire with him. When she begged off at the last minute from an important Arsenal–Tottenham derby match he'd bought tickets for, that was it. *Sacrilege!* She didn't see him again; he hadn't even bothered to phone to tell her why he didn't want to see her anymore.

Josie showered, dressed and put on her make-up. She was out of the door within fifteen minutes.

But getting feedback from Lanham on the Colin Payton case and this new information from a Polish journalist proved difficult that day. A constant cycle of fresh stories breaking and emergency meetings meant it wasn't until the end of the day that he was able to broach the subject with her.

He poked his head into her cubbyhole towards the end of the day; practically everyone else had already left the office.

'Sorry if it seemed like I was avoiding you. It's been one of those days.' Lanham rubbed his forehead. 'But I wanted time too, to think this through, plus tie it all into something else that's come in.'

Josie's brow knitted. 'What's that?'

'Fresh lead that's just come in on the Daniel Clough case.' Lanham held a hand out as if to quell the rising excitement in her expression. 'But let's not be too hasty. It might be just a coincidence and end up being nothing. But if it is of substance, it could be an important breakthrough. Could provide the ideal cherry on the cake on the Colin Payton case you've been championing all these years. We've also got the jump right now on everyone else. She apparently hasn't gone to any other newspapers yet with this, or to the police.'

'And you're giving this to me?' Josie found it hard to keep the incredulity out of her tone. Exclusive story breaks on prime, current disappearance/murder stories were like hen's teeth for young reporters.

'I think you're due, don't you?' Lanham's tone also held a degree of questioning surprise. 'After all, you've pursued this case with more dedication than anyone else.'

Josie smiled tightly in acceptance. She was glad Lanham hadn't used the term 'obsession'. She took the piece of paper Lanham handed her: Brenda Kirkbride, at an address in Plaistow, east London. Josie wondered whether the Scottish name was significant; the group Farren described had originated from Scotland.

'I know it's a late call, 9.30, but she works shifts as a nurse, and that's apparently the best time to see her.'

'No problem. Not too far from where I live, in fact.' She'd have time to eat, freshen up and still have forty minutes spare. 'No phone number, I see?'

'That's right.' Lanham grimaced. 'She feels this is delicate information, so she only wants to do this face to face. Doesn't want to risk talking about it over a phone line where others might be listening in.'

Josie nodded. She perfectly understood that; had dealt with many similar stories where people were nervous speaking over the phone. Or often the account was so long and complex that the journalist would immediately opt for a face-to-face meeting. True also of human

interest stories, where the details might be too emotional and personal to deal with over a telephone line:
reading reactions, facial expressions and mannerisms
became as important as the words imparted.

'Okay. I'm on it,' she said, folding the piece of paper
and putting it in her pocket. 'I'll let you know how I get
on first thing tomorrow.'

Almost two hours later, at precisely 8.59 p.m., Josie was
ringing Brenda Kirkbride's bell. An end-of-terrace house
set four yards back from the pavement, what little garden it had in front was heavily overgrown, with some
bushes to one side half-overshadowing the pathway. It
appeared to have been split into two flats, the upper one
of which was Kirkbride's. From the heavy dust on the
front window, it didn't look as if the downstairs flat had
been occupied for a while.

Josie could see a faint light seeping down from the
top of the stairs, but there was no light appearing in the
hallway or on the stairs themselves to indicate anyone
was coming down to open the front door. No entry-
phone buzzing sound either. She rang again, looking to
see if there was an intercom mouthpiece she'd earlier

missed. No grill in sight, and still no other light coming on inside apart from that faint glow from the top of the stairs.

Josie left it a moment more, then rang again and knocked sharply three times in case the bell wasn't working. Still nothing.

She took a couple of paces back, looking up at the upstairs window. A faint backroom glow was discernible there too – probably the same light that was showing at the top of the stairs – but nothing else. She counted off thirty more seconds, then called out, 'Brenda, it's me! Josie Dall—'

The last word was cut off and muffled as a hand from behind clamped a piece of cloth hard over her mouth. She was startled, breathless with shock. Whoever it was must have come out from the cover of the bushes to one side. But she'd looked around a second ago, panning the small garden and checking towards the park on the other side of the road – and hadn't seen or heard a thing. They'd moved silently, like a *ghost*.

She tried to swivel around to see her attacker, but the grip was too tight; she was braced hard. And then the smell of the chloroform on the cloth overwhelmed her sinuses and she sank into darkness.

Chelmsford Crown Court, Essex
June 2014

Lapslie's legs felt shaky as he left the courtroom, his stomach dancing wildly.

Judge Cleveley had adjourned for a break straight after the questioning, and half the public gallery had spilled on to the corridor outside: a confusing mass of barristers, solicitors, press, relatives and parties concerned on either side. A kaleidoscope of sounds which ignited a mass of conflicting smells and tastes in Lapslie's throat.

He pushed desperately through the group, his eyes searching for Bradbury. He finally spotted her, eight yards beyond the main mass of people; far enough away to get some privacy for her phone conversation, but still close enough to see him exit. From her expression as she put her mobile back in her pocket, he could tell it was bad news.

'There's been another one,' she said simply, flatly, as he approached.

'Oh, God.' He closed his eyes for a second. 'Where?'

'Near Bicknacre. Only four miles from where Ben was found. They discovered the body within twenty-four hours of the missing alert coming in.'

'How old?'

'Only twelve.'

Lapslie closed his eyes again for a second, but suddenly it was all too much: the kaleidoscope of sounds and tastes, and now the news of this fresh horror on the back of Sinclair's grilling.

He dived into the toilets to one side, unsure with his shaking, unsteady legs whether he'd make it to the sinks in time.

The surge of vomit flew up and he stayed there, braced over the sinks, vomiting another three times, eyes watering, his reflection bleary in the mirror as he straightened up and became aware for the first time of Giles Crawford washing his hands two sinks away.

'I'm afraid Sinclair often has that effect on people,' Crawford commented.

'It's not just that,' Lapslie said, swilling his mouth briefly under the cold tap. 'More the effect of the crowd now outside the courtroom triggering my synaesthesia. All those sounds and tastes colliding.'

'I understand,' Crawford said.

Though meeting Crawford's gaze, Lapslie sensed there was probably a limit to Crawford's understanding, given that it might now be the main thing to have destroyed their case. Lapslie decided to withhold sharing the news that there was another boy victim in the same area until he'd gained more details; after all, if there were no MO similarities, it would have no bearing on the Tovey case.

'And of course, recalling what happened to poor Ben Tovey no doubt didn't help,' Lapslie said. 'All those images flooding back.'

'Of course.'

3

Stratford, east London
September 2013

Orange light-bars played intermittently across her legs, coming through a small window at the back of the van as they passed street lights.

And as Josie craned her neck the other way towards the front, she could see the left arm and shoulder of her abductor in the driver's seat of the van. What was that tattoo? A snake or an ostrich's long neck? Before deciding, as the next light-bar hit the arm, that it was a swan's neck.

Her hands were tied behind her back and her ankles tied too. A gag was pulled tight across her mouth, her abductor obviously more concerned that she might call or scream out and draw attention – otherwise a hood might have been opted for.

But then the connected thought quickly hit home and made her heart sink: there was no concern that she might see where she was going or view her abductor, because they had no intention that she'd later be able to tell anyone.

Josie knew in that moment that she was about to die. Quick trip to a deserted woodland or field, then battered with a crowbar or shovel and buried. Or buried alive.

She was reminded that in most of the cases John Farren had talked about, the boys' bodies had never been found.

She felt her stomach dive at the hopelessness of her situation, an empty feeling flooding through her. Her hands and ankles were bound tight, no possible movement there. But as she arched back, she realized she could almost reach her ankle tie with her hands.

Almost. Frustratingly, she was still an inch short. She arched and stretched harder – suddenly stopping midway through as she noticed Swan-Tattoo looking in his rear-view mirror.

She kept perfectly still. Played dead again.

Then, as soon as she was sure he was looking straight ahead again at the road, she started trying once more. One hard arch backwards and she might be able to reach the ankle tie.

The Bell public house, Essex
June 2014

Sir. We need your help with this one. Like I said before, it needs your ... your magic touch. It would be a shame to finally let the real culprit slip through the net.

Lapslie put his mobile back down on the table. The fourth phone message along similar lines from Bradbury in the last forty-eight hours, and two or three text messages too. All that had changed was that 'insight' and 'assistance' had been elevated to 'magic touch'.

He took another sip of his beer, sneering. What 'magic touch'? It had been his own personal condition with synaesthesia which had helped destroy the case against Alistair Tulley. Two days after his testimony, Toby Sinclair had made his closing presentation to the jury, zeroing in on his synaesthesia and the illegal search without warrant as crucial points. The jury took only six hours to deliberate: *not guilty*. He'd let the side down. What use would his 'magic touch' be with another suspect? He'd no doubt screw that up as well.

'Carpet slippers, eh? I didn't realize this was the new fashion.'

Lapslie looked towards the voice: Charlotte, his girl-friend, though three years into their relationship they still hadn't moved in together. Lapslie wasn't sure if that was because of their respective busy schedules or because he feared that living day to day with his synaes-thesia would prove too much for Charlotte, as had been the case with his ex-wife Sandra.

He glanced down at his feet with a wry smile. 'Sorry. Didn't even realize I still had them on. One advantage of a pub within walking distance, I suppose.'

The Bell, Lapslie's local, only three hundred yards from his home, had seen better days, and Lapslie could recall Friday and weekend nights when it would be heaving. But its quietness these days suited him, though he'd still chosen a secluded alcove. It was away from the main throng, which usually wouldn't descend for another hour at lunchtime, at which time he'd planned to leave.

But obviously Charlotte knew the pub and his favour-ite alcove, because he'd brought her here a couple of times.

'What are you doing here?' He arched a brow, and as she contemplated him steadily, he held out a hand. 'Please . . . take a seat. What can I get you?'

'Thanks – but I'm okay for a drink.' She sat down

opposite him at the oblong table for four. 'I thought you might be here.'

'You went to my house first?'

'Yes.'

Lapslie nodded thoughtfully. 'Did Emma Bradbury send you?'

'More *asked* if I'd see you than sent.' Charlotte sighed. 'She thought I might have more luck than her talking you round.'

'I see.' Lapslie sipped at his beer. 'You could have phoned.'

'And would you have answered me? You haven't answered Emma so far.'

Lapslie didn't say anything, wasn't entirely sure whether he'd have answered for anyone in his present mood.

'Besides,' Charlotte said, 'with our hectic schedules, when do we ever get time for meaningful conversations on the phone? It's usually just to arrange a time to meet, then the rest is saved for when we're face to face. Like now.'

She looked at him searchingly, and with the intensity of her gaze he felt uncomfortable, sought refuge in contemplating his beer. With Charlotte's work as a doctor and his police work, their telephone conversations were usually brief.

'So, Mark. If you're done with feeling sorry for yourself, are you going to help your colleagues with this investigation?'

'What would be the point? Look how I messed up last time.'

'Don't you think Emma and the rest of the team took that into consideration when they asked you back? How many calls and texts has Emma sent you now?'

'Six or seven. I've lost count.'

'And doesn't that tell you something?'

'Yes. That she can be persistent to the point of annoyance.' He smiled crookedly. 'And doesn't know when to give up.'

But it backfired as she met his smile challengingly. 'Sounds like someone else I know. So at least you have that in common.' Her smile dropped. 'Or should I say *used to* know. You used to hate that trait in others – making excuses, throwing in the towel too quickly – and now you're displaying it yourself.'

Lapslie nodded dolefully after a second as the words sank in. He held out a palm. 'You don't understand. It wasn't just the personal mauling I got from Sinclair, it was the fact that I'd let not only my own side down, but also Donovan and Marianne Tovey. You didn't see the look they gave me across the courtroom.'

She gave a pained, understanding smile. 'Losing a child is never easy.'

Lapslie nodded. Experience rather than conjecture; Charlotte had seen more than her fair share of infant and child losses in hospital to know.

'And murder is even more difficult to accept – but at least when there's justice at the end of it, it gives them something to cling on to.' Lapslie took a sip of his beer. 'But I robbed them even of that.'

Charlotte held his gaze for a moment. 'And how would letting them down now, a second time, by not catching their son's real killer help?'

Lapslie grimaced awkwardly. 'Maybe that's what I fear. Letting them down a second time. I couldn't face that.'

'But with you not involved at all, that failure is almost a certainty. Or, at least, that's how Emma and the rest of your team obviously feel. At least with you back heading the investigation, there's a chance of success.'

Lapslie ran one finger absently along the table by his beer. 'Maybe they're wrong.'

Charlotte sighed. 'From what Emma tells me, the MO on this second boy is identical, and there are some likely links as well between the two victims. Also, Tulley couldn't have killed the second boy because he was in custody at the time. So even if the case against him had been won, without doubt there would have been an appeal – which, looking at the facts, would have been successful. So how can you blame yourself for letting Ben Tovey's murderer go free? It's only your actions now which might be guilty of that – sitting in a pub feeling sorry for yourself while the murderer of those two boys roams free.'

Lapslie felt the jolt of Charlotte's words, her pointed tone and his own feelings of guilt giving rise to an acrid seaweed and cherry taste in his throat. He could see now why Emma had asked Charlotte to talk him round. Having to be so blunt and forthright, Emma Bradbury would no doubt have felt she'd be overstepping the lines of their professional relationship.

Their alcove was separated from the rest of the pub by a bookshelf crammed with old books, no doubt picked up from boot sales and charity shops – so none valuable enough to be worth pinching. And at the centre was a wood panel with a mirror in an ornate gilded frame. Lapslie caught his own reflection for a moment: three days' growth, sullen expression, eyes lost, unfocused. *Feeling sorry for himself?* She didn't know the half of it.

But perhaps at that moment she sensed him swaying, because she said, 'Look, Mark, if this is going to take a while – perhaps I will have a drink after all. A white wine spritzer, thanks.'

Stratford, east London
September 2013

Josie's abductor was known as Mandrake, a moniker gained due to his silent and graceful swan-like movements during a past sortie in Afghanistan.

Compared to that mission – killing four Taliban within their own camp in the dead of night – grabbing this rookie journalist and disposing of her should be a cakewalk. A 'skate', as they said in the army.

He'd already pre-planned where he was going to dump and bury the body. A new apartment block, one of many that had sprung up in the wake of the 2012 Olympics. Several support columns were already partially filled with concrete, and Mandrake had chosen one with a cement hopper suspended above it. He'd snap her neck with a sharp tug, dump her in the half-filled column, then release three foot of wet cement from the hopper on top of her.

It would set within a few hours, and the workers in the morning wouldn't spot the extra fill – there were too many columns, with varying levels of fill in each.

Paradoxically, she'd be buried only a mile from where she lived. They were now heading back the way she'd come earlier to see Brenda Kirkbride – who'd never in fact existed. They should be at the building site in another twelve minutes or so.

Mandrake looked sharply into his rear-view mirror. He thought he'd heard some movement from her earlier, but when he'd checked in the mirror, she was lying still. Now he thought he'd heard some faint rustling again, but it was too dark in the back for him to see clearly – until the next bar of orange light struck as they passed by a street lamp.

Then he tensed, nerves jarring as he saw in the mirror how she was bent back into an impossible position, hands fiddling with her ankle tie. The view as quickly sank back into darkness as the street lamp receded.

'What the fu—?'

The word was abruptly cut off in his throat by the bang on the side of the van, and suddenly everything was spinning, a shower of white cubes from the shattered windscreen flying around them like a blizzard of snowdrops.

With the distraction of looking back, he hadn't seen the lights changing ahead, had sailed through on red. He was hit broadside by a truck doing a steady thirty, which had hardly bothered to cut its speed with the lights kindly changing to green on its approach. The driver braked at the last instant as the white van suddenly loomed in front of him, but only managed to cut his speed fractionally before impact, shunting the van back six yards and turning it on to its side.

As Mandrake's vision cleared, he wasn't sure how long he'd blacked out for. Five seconds, six? He could feel dampness on his head and one cheek, and see some of his own blood on his shirt.

He looked instantly into the rear-view mirror. The girl appeared to be in a similar state, bloodied and bruised, although he wasn't sure if she was still unconscious or not.

Then, as if in answer, he heard a faint groan from her. But what suddenly alarmed him as she started stirring was that one leg appeared to be stretching out beyond the other. She'd released the ankle tie!

Slow to stir at first, it was as if her prior predicament only hit her in that moment. Then suddenly she was galvanized into action, shifting quickly towards the back of the van and kicking out at its back doors.

On the third kick, the doors burst open, and she was out.

Mandrake responded quickly. But his side door was directly above him and had been heavily dented and mangled by the collision. After a rapid succession of hard kicks, it simply wouldn't budge. The lock was jammed tight. In the end, he knocked out the last of the broken windscreen with the back of one hand and clambered out.

4

Emma Bradbury parked in the car park at Chelmsford HQ and, after keying in her entry code, started making her way up to her second-floor office. She glanced at her watch. That morning's meeting was scheduled to start only fifteen minutes from now.

A love–hate relationship? In the end, her relationship with Mark Lapslie was probably neither, she contemplated. Probably more admiration–resentment. Others in the squad would comment now and then, 'How do you put up with him?'

Certainly, Mark Lapslie's temperament would seem abrasive to most people who didn't understand him, and perhaps 'understanding him', which she felt she did more than anyone else on the Chelmsford force, gave her an edge. Put her closer to the centre of the power structure that radiated out from his leadership of the squad. So she found herself often explaining Lapslie's curt, abrasive attitude – to her and to others – although she was sure many interpreted that as 'making excuses for him'.

At the heart of that 'understanding' was without doubt Lapslie's synaesthesia. The conversion of sounds and words into taste and smell in his mind. That gave him a distinct edge in some cases, acted as a drawback in others.

But most of all it must be a tremendous burden for him to work with and through on a day-to-day basis. Sympathy would be the last thing Mark Lapslie would have wanted, and so she found herself for the most part admiring how he coped with it, many times even managing to turn it to his advantage in investigating cases. She wouldn't have been able to do the same burdened with that condition. She'd have repeatedly called in sick for a few months, then finally thrown in the towel and handed in her resignation. And there had been pressure too from his boss, Chief Superintendent Rouse, and from others at times for him to do just that.

So that admiration for him 'battling through against all odds' was at the root of her understanding of him;

and from that stemmed her habit of making allowances for him, or making excuses as some might say. She knew that when he was abrupt or impatient, sometimes downright rude, he didn't intend his words as personal slights – he wasn't at all a malicious or uncaring person – it was because the synaesthesia had been niggling away at his nerves, flooding his senses with strange tastes and smells.

And possibly too that was his defence mechanism against his condition, rather than simply admit he wasn't feeling well; he'd hate the sympathy, and so, faced with Hobson's choice, the acrimony was seen as preferable. He was less troubled that people might not take to him or find him rude.

But now she'd seen Mark Lapslie's vulnerable side. Toby Sinclair had directly attacked his synaesthesia in the courtroom, made a mockery of it; and now the protective house of cards Lapslie had built around it had crumbled.

She only hoped that Charlotte had been successful in lifting him out of his slump. Charlotte had spoken to him shortly afterwards and he'd said he was 'better now' and promised he'd be in that morning. 'Hopefully not long after you've started the meeting.'

But she wondered. If Lapslie didn't show within half an hour, he probably wasn't coming in. She'd just have to accept they'd lost him for a while longer.

'Okay, let's recap on what we know about this new boy, shall we?' Emma Bradbury glanced at her notes before looking up, her gaze sweeping slowly across the dozen detectives assembled in the squad room. 'Chief Inspector Lapslie will be here shortly to take over, but meanwhile he's asked me to get you all fully up to date on what we've discussed with regard to the case over the past two days.'

DC Barrett lifted a hand halfway, as if what he had to say was too tentative to be deserving of a bold, full lift. 'And he's okay now?'

'Yes. As I said before, it was just a touch of flu. Meanwhile, he's been running the case as best he can from home, and we've been in touch fully throughout.' Bradbury noticed a couple of looks being exchanged around the room. From Lapslie's first day away, she had invented a cover story to satisfy Rouse, and so it followed that she had to keep to the same story with everyone. She felt it might be too damaging career-wise if it became known that Lapslie's absence was connected with the mauling he'd got from Sinclair and the case subsequently collapsing. Lapslie had thanked her for the cover story when he'd phoned her shortly after meeting Charlotte, and she'd brought him up to date on events. She only hoped her claim proved true now and he *would* show up. 'So, much of this follows Chief Inspector Lapslie's initial thoughts on the case, and then we'll open it up for comments. And, as always, let's keep things *sotto voce* when he arrives.' She held out a calming hand to illustrate.

They started getting to grips with the main details of the case: twelve-year-old boy, James Lewis, reported missing by his family after eight hours; body found twenty hours later; family live in a semi-detached house in Hazeleigh; body found in a field six miles away from the Lewis family home.

'And how far was that away from where Ben Tovey's body was found?' DC Pearce asked.

'Eight miles,' Bradbury said.

The questions and comments began to flow, and at one point Bradbury glanced at her watch, concerned that they might run into areas she hadn't so far covered with Lapslie, and the lie would show. The worry also surfaced again that he might have got cold feet and wouldn't show.

DC Kempsey held up his hand. 'And does the distance between the two bodies, and the fact that this second boy is from a normal rather than a traveller family, lead us to believe we might be looking for a different murderer? That there's no connection between the two.'

Bradbury flinched slightly at the word 'normal', a reminder again of how much travellers were seen as outcasts from society, even in politically correct, sanitized – as should be the case, after all these years – squad-room comments.

'No,' she answered. 'There are reasons to believe we're looking at the same murderer for both boys. The method of killing is almost identical: part strangulation, probably to render them unconscious, then a clean neck snap. Almost like you would do if you were killing a chicken . . .'

'. . . and also, don't forget, the severed limbs,' Lapslie's voice came from the side as he entered the room. 'Young Ben Tovey had his right arm severed from the elbow joint down, and James Lewis the same. And both have portions of abdominal flesh and an organ missing. Ben Tovey, the liver, and James Lewis, one kidney.'

'I thought there was a suggestion that this might

have been caused by some farm machinery, such as a combine harvester,' DC Parkin offered.

'That was something initially suggested by the Sinclair defence team, yes,' Lapslie said. 'They were trying to paint a convincing picture that the murder and the body-mangling might have been separate, and that Tulley might have simply come across the severed body part by accident. But the cuts in both cases were too clean.' The reminder of Sinclair still left a sour taste in Lapslie's mouth, though more specific than with most: a sickly blend of overripe plum and vinegar. 'And now, with two bodies, that becomes even less likely, and of course Tulley was in custody at the time, so it couldn't be him.'

The reminder of the collapsed case against Tulley hung like a cloud over the squad room for a second, then Kempsey commented, 'Good to see you back, by the way, sir.'

'Thanks. But it was only a touch of flu, not a heart bypass.' Lapslie smiled tightly and swung his gaze around the rest of the squad room. 'Now, what else do we know about this case and what it might indicate? What other questions does it raise?'

Silence for a second, then DC Rebecca Graves ventured, 'So while this boy's not from a traveller family, did he have similar issues with running off for hours at a time?'

This was one detail Lapslie hadn't been brought up to speed on.

As he paused, Emma Bradbury interjected, 'Not from what we've found out so far. His parents say it was unusual for James to wander off like that. He'd go off with a friend from across the road, Patrick Astley, to a nearby park or local shops, but that was about it.'

'That's why, no doubt, we got the alert after only eight hours,' Lapslie added in support.

'Did he see his friend that day?' Barrett asked.

Bradbury answered. 'Earlier, yes. But when his parents checked later, Patrick said they'd split up a couple of hours before and he thought James had gone home. They checked the local shops and a couple of other places he might have gone, then called us.'

Kempsey had his hand up again. 'So if this second boy is not from a traveller camp, are there any other links between them?'

'No,' Lapslie said, relying on the details Bradbury had filled in. 'We checked all the obvious: schools, youth clubs, scouts, etcetera. No crossover links between the two boys.' As Lapslie observed most of the detectives in the room lapse deeper into thought, he added, 'But that by no means suggests that's an area we should stop exploring, because it could provide a vital breakthrough. If these two are just random, unconnected victims, it makes the investigation that much harder.'

They spent a while discussing details and minutiae from forensics and autopsy, concluding that the strength needed to break the victims' necks would likely indicate an adult male, then Rebecca Graves, thoughtful through-out the exchange, returned to the subject of possible links: 'If none can be found between the two boys, then perhaps it could be between their parents?'

'Unlikely,' Lapslie said. 'The Toveys and Lewises move in completely different circles. But, as I say, anything's worth exploring. We shouldn't at this stage discount any possibilities out of hand.'

Bradbury nodded, adding, 'But without any link between the two boys or their families, we might have to accept that the only common factor will be the iden-tity of their murderer.'

'Or *murderers*,' Lapslie swiftly added; when Bradbury had earlier made it clear that she believed it was the same murderer because of their identical MOs, Lapslie had raised this issue. 'It could be that we're looking at *two* murderers working closely in conjunction, and that's why the MOs – with strangulation, neck-breaks and cleanly severed limbs – are so similar.'

It took a second for the significance to settle with the squad room.

Parkin raised a quizzical brow. 'So we might have got it right with Tulley all along?'

'Yes, we might have.' Observing reactions, Lapslie hoped his squad saw that as a distinct possibility too, rather than just going with the flow while privately thinking that their boss was only clutching at that straw to salve the personal sting of the collapsed case against Tulley. He took a fresh breath. 'But Tulley has been cleared, so that's an avenue which, under *Ladd* v. *Marshall* rulings, can only be pursued on the basis of fresh evidence. So let's go to it and see what this second murder might uncover.'

Stratford, east London
September 2013

Josie felt her chest heavy, her breath rasping as she ran.

The gag around her mouth restricted her breathing, and she felt something burning her throat. Not sure if it was phlegm or blood, she felt herself almost choking, retching with it.

Her left shoulder was throbbing and ached – it was probably dislocated – but she ran on blindly, tried to ignore the pain.

It was an awkward running motion, with her hands tied behind her back, and she felt herself naturally tilting forwards, almost falling over as she took the first few strides before finding her balance. She'd glanced back twice, frantically, during her run. She appeared to have a good sixty yards on Swan-Tattoo before he clambered clear of the stricken van and started after her.

She saw some terraced houses fifty yards to one side, but they didn't appear to have much life in them. She couldn't risk trying to raise someone before her abductor was upon her.

The truck driver had been slow to rouse from the impact, and looked badly injured. But looking back she'd seen another car pull up at the junction shortly after the collision, and pinched herself that she might have missed an opportunity. But her first instinct had simply been to get away from her abductor as quickly as possible.

But it now sparked the thought in her mind: *passing traffic*. There was none on the road she'd just crossed, or on the short side street now, but directly ahead was a forty-yard-wide oblong of greenery with some trees, the road beyond that quite busy with traffic. The houses on that far side also appeared to have more life in them. But could she make it across before he caught up with her?

She pounded on hard, her strangled breath seeming to bounce back in hot, aching waves from the gag around her mouth.

She looked back desperately: he appeared to have gained twenty yards on her already, maybe more. She willed herself on, running flat out, and as she reached the very edge of the stretch of parkland, she glanced back again. Just over thirty yards behind her now, she could almost hear the pounding of his feet.

She became frantic. At this rate, she would barely get to the far side of the park before he reached her. Unless the first cars she came across stopped to aid her, she was sunk!

She tried to put on an extra spurt, every muscle in her body aching for release. She daren't risk another glance back, aware that the awkwardness of her half-turn with her hands tied behind her back slowed her down. So she had only the sound of those pounding steps from behind as her guide, moving closer . . . *closer*. And as she came to within ten yards of the road ahead, even that guide-sound was lost, merging with the traffic noise.

He was only ten yards behind her, bearing down fast, as she stumbled into the road. But the first car simply caught fright, blaring its horn and flashing its lights before swinging around her. The next car was forty yards behind. She ran towards it, still in the middle of the road, not caring.

The pounding steps shadowed her from the pavement behind.

Seven yards, six . . .

The approaching car slowed and flashed its lights, and for a moment Josie feared it too would beep its horn and swing around her. But it pulled to a stop and the passenger door opened, a thirty-something man with dark hair calling out, 'Are you okay?'

'Pleeeease, heeelp . . . heeelp!' A garbled, muffled shout through her gag. All she could manage.

The footsteps behind shuffled to a stop five yards away. Uncertain, assessing.

She ran towards the car that had stopped. Another car behind had now pulled up, and barking came from a Labrador being walked by a woman at the edge of the park. Her abductor appeared to think better of it, turned and ran back into the shadows. Too many people, too much commotion.

'Was he chasing you?' her passenger-saviour asked.

She nodded mutely.

And halfway through the reassurances from him and the car driver – 'Don't worry, you're safe now,' 'Let's get these off you, shall we?' – she found she had no emotional reserves left for an explanation. As the gag came off, after a few welcome gasps of fresh air, she collapsed into tears; heart-racking sobs which shook her whole body.

Hazeleigh, Essex
June 2014

As Lapslie got deeper into the interview with Bernard and Catherine Lewis, young James's parents, he wondered why he didn't delay his questioning by a few days as a matter of course in murder enquiries. The few days' grace meant their recall wasn't so addled by grief, and while going over the same ground might have seemed tedious, it helped clarify some finer details from their earlier interview with Bradbury and the family liaison officer. Lapslie knew that early interviews were always urged – while everything was fresh in the minds of family and any contacts – but he couldn't help reflecting that abject grief obscured clear thought for a while. Certainly that appeared to be the case with the Lewises.

He'd made his excuses at the door about not being able to visit earlier.

Catherine Lewis had answered, 'That's okay,' with a strained smile; it was as if she'd almost been relieved that he hadn't intruded earlier. 'I'll just get Bernard. He's out the back in the garden.'

She showed them into the living room, and through the back French windows Lapslie and Bradbury could see Bernard Lewis tending to a rhododendron bush on one side. *Strange*, he'd always thought, *the various ways that people handle grief.* As a young rookie, he thought it callous that people might continue with mundane, day-to-day chores, as if nothing had happened. But having seen it so often over the years, he now realized that invariably they did it as a distraction, a way of keeping going; that if they didn't, they'd have to face up to the fact that something tumultuous had happened which, if they dwelt on it for any length of time, would eat them away, destroy them. He could almost see it with each of Bernard's pruning strokes. Push it away ... *keep it at bay.*

Perhaps reading his thoughts, Catherine Lewis commented as she walked back in, 'Things got left for a few days, as you can imagine. So Bernard felt he should go out there again.'

'I understand.' Lapslie didn't want to start without both of them present, so he briefly perused the photos on the sideboard – James with his parents and an older girl by a beach donkey ride, young James smiling over the top of a swimming certificate with a dolphin logo – while Bernard washed his hands in the kitchen and came through. Lapslie extended his hand into a shake as he introduced himself. 'I'm sorry if much of this goes over ground you've already covered with Detective Bradbury, but if anything additional is uncovered – however small – it will have been worthwhile.'

That same ground covered in the first fifteen minutes of the interview was mainly a refresher for Lapslie, to get him focused on the key elements: where James had last been seen; how long he'd been missing; where else they'd explored when looking for him, before calling the police. They didn't hit on anything particularly enlightening until Lapslie mentioned James's older sister. 'It might be a good idea if she was also interviewed at some stage. Where is she now?'

Bernard and Catherine exchanged a glance before Bernard answered. 'She's at Norwich University now.'

'So can we visit her there, or is she due a visit home anytime soon?' As Lapslie observed them exchange another awkward look, he prompted, 'Why – is there a problem?'

The look was repeated before it was obviously decided that Catherine should answer. She sighed. 'Not exactly a problem. It's just that, well . . . Julie was very close to James, and she partly blames herself for his death.'

'Oh. And why is that?'

Catherine went on to explain that she herself had stayed home and taken care of James for all of his first years, but she'd always been keen to return to work if possible. 'I'd trained as a cardiac unit physio, and there was always strong demand. So in part there was the sense of vocation – that those patients needed me – but also the fact that I'd be able to help out with Julie's school and future uni fees.' She fired a taut grimace at

Bernard before continuing. 'Then, when Julie was four-teen, the opportunity arose for me to return to work, because she was there to take care of James more. But that obviously stopped when she went to university.'

'I see.' The latch-key kids who were an increasing fea-ture of British society, particularly with the pressure for both parents to work to afford a mortgage. 'But if you were then back home again to take care of James, why should your daughter Julie blame herself?'

'Because she used to go out with James and do more with him than I do – particularly to the local park. She had friends she'd meet at the park too, so she was happy to go with him. Whereas I often had much to do at home, so would only be happy for James to go if he was with his friend from across the road, Patrick. Which is what happened on the day in question. So perhaps I partly blame myself too.' Another taut grimace.

Lapslie watched Bernard reach out and gently clasp his wife's hand in support, obviously sensing that tears were close, but also reassuring her: *No, don't blame yourself.*

Lapslie homed in on the mention of Julie's friends. 'Might Julie's friends – the ones she'd see at the local park – have also got to know James?'

'Yes, they did,' Catherine answered. 'Well, a few of them at least.'

'And might some of them have been at the park on the day he disappeared?'

Catherine exchanged a look with Bernard, suddenly seeing where Lapslie was headed. 'Yes, well, one or two of them, perhaps. It was a regular haunt for them, even as they got older. And some of Julie's group of friends were a year or two younger, so they're still at local secondary schools.'

'In a situation like this, one might indeed be enough.' Lapslie smiled tightly and nodded towards Bradbury.

She took out her notebook.

'So I wonder if you have their names?'

Straight after the interview with the Lewises, Lapslie went with Bradbury to the crime scene. It was his first visit, and now – three days after the body of young James had been discovered – there was only one constable standing by the blue-and-white taped-off area rather than the two or three who would no doubt initially have been there. A forensics tent had been erected at first, while every surrounding blade of grass and clod of earth was examined, but that had been gone since late the night before.

Lapslie cast his eyes around the surrounding field before bringing his gaze back to the area where it dipped down at one side, by a hedgerow. He'd worked out everything in advance so that they arrived there at a specific time.

'So is this, more or less, the time when young James Lewis's body was discovered here?'

'Yes, well, we're about ten minutes short, sir – 7.38 is the time we have it logged for. A man out jogging was first to see the body. But from the forensics and autopsy reports, it looks like the body was put here a good two to three hours before that, and the boy killed at least ten hours before he was transported here.'

Lapslie looked towards the far treeline. The sun was close to dipping down behind the branches, the light fast fading. The temperature was dropping too, and Lapslie felt a chill run through him. Though that might have been as much from what he was now looking at – the place where James Lewis's mutilated body had been dumped. The photos in the crime scene file flashed through his mind, superimposing images on the patch of earth beyond the cordon.

As they'd left the Lewis home, he'd reassured them: 'Don't worry, we'll find whoever has done this to your boy.' But after the fiasco with Ben Tovey and the court mauling from Sinclair, he wondered whether he was mostly reassuring himself. Because now, looking across this cold, damp field, it felt like a desolate hope, out of reach.

'So, not far short of dusk when he was spotted?'

'Yes.'

'But two or three hours before ... that would have meant the body was dumped here in broad daylight.'

'Yes, sir. But it was raining heavily that day, so few people would have been using the path then. The rain didn't clear until almost 6 p.m.'

Lapslie nodded. Then, struck by a fresh thought, he paced towards the path. Bradbury followed after a second, and Lapslie waited for her to be alongside him on the pathway before confirming that this was the spot from where the body had first been seen by the jogger.

'Yes, sir. More or less this position.'

Lapslie strained his eyes in the fading light as he looked back towards the patch where the field dipped.

'Not easily seen from this point. Was there any bright clothing on the body?'

'No, sir. It was wrapped in a brown blanket, with what forensics have determined was farm manure sprinkled on top.'

The brown blanket was the same as last time, the manure covering different, Lapslie reflected. Last time they'd simply spread some rubbish on top of the body. But then, while there were similarities between the two fields – and Ben Tovey's body had been left in a ditch – the last site had been a notorious fly-tipping area. Forensics couldn't even determine whether the rubbish covering the body had been brought there with Ben, or had simply been gathered from surrounding rubbish. But the brown blankets on both occasions, were they also part of the camouflage? Or simply showing modesty – respect for the dead?

Green growth was sparse since the field had last been furrowed, Lapslie noted. So would a concentrated brown patch have stood out? 'Aside from the brown covering possibly merging in, the angle is difficult too.'

'The jogger who first saw the body was fairly tall: six-two or three. And by then the rain had washed away some of the manure. So part of the blanket was clearly visible.'

Lapslie took a fresh breath as he led the way back to the taped-off side of the field. 'So, let's recap on what we have. A number of similarities in the two murders with the age of the boys, method of murder, and body parts removed. Plus also the same, or similar, blankets used to cover the bodies. Any leads from forensics on those?'

'Same type of wool and colouring on both, but forensics found horse hairs on the first one, as if it had been used under a strap-on horse-blanket, whereas on this second blanket they found cow hairs.'

'So, a very small difference between the two murders there. But there is one big difference between the MO on each.'

'What's that, sir?'

'Little James Lewis disappears from the local park or shops between five and six one evening. He's killed and some body parts are severed and removed within four to five hours – then twenty-two hours later his body is dumped in a field. With Ben Tovey, there was a two-to-three-day gap between his murder and his body being dumped.'

Bradbury raised a tame eyebrow after applying thought for a moment. 'That might just be a random factor, the timing of body disposal not that important to him. Or it might have simply been when the first or best opportunity arose to dispose of each body.'

'Yes, but either way – whether purely random or there being a good reason – it will tell us something about the killer that we don't as yet know.'

5

Beernem, Belgium
May 2013

Young Luke Meerbecke had always been told by his mother never to cut across the field, which confused him. When they'd gone out for walks together or for picnics in the countryside close to their home, she'd remarked on the beauty of the field.

She'd told him about the fields only a few miles south covered with the same blanket of poppies and bluebells in the summer, and what the poppies were meant to symbolize: the blood of the many young soldiers who'd lost their lives there.

It was difficult when you were only twelve to relate to a war that had taken place sixty years before you were even born, and his parents had never explained what the bluebells represented. One day he'd asked whether it was because of all the kings and queens who'd died there? 'All that royal blood.'

His parents had laughed, his father's bellowing laugh heartier than his mother's as he'd reached out and ruffled his hair. It saddened him, thinking about it now. Two years since his parents had split up and they'd returned to his mother's home town, leaving his father in Spain – where both he and his younger brother had been born. And six months now since his father's last visit to see him and Justin.

He'd had trouble understanding the split, and it had hit Justin even harder. His younger brother had cried himself to sleep almost every night for three months after they'd left Spain. That's why Luke was heading across the field now. It was Justin's seventh birthday tomorrow, and Luke knew just the present to put a big smile on his face: the stamp album he'd seen in the charity shop at the edge of town. Justin's interest in collecting stamps had started not long after his own interest in them had waned, over a year ago. So he'd given him his own album and Justin had added to it month by month, but it was slow going. Then, just a few weeks back, he'd seen a bumper album full of old and exotic stamps at the nearby charity shop. But at eight euros, it had taken him a couple of weeks to save up for it.

Then, with the money finally saved, first thing that morning he'd headed across the field to town, heart in his mouth, desperately hoping that the album hadn't already been sold and was still there. It was!

He'd handed over the money and the shop assistant had put the precious album in a bag with a smile. 'You might find some rare ones there.'

'I hope so. It's for my brother's birthday.'

So now he clutched the bag with the stamp album as he made his way back briskly across the field. He couldn't wait to get it home and get it wrapped, already anticipating the big smile tomorrow as Justin opened it.

In the winter the field would be shrouded in a cold, damp mist, and he'd follow his mother's advice and *never* venture into it. But in the summer the field came alive and reminded him of his childhood days in Spain – when his mother and father were together. Besides, the field was a handy short cut to the shops at the edge of town. For the shops at the other side of town, he'd follow his mother's instructions and walk along the road.

It was then that Luke noticed the man by a camper van in the woods at the edge of the field. He had a dark jacket with a red poppy on it, and there was also a red streak in his mid-brown hair; the two red patches looked like a continuation of the poppies in the field for a moment. As Luke got close enough to be able to see the man more clearly, the patch of red hair struck him as particularly out of place, because the man looked too old to be a punk rocker or a goth.

The man appeared to notice him then too, before his eyes drifted to one side, fixing on a position behind Luke. The man started across the field, following the direction of his gaze. But as Luke looked back, he couldn't see anyone there. Perhaps the man was heading to the shops too. With the path he was taking, he'd pass about eight yards to Luke's side. Which indeed was the line the man kept to – until the last minute.

Luke's breath caught in his throat as the man lunged towards him.

Luke started to run, but the man had the advantage of momentum and caught up with him after only six yards, pulling him to the ground amongst the grass and poppies.

The man was strong, pinning him down by the chest with just one hand.

'Don't take my album,' Luke said breathlessly, clutching the bag tightly to his side.

The man's brow knitted curiously. 'What on earth would I want with your album?'

'It's for my brother's birthday,' Luke said, eyes fearful, and still catching at his breath. 'I saved up my last two weeks' pocket money for it.'

The man smiled faintly, and Luke couldn't tell if he were teasing or sympathetic.

'You're obviously a good boy. I'll do my best to make sure your brother gets the album. You have my word.'

Hazeleigh, Essex
June 2014

It took a further five days to go through the list of all those who might have seen young James Lewis during his last hours, then to locate and question them.

Only one of Julie Lewis's friends from the park had been there on the afternoon in question. When James's friend Patrick left the park, she saw James playing for a while with another blond boy, who looked slightly younger. Both boys then headed off together after about twenty minutes. Lapslie asked if she knew the other boy.

'No, I've seen him in the park before, but I don't know his name.'

'So that would have been about, what – 5.10, 5.20?'

'Yes, about that. Maybe slightly later.'

They discovered the other boy was a ten-year-old, Lucas Naylor, who lived just around the corner from the park. But when they questioned him at his house, with his parents present, he said that they'd planned to go to the local shops together, but his mum was halfway to the park to get him, and so James went on to the shops on his own.

Mrs Naylor supported her son and shook her head eagerly.

Lapslie asked at what point she'd met up with the two boys to take Lucas home.

'Oh, only about fifty yards from the park entrance, I would say.'

'And did you keep young James in sight for much time beyond that, as he continued on to the shops?'

'Only another thirty or forty yards, as by then we had to turn the corner towards home.'

'And you saw nothing untoward during that time – no cars or other people approaching James?'

Susan Naylor thought hard for a moment before shaking her head resolutely. 'No, nobody that I could see.'

Lapslie did a quick calculation: a half-mile to the local shops, with James in view for, at most, the first 100 yards. That meant 750 to 800 yards in which he was out of view and on his own.

He put a team of six, assisting himself and Bradbury, checking again with the local shops. Then they went on a door-to-door of all the houses in that 800-yard stretch.

Nobody had seen James. In those 800 yards he'd simply vanished. It reminded Lapslie of how quickly some opportunistic abductors and murderers struck: a mother turns away for a moment to look at a dress or a new pair of shoes, turns back and her child is gone. A father is five minutes late for a normal pick-up time, and his child is no longer there when he arrives. Those instances were the most heartbreaking of all, because the parents forever blamed themselves. *'If only I hadn't been distracted . . . if only I hadn't been a few minutes late.'*

Eight hundred yards. Where had young James Lewis gone? Or what was it in that 800-yard stretch that they were missing?

Stratford, east London
September 2013

When Mandrake saw one young guy, no more than nineteen, in royal-blue-and-white football strip, outside Josie's ground-floor flat – one of three in a converted terraced house – he thought it out of place. Football strip at 9.30 at night?

When he saw three more teenagers in the same strip appear, he thought it decidedly odd. But when he noticed that one of the second group was carrying a plate with a small mound of food on it, he thought he knew what was going on. The only oddity remaining was how she'd got hold of half a football team at this time of night.

He was waiting, seventy yards and ten parked cars back from the entrance to her flat, slumped down out of sight in a dark-blue Nissan Micra he'd hot-wired early that morning. The van yesterday had also been stolen, and if he was still maintaining a vigil outside her place tomorrow – looking increasingly unlikely, given current events – he'd no doubt have to steal another car.

The boy with the plate knelt and put it down, halfway up the short path, calling out, 'Here, Creampie ... Creampie! Your favourite!'

Mandrake suspected she'd come back for her cat at some stage; what he hadn't banked on was her turning up with half the Chelsea youth squad!

There was a lengthy pause though now, as they waited to see whether Creampie would take the bait and slip through the cat flap towards the plate. He might only respond to food being offered by his owner.

The boy called out again, 'Creampie!' But with no cat appearing after a moment, he looked around anxiously, waving to one of his backup team further along the road.

Following the direction of that wave, Mandrake saw another blue shirt emerge, along with two lads in crimson football strips. He was able to pinpoint where they emerged from: a minibus parked forty yards beyond her flat.

Mandrake sat up – sharper, keener – as he saw the last person to emerge: *Josie Dallyn!* She obviously felt brave enough to return with half a football team guarding her. Her left shoulder was strapped up, and there was a plaster on her forehead on that same side.

She started calling out as she made her way up the pathway, 'Creampie . . . it's me!' One hand delved into her pocket for her keys, in case she actually had to go in.

But at that moment a custard-coloured ball of fluff emerged, and she joyfully scooped her cat up into her arms.

'Let's go!' One of the teenagers said, looking around anxiously. Someone who needed seven fit teenage body-guards to warn him off was obviously a force to be reck-oned with. The youngster didn't want to hang around.

Mandrake took a deep breath, rested easy. He wasn't going to risk confronting them now. He'd wait for them to pull out, then follow at a distance. Find out where she was staying now and simply bide his time. Choose a moment to take her out when she wasn't guarded by half a football squad.

He watched them hustle their way back into the mini-bus. Heard it start up, and hit his own ignition a second after.

As they pulled out, he tapped one finger on his steer-ing wheel, timing his own pull-out for when they were thirty yards on and he wouldn't be noticed following.

But as he finally pulled out, he had hardly gone twenty yards when an old BMW saloon car pulled out directly in front of him, turning sharply to an angle so that, with the cars parked each side, it blocked the road. He couldn't get past.

Mandrake beeped his horn once, twice . . . and flashed his lights.

The minibus was almost out of sight now, turning off into another street.

He looked frantically behind. Too far to back up and swing around the block from the next turn. The minibus would be long gone by then.

He beeped and flashed again, and in answer two middle fingers appeared by the rear window from two separate blue- and crimson-clad arms.

Clacton-on-Sea, Essex
July 2014

Doldrums.

Lapslie looked out from the deck of his boat at the flat, grey sea. He'd used the 24-foot Mazury's small motor to get him out of Clacton harbour, where the boat was permanently moored, but even clear of the headland there was no wind; no point in even unfurling the sails. But Lapslie had taken the boat out mainly for the quiet and solitude. So, having cut the engine, he was quite happy to just let it bob and drift along with the tide at only one or two knots.

The door-to-door enquiries along the stretch of road where young James Lewis had last been seen spilled over into two days. A few people hadn't been in when officers first called, so they'd had to revisit the next day. They'd also checked some extra shops in the local high street, in case James had visited a shop he hadn't previously gone to.

Nothing.

Nor anything in the past week from photo-print pictures and details of where James was last seen, which they'd displayed in various local shop windows and on lamp posts within a half-mile radius. Nothing too from the story they'd run with James's picture in the local and national newspapers. A few false leads, and the usual bunch of nutcases, but nothing of substance.

Earlier that day, Lapslie had gone out again to the field where James's body had been found, then the section of street where he'd last been seen – looking back and forth, his eyes desperately searching for answers, for anything they might have previously missed.

He found himself now scanning the sea and horizon from his boat in much the same way, but it seemed just as grey, empty and unyielding. His part-time captain, George, a retired Royal Navy man who tended to the boat, had advised that it was due in dry dock within the next two weeks for maintenance and a repaint, so this might be his last chance for a sail this year. Usually being out at sea, away from work and distractions – and, most of all, the *noise* which threatened to unbalance his senses with unwanted tastes – his thoughts would be freer, and he'd find it easier to focus.

But he found it slow going today, the doldrums of the seascape before him uncomfortably mirroring the case: no movement, not heading anywhere fast. Lapslie knew that the first few days of a case were the most vital. If no clues were hit upon in that time, no leads or sightings, then often they had to be prepared to settle in for the long haul. Now it had been ten days since young James Lewis had disappeared, and they were no further ahead than on that first day.

First thing that morning he'd laid out every file on the case on his desk, going meticulously through them for anything previously missed or a possible fresh angle. But after a while he found himself rereading the same lines without absorbing anything, the noise and activity of the squad room beyond his office partition cramping his thoughts. After a while, he packed all the files under one arm and headed out.

'I'll be gone a couple of hours or so,' he announced to Bradbury halfway across the squad room. 'Get me on my mobile for anything urgent.'

For the first hour after cutting the boat's engine, he made himself tea in the galley, spread the same files out on the dining table in the galley alcove, and went through them again. Even with his mind more settled and receptive, his focus sharper, nothing leapt out at him.

So finally he'd come back up on to the open deck to see if that might help him to settle, give him more clarity. The main points of the case were still spinning in his head: young James goes to the local park, two hundred yards from his home, with a friend, Patrick; Patrick goes home and James plays with another boy, Lucas Naylor, for twenty minutes, then both boys head from the park towards the local shops. But fifty yards from the park entrance, Mrs Naylor meets Lucas and takes him home. James continues on the remaining 800 yards on his own. No shopkeepers saw James later that day, and there were no sightings in that 800-yard stretch from neighbours. Not even the usual *'We saw a car or van just along from our house we hadn't seen before. Thought nothing of it at first . . .'*

Ten days in and they had no leads, not even slim ones. *Nothing.*

Where . . . *where?* Lapslie noticed he was gripping his teacup too hard – his second cup, made to take up on deck. The sea air was brisk, so the extra warmth was welcoming.

He wasn't sure how long he'd been sitting there staring at the flat unyielding sea when his mobile started ringing from the galley below: the first bars of 'Knights in White Satin', one of his favourite songs, but he'd chosen it because it brought on the smell and taste of coffee, made him snap to, suddenly alert. Although now, mixed with tea, the taste wasn't quite as welcoming.

Emma Bradbury's number showed on his display. 'Hi, Emma. Tell me.'

'Sir. A lead has just come in which I think is worth checking out. A comment about a labourer who was doing some asphalting on the Lewis family's driveway earlier this summer. Said they observed him taking a special interest in the boy, which they found odd.'

'Who was this from? A neighbour?'

'I suspect so. The call was put through to me – but the caller, a woman, didn't want to give her name. The call was made anonymously.'

'Have we been able to trace it to a mobile or land-line?'

Out of the seventeen calls about James Lewis, none of which had so far borne fruit, five of them had been anonymous; but two of those they'd been able to trace back.

'Afraid not. It was made from a payphone at a local supermarket. One of the few still around.'

'I see.' Anonymous call from a payphone; Lapslie suspected the worst. 'Probably just a crank call.'

'That was my first thought too, sir. Until she mentioned the reason why she was keen to remain anonymous.'

'Oh. What was that?'

'She said she thought the asphalt crew laying the Lewises' driveway were travellers, and that you can't be too careful with them: "Don't want to find my car with no wheels one morning." '

6

Central Library, King's Cross, London
May 1998

It wasn't until her fourth visit that librarian Christopher Wilmott paid any attention to the lady who took up a seat at a table three away from his central desk in the newspaper archive section.

Much the same time of day too, he noted, looking briefly at the clock on the side wall: mid-morning. And it had been a Tuesday last time she visited, if he remembered correctly.

She looked like a bag lady, which was why he'd paid her only scant attention the first time. The library was only a few hundred yards from King's Cross Station, and many of the vagrants and tramps who'd spent the night under its surrounding archways and bridges would often drift into the library, particularly in cold weather.

But usually they'd just take a seat and nap or look aimlessly through recent newspapers and magazines. Some, on occasion, might splash out on a tea or coffee and bring it into the reading room – but as long as they didn't make a noise or disturb other readers, librarians and security generally let them be.

She was in her late fifties, he guessed, though street life had probably added on a good eight or ten years. She had straggly light-brown hair, heavily greying. Her hands were slightly bent with arthritis and looked as if they hadn't seen a manicure in many years. She wore the same dark-brown herringbone coat each time. On her first visit it had been cold and so he could understand it, but today it was nearly 70°F and she was still wearing it.

But apart from her dress, she was different from the other visiting vagrants. She'd spend her two or three hours there voraciously looking through articles and microfiche files, her eyes glued either to hard copy or screen, all but oblivious to her surroundings.

So when he did decide to go over to her table that day, she was slightly startled at first.

'I'm not causing any trouble, am I?'

'No, not at all,' Christopher Wilmott assured her. 'It's just that I've seen you in here before, and if there's anything I can help you with, point you in the right direction of, please let me know.'

'Yes, yes, I certainly will. Thanks.'

Though it wasn't until three Tuesdays later that she finally asked his assistance and opened up a bit about what she was researching.

'I was looking for articles about the disappearance of a young boy in 1974, David McCauley. I wondered where I might find articles from the Dumfries area?'

'Section twenty-two, index one-four-nine,' he confirmed after checking on his computer. But after a moment an oddity struck him about this request. 'But you've been searching through articles for a while now. Surely you'd have found ones for the Dumfries area already.'

'Ah, yes.' She eased a gentle smile. 'I've been looking so far in the national press and the Peterborough area, which is where we lived when David disappeared. Also for articles about those who might have been responsible for David's disappearance. Dumfries was where we used to live before David was born. I wanted to see if the way it was reported was different there.'

'I see,' he said, even though he was unsure of the significance of that. 'Someone special to you?'

'Yes. David was our son.' Her shy smile became drawn. 'It was in all the national newspapers at the time.'

'I'm sorry to hear about your loss. How old was your son when he disappeared?'

'Only twelve.'

Ashingdon, Essex
July 2014

'When was it that you did the asphalting on the Lewis family driveway?' Emma Bradbury asked.

Harvey Reid thought for a moment. 'Oh, that would have been back in late April, maybe early May.'

'And who else was on the work team with you, if you recall?'

'Frank Crosby, Chris Logan and ... uh, "Tumbleweed".' Reid gave a cramped smile. 'That's our nickname for him. Sorry, never can remember his actual name.'

Emma Bradbury glanced at Lapslie, then at her notes again. 'That would probably be Lee Bateman.'

'Yeah, that's him.' Reid's smile became more open. 'We call him Tumbleweed because his hair is always so wild.'

Lapslie followed a second after Bradbury in nodding his accord. They knew it was Lee Bateman by process of elimination, having already questioned Catherine and Bernard Lewis about the asphalting crew the day before. The dates Reid had given for the asphalting being done also correlated with what they'd already learned from the Lewises. But they'd decided to interview Reid first because, when asked the key question – 'Which one of the work team seemed particularly friendly with your son, James?' – the Lewises had shown no hesitation in singling out Harvey Reid. Catherine Lewis had added, 'It was almost like they had a special bond, spoke the same language. It was a delight to watch.' Then, after a moment's reflection, she'd put one hand to her mouth in horror. 'You don't think . . . ?'

'No, we don't,' Lapslie had been quick to reassure. 'It's just one of many leads we're following.'

It had taken them another forty-eight hours to track down Harvey Reid's whereabouts. He hadn't stayed at the traveller's camp for over a year and now lived with his aged aunt in the small village of Ashingdon, five miles from the coast. Except, that was, for three or four months in the summer, when he was allowed to sleep in the barn of the farm where he did casual labour. Lapslie thought that an odd arrangement. When he'd asked the aunt's neighbour who'd supplied the information – neither Reid nor his aunt had been in when they first called – she'd conjectured, 'Maybe it's because she does a bit of bed and breakfast in the summer months, so there's not the room. But I'm sure she's keen not to let the taxman know about that – so if it comes up, you didn't get the information from me.'

Neighbours and past fellow travellers of Reid's were also useful in giving some guide to Harvey Reid's character. One former workmate commented, 'He's not by any means a violent character, or I've never known him to be. But he does at times seem odd. Maybe it's those eyes of his that do it.'

His aunt's immediate neighbour had been more specific about his 'oddness'. 'You do know that he's got learning difficulties, don't you? His mental age has probably never risen above that of a twelve-year-old.'

Lapslie made sure that wasn't entered into the notes. If it was, they'd be required to contact a special liaison counsellor before interviewing Reid, and that would have hampered an open and frank interview.

A past fellow traveller had been less kind in referring to Reid's condition. 'So, Simon's in some sort of trouble, is he?'

Lapslie had corrected him. 'Don't you mean Harvey?'

And the traveller had informed him that Simon was the camp's nickname for him. 'Simon . . . as in "Simple Simon".'

Reid was in his late thirties with lank, reddish-brown hair, though he looked almost ten years older, his hair heavily greying at the sides and his skin rough and pitted. He was thickset with a slight paunch and no more than five-foot-eight. They'd heard that he went through a wild period of drinking cider with meths. But sleeping rough and in farm barns might also have been a contributor, Lapslie reflected, looking at Reid now. This 'wild period' had also been mentioned by way of explaining Reid's left eye being slightly frozen and not fully following the motion of the other: 'Before his heavy drinking period, we hadn't noticed that.'

Lapslie had arranged to interview Reid at the aunt's house. He agreed in advance with Bradbury that she would ask all the initial 'scene-setting' questions, then Lapslie would take over for the more pointed, sharper part of the interview.

Reid's aunt, Hilary, offered them tea upon arrival. Lapslie had just finished a take-out Costa coffee ten minutes before they'd pulled up, but he said yes, keen to keep the aunt away from the interview for as long as possible. She hadn't made any direct reference to Reid's condition before going to make the tea, simply commenting, 'It sometimes takes him a bit of time to get things clear − so you'll have to be patient with him.'

As the sound of tinkling cups drifted from the kitchen, Lapslie leaned forward. 'Now on that asphalting job at the Lewis home, you met young James Lewis, I understand?'

'Yes, I did.' His countenance darkened as he shook his head. 'Terrible thing that happened to him. Terrible.'

'Yes, indeed.' Lapslie glanced at Bradbury.

She was making a note; no doubt recording that Reid was obviously aware of what had happened to young James Lewis, and logging his reaction.

'I would imagine it came as something of a shock to you. Especially as you'd become quite friendly with the boy.'

Reid's expression slowly brightened. 'It was only a three-day job. But, yes, I suppose I had. Lovely boy.'

'So when you heard what had happened to young James on the news, you had no trouble remembering him?'

Reid's brow knitted. 'Of course not.'

'And while nobody would disagree with your description of James as a "lovely boy", what do you recall specifically about him from that short time you spent working at the Lewis house. What stuck in your mind about him?'

It took a moment for Reid's brow to ease, like a tide swilling in as his thoughts cleared. 'Well, he had such a happy smile all the time. He showed me some of his DS games one day, and we played them a couple of times. In the lunch-break, mind. Don't want to admit to skiving off.' Reid eased an impish smile, as if he himself were a kid caught raiding the cookie jar. 'We had some real good laughs together.'

'Yes, I can see that. And was young James as friendly with anyone else in your work crew?'

Reid's smile quickly faded, as if suddenly reminded of what had happened to 'happy, smiling James'; or perhaps simply exhausted by the effort of applying thought. 'No, he wasn't, now you come to mention it.'

Lapslie felt a twinge of guilt asking the question. Reid might not be aware of his own disability at that sort of level: that the reason a twelve-year-old boy had formed a 'play bond' with him was because they were on the same wavelength and developmental level. And that, in turn, was why his work colleagues had not formed the same bond with young James.

After a second, Reid continued. 'Thing is, I think he was unsure of me at first. What with my eye an' all.' He pointed to his left eye. 'But I told him that it let me keep one eye on my work and one on the crew boss at the same time. That made him laugh.' Reid's smile as quickly returned with the memory, verging on a chuckle.

It was strange, Lapslie reflected, like a tide of emotions swilling in and out, with Reid having little control over it. Could Reid's affection for young James hint at something more sinister that had later led to him returning and killing the boy? Or was it just innocent: a man and a boy on the same twelve-year-old wavelength because of Reid's disability.

Aunt Hilary, touching seventy, came back in with their teas on a tray at that juncture, so Lapslie changed the topic.

'I understand you were previously at the Everdale traveller's camp. How long now since you stayed there?'

'Oh, about a year or so.'

'And if you can recall: were you at Everdale camp when Ben Tovey disappeared?'

A longer application of thought this time. 'No, I think

I'd just left then. But it was all over the news and the talk of people I knew at the camp – so of course I knew about it.'

'Of course.'

Hilary Reid looked up pointedly. 'Milk . . . sugar?'

'Uh, milk, no sugar. Thanks.' For a moment Lapslie had been afraid that Aunt Hilary had made the connection and was about to intervene. But then of course she hadn't been in the room when they were discussing James Lewis. Bradbury went for the same with her tea and Lapslie waited for her to pop in her usual Sweetex before resuming. 'And since then you've been staying here with your aunt?'

'Yes.'

'Apart, that is, from the summer months, which you apparently spend labouring on local farms. And which farm have you been working on this summer, by the way?'

Reid exchanged a look with his aunt. Had Lapslie's question hit a nerve? Or was it just surprise that the police knew, and some concern related to her B & B work?

'Uh . . . Milford Farm,' Harvey Reid said at length. 'Just outside Purleigh village.'

Milford Farm? The name rang a bell from somewhere,

but Lapslie couldn't recall from where. He did a quick calculation: Purleigh was eight or nine miles from Everdale camp where Ben Tovey had disappeared, but only two or three miles from the field where James Lewis's body had been found. The aunt's house, towards the coast, where they were sitting now was over fifteen miles away.

As if reading his thoughts, Bradbury, who had been making periodic notes throughout, asked, 'And when do you intend leaving Milford Farm this season and returning to your aunt's house?'

'Oh, I'll give them a hand getting the hay in this season, so I'll stay on to help out with that.'

So Reid appeared to have no intention of returning to the travellers' community, Lapslie thought. But with the past connection to Everdale camp, Lapslie wondered whether the other connection might be made: whether, with Alistair Tulley in prison when James Lewis had been abducted and killed, the two of them were somehow working together.

'And do you happen to know or have been associated with a certain Alistair Tulley at any time?'

Harvey Reid jolted slightly at the mention of the name. 'What? You mean the suspect that got off with Ben Tovey's murder?'

'Yes, I do. One and the same.' Lapslie kept his gaze steadily on Reid, watching every nuance of his countenance.

'Well, not in the way you mention now.'

'What do you mean, "not in the way"?' Lapslie pushed. 'So were you friends or not?'

Reid almost laughed. 'Far from it. Only met him the once.'

'Oh. When was that?'

Again Reid had to pause to apply some thought. 'About a year ago, when we did a job asphalting his drive. Like we did at the Lewises.'

Stratford, east London
September 2013

Josie waited until they were over half a mile from her flat – with the Nissan Micra that had been blocked in nowhere to be seen behind them – before she did a mini-celebration of a high-five with Jake and a couple of his mates and gave him a hug.

She'd met Jake that morning over breakfast at the YMCA she'd checked into. She'd heard they were good for transients looking for a bed for the night. She'd probably stay at different YMCAs for a couple of weeks, keep on the move, then decide on a longer-term plan.

She'd told Jake a variation on her predicament. She'd just escaped an abusive relationship, thus the head and shoulder injuries, but the problem was she'd left her pet cat in her flat: 'The only love of my life remaining.' She'd pushed an awkward smile.

'And you're nervous about going back for him?'

'Yes, very much so.'

Jake nodded thoughtfully, a tentative smile rising. 'I can go back with you, no problem.'

Josie had a sudden horror image of Swan-Tattoo killing both her and Jake and dumping them in shallow graves. But she didn't want to come across as ungrateful or hurt Jake's pride. She reached out and touched the back of his hand. 'But he can be unpredictable and violent. So we might need to give him a bit more of a warning off.'

Jake's eyes darted a moment more before he hit a possible solution. 'I play regular six-a-side football and tonight's one of our training nights. I can ask whether some of the other guys want to come along too. You know, just for a laugh.'

'Yeah, just for a laugh.' Her easy-going grateful smile didn't give away that it might take five or six of them to deter Swan-Tattoo.

In the end, Jake had not only managed to convince most of his own team, but also part of a team training on the adjoining indoor pitch.

'Thanks, Jake. You're a star.'

As they approached the YMCA, she took a slip of paper from her pocket and looked again at the name written on it: Tom Barton. A two-fisted journalist/editor in the true sense of the word. Barton was editor of a fringe journal and blog site, and she'd been given his name by a fellow journalist as 'one of the few editors I know brave enough these days to run with a really controversial story.'

She should have taken heed of that – or, indeed, of John Farren when he'd said that this group's tentacles reached into 'all manner of leading institutions, including the police, the legal establishment, media and government.' She'd been naive to think that the *Daily Post* might be sacrosanct. So right now she didn't see contacting the police or any other mainstream media as an option. At least, not a safe one.

The only question remaining, now that she had her cat back, was should she leave London Dick Whittington-style – since she had hardly any personal possessions and daren't risk returning to collect more – or contact Tom Barton and fight on?

7

Milford Farm, Essex
July 2014

Lapslie let himself under the taped police cordon and walked towards the SOCO tent twelve yards away. White canvas and fifteen-foot-square, it shone brightly, lit up by the two arc lamps inside. Another two lamps were beyond the tent, illuminating the remaining few yards in front of the barn where Harvey Reid had been spending most of the summer. Lapslie knew that there were also another three or four powerful arc lamps inside the barn itself where a dozen SOCOs were busy going meticulously over every inch of ground and hay bale.

Just past 3.40 and the light was already fast fading at the approach of a summer storm, the light from the tents and the barn beyond appearing brighter, starker. When they'd first set the area up, just before midday, the lights hadn't seemed that much stronger than the sunlight. Lapslie had stayed with the SOCO team for the first two hours, then grabbed a late lunch.

Lapslie had suddenly recalled where he'd heard the mention of Milford Farm before. One of the five anonymous calls they'd received had mentioned seeing a boy fitting James Lewis's description near Milford Farm. The farm was fairly remote: the farmer himself hadn't seen young James, nor had anyone among the eight stone cottages approaching the farm. Outside of that, they'd have been in Purleigh itself, which would have meant canvassing hundreds of homes.

But then, with Reid's mention of Milford Farm, they'd decided to go in with a sniffer dog who'd already got the scent from James Lewis's clothing. The dog had started straining at the leash by the barn entrance. They couldn't risk the dog contaminating a potential crime scene, so Lapslie had called in Thompson and his SOCO team to conduct a search from that point on.

Emma Bradbury greeted him as he approached; she'd taken her lunch an hour beforehand, before returning to the barn. This meant there was always one of them on hand to answer any key questions which arose – their standard switchover routine during the early, crucial stages of SOCO examination of a crime scene.

'There's been a development, sir.'

'Always the way.' Lapslie smiled tightly. 'All the excitement while I'm away.'

She nodded towards Jim Thompson, head of the SOCO team, six yards behind them at the barn entrance talking to three others in his white-polyurethane-suited team. 'They found it just fifteen minutes back.'

As they approached, Thompson looked up and broke a couple of paces away from his group. The taste and smell of petrol swilled the back of Lapslie's throat, but it wasn't pungent or unpleasant; in the same way that some people liked the smell of asphalt. Or perhaps it had just mellowed over the years of Lapslie working with Jim Thompson.

Thompson gestured back towards his team. Upon the prompt, one of them lifted up a large, clear plastic evidence bag, and Lapslie saw for the first time what 'it' referred to: a fifteen-inch-long object wrapped in white paper. All but one end of the paper had been permeated a dark crimson, the other end was partly unwrapped.

'It was buried almost two foot down in a hay bale at the back,' Thompson said. 'Which is why it wasn't found quickly.'

Lapslie nodded as he studied the package. 'Have you already looked inside the paper, Jim? Or was it discovered like that?'

'We looked inside,' Thompson said, his expression heavy. 'It was important we quickly discount any other possibilities: someone wrapping up a leg of lamb or some meat to take home for their dog.'

Lapslie nodded. He knew Thompson would have ensured his team had been careful and methodical. The wrapping would have been tweezered back inch by inch. Even though Thompson's expression had all but given him the answer, he had to ask, 'And is it what I fear it might be?'

'I'm afraid it very much looks like it: the hand and lower forearm joint of a child.' Thompson held out a palm, as if balancing. 'Or at least certainly not that of a fully grown adult. Though of course we won't know for certain until we get it back to the lab and do all our measurements.'

'And then we'll know as well if we might have a match with little James Lewis?'

'Yes, that too . . . and the paper it's wrapped in might have a tale to tell.'

It took a second for Lapslie to catch Thompson's inference. 'I see. In perhaps matching the wrapping used to parcel up Ben Tovey's limb that we found in Alistair Tulley's cupboard?'

Thompson grimaced his accord. 'And while the two murders are thirteen months apart – so we perhaps wouldn't expect to find the exact same type of paper – I see in this case that there's a mixture of newspapers and greaseproof paper used. The newspaper might carry a date, or perhaps that can be determined from its articles.'

Lapslie recalled that with Ben Tovey just greaseproof paper had been used; no newspaper. 'But it would be something if the same greaseproof paper was used in this case. Another item to tie the two murders together.'

'Yes, it certainly would.'

'And where was it found?' Lapslie asked.

'Right side of the barn.' Thompson pointed, only half-looking around. 'Again towards the back.'

Lapslie scanned the length of the fifty-foot barn for a second. 'Far from where Harvey Reid bedded down?'

Thompson looked nonplussed for a second.

Bradbury interjected, 'About six or seven yards away.'

Lapslie nodded thoughtfully. Bradbury had been the one to initially get the farmer's directions as to where Reid had bedded down. 'What's left to be done now?'

Thompson took a fresh breath. 'In the last twenty minutes since discovering this, I've had three people on an intensive search of the ten feet surrounding where it was found. Every possible fibre, or indeed any strands of hay which appear to be discoloured.'

'Any of Reid's clothes or personal effects found in there?' Lapslie asked.

'No, nothing, I'm afraid.' Thompson was struck with an afterthought. 'Oh, but we did find a blanket towards the back of the barn. Though it might be simply one of the blankets from the cattle shed over there, and not Reid's own personal blanket.' Thompson nodded towards the cattle shed sixty yards to their left. 'One of my men brought one over and they certainly look the same.'

Cow blanket. Lapslie's nerves tingled. Another possible link. 'Could you bring both in for examination to check, plus also to see if we might have a match with the blanket young James Lewis was found wrapped in?'

'Of course.' Thompson smiled tritely. 'That was already high on my checklist.'

Lapslie nodded. He should have known that Thompson would tick every possible box. 'Sorry. Old habits die hard: suggesting belts when it's clear everyone's already wearing braces.'

'Yes, well. I'd better get back to my team, otherwise I will be guilty of letting my trousers slip.' With a final curt smile, Thompson rejoined the group of three, then after a moment's discussion he headed with the man holding the evidence bag towards the inspection tent while the other two went back into the barn.

Lapslie surveyed the area for a second, looking from the hay barn to the cattle shed on the far side. The area appeared even more ghostly-white now under the arc lamps as the daylight faded fast. The scene was also strangely serene and still, despite the white-suited team of a dozen SOCOs examining every yard. They too were moving like silent ghosts, careful not to disturb any vital evidence. Or perhaps it was the body part being found that had changed the mood of the scene.

Bradbury's voice broke Lapslie from his contemplation. 'What now?'

'I think time to bring in Harvey Reid for more questioning.' Lapslie grimaced. 'And while he's in the station, we'll have Thompson's team here trawling over every inch of his aunt's house.'

'So tell us about the package. When did you put it in the barn at Milford Farm?'

Lapslie and Bradbury were on one side of the inter-view table and Harvey Reid and his solicitor, Roland Mattey, were on the other. As soon as the introductions had been made and the time set on the interview tape, Lapslie went in with the key question.

Harvey Reid looked vague, shrugged. 'What package? I don't know anything about a package.'

'Oh, come on now,' Lapslie pressed. 'It was there only yards from where you've been sleeping in the barn most of the summer. So don't tell me you don't know any-thing about it.'

Harvey Reid looked towards his solicitor, as if for inspiration.

Roland Mattey maintained a perfect poker face; he knew better than to guide his client at such a crucial juncture. He made a quick note on his pad before looking back steadily at Lapslie across the interview table.

Reid shook his head. 'Told you. Don't know nothing about any package. Is this something my farm boss Chris Milford might have given me?'

'I very much doubt it.' Lapslie suppressed a wry smile.

'So what was meant to be in this package?'

'I think you know all too well what was in it.'

This was met with a vacant expression, Reid's mouth slightly open as his mind searched for an answer.

Lapslie added, 'But I'm afraid I can't prompt you at all about this package and its contents.'

Reid held Lapslie's steady gaze a moment longer with the same vacant expression before shaking his head again, this time more resolutely. 'But I told you – I don't know anything about any package.'

Lapslie sighed. 'I'm sorry, but it beggars belief that you knew nothing about it, with it being so close to where you slept in the barn. The smell alone would have alerted you.'

As Reid continued to look perplexed by the question, one hand clenching and unclenching on the interview table, Mattey cut in:

'My client has made it clear that he has no knowledge of the package in question. So I don't feel it correct that he should be pressed further on the issue – especially given his condition.'

'Understood. But as I'm sure you appreciate, what has to be ascertained here is whether with your client's condition he simply can't recall the package in question, or whether he's selectively blotted out any recall of it.' Lapslie smiled patiently. 'Which would be perfectly understandable, given the horrors of what happened to young James Lewis and what the package contained.'

Harvey Reid's eyes flickered uncertainly for a moment as he made the connection. 'What? You're saying that the package had something to do with James Lewis?'

Lapslie held Reid's gaze evenly, not only to avoid giving any prompt, but also trying to discern if it was just an act. Could Reid simply not recall, or had his subconscious separated his more horrific actions from his conscious mind as a form of protection? Lapslie could feel Mattey's eyes on him, annoyed that he'd slipped in the inference. Roland Mattey's experience included dealing with vulnerable adults, those with special needs, and asylum-seekers; if a 'non-specialist' solicitor had been chosen, they'd have had to ensure somebody from social services was present.

After a moment Lapslie said simply, 'You tell us. It's *your* package.'

'And, like I told you before – I don't know nothing about any package.'

Lapslie couldn't tell whether Reid was being cute or simply couldn't remember, and he was rapidly losing patience. He looked directly at Roland Mattey.

'Whether by design or default, since your client

professes no knowledge of the package in question, nothing is lost or gained by revealing its contents – a body part of young James Lewis.' Lapslie ignored the visible flinch from Reid as he continued. 'Indeed, with it revealed, he can hardly argue later that he was tricked into admitting its contents. So in that regard, the information being brought out now can be viewed as acting in his favour.' Lapslie smiled thinly.

Mattey's thoughts appeared to be in conflict: annoyance at the revelation battling with the not-fully-accepted 'to his client's advantage' factor Lapslie had used to soften it.

He nodded after a second. 'Very well, Chief Inspector. It's done now.'

Reid's mouth was half-open; perhaps at the revelation, or the brief exchange – wondering why his solicitor hadn't protested more. 'You're saying it was a body part of young James in that package found in the barn?'

'Your hearing's good,' Lapslie said curtly, 'if not your memory.'

Reid shook his head. 'I know nothing about it. Would never dream of doing anything to little James. I liked him a lot.' He held one palm out, almost a plea. 'I became very close to him . . . we were *friends*.'

'Possibly too close to him – too friendly.' Lapslie ignored the skewed-mouth frown from Mattey, kept his stare directly on Reid. But the inference seemed lost on Reid, or perhaps it was all part of the act.

Reid shook his head more resolutely. 'I would *never* have harmed the boy. Was as upset as everyone when I heard the news. Probably even more so – what with us being friends.'

'So you say,' Lapslie said, briefly consulting his notes. 'So if you claim no knowledge of the package, how do you suggest it got there, only feet from where you've been sleeping?'

Reid considered for a second. 'I'm not in the barn all day, I'm out doing farmwork. Or doing driveways – like at the Lewises'.' Reid's eyes flickered for a second. 'So maybe someone put it there.'

Lapslie discerned the trace of a smile, which quickly died. Was Reid being cute again, or simply pleased with himself for thinking of that? Perhaps he'd suddenly recalled that had also been Alistair Tulley's excuse.

'But the Lewises' wasn't the only driveway you did, was it?'

'No, no. Me and the gang do a fair few of them. Sometimes eight or ten a year.'

'Including that of Alistair Tulley,' Lapslie said.

Reid appeared vacant for a moment before a fresh thought hit him. 'Do you think the same man that planted something at Tulley's place might have done the same with me at the barn?'

'Unlikely, given that the only connection between you two is you doing Tulley's driveway last year. Few people could have possibly known about that. But that does bring us round to the question of whether you went inside Tulley's house while doing his driveway?'

'No . . . well,' he shrugged. 'Only to get tea from him when he called out it was ready.'

'You didn't ever go upstairs at his place?' Lapslie pressed.

'No, not that I recall.' Reid's expression went from faintly quizzical to incredulous as it dawned on him what was being suggested. He shook his head. 'No . . . *no*. You're not laying that one on me.' But it was said with a jocular leer, as if he'd been the butt of a poor joke rather than a vital factor in a murder investigation.

Lapslie looked towards Bradbury. 'When is it we're expecting results in on the fibre tests?'

Bradbury looked up from her notes. 'Late tomorrow. Thursday at the latest.'

Lapslie nodded. They'd both known the day before that the fibre tests would take that long, but Lapslie hadn't wanted to delay confronting Reid about the package; better to hit Reid hard with an early interview, then arrange a second when the fibre results and any other late findings came in. Though as part of his tactical play, he'd prearranged with Bradbury to enquire about the fibre results halfway through: get Reid and his solicitor sweating in advance about that. Lapslie took a fresh breath as he changed tack.

'Are you a gambling man, Mr Reid?'

'Well, I like a little flutter now and then.'

'And what form would that take: bingo, casinos, something else . . . ?'

Reid smiled crookedly; no doubt the image of himself in an 007-style tuxedo had tickled him. 'The gee-gees. Horses.'

'And do you get some idea of the "form", as they call it, yourself – down at the bookies, talking to others, or by some other means?'

'Some chat and tips from down the bookies now and then, or from lads at work – but my main guide is from the *Racing Post* every week.'

'I see.' Lapslie folded his hands on the desktop. 'Would

you care to read from your notes, Detective Bradbury, the forensic results regarding the package containing young James Lewis's forearm?'

'From forensic report number 895632XM, dated the twelfth of July, prepared by examiner Jim Thompson . . .' She looked up briefly. 'There follows quite extensive medical notes regarding blood type, suggested method for the limb's severing, and the period after death that the limb had likely been severed – so for the purposes now, I shall go straight to the latter part of the report.'

Perfunctory nod from Lapslie, and with the same from Mattey a second after, she continued reading:

'The wrapping of the package was comprised of two A3 sheets of 100-gram greaseproof paper and three pages of the *Racing Post* from week commencing 7th May. The greaseproof paper formed the innermost wrapping and the *Racing Post* three pages the outermost – so for the most part the blood infusion with these outer pages of newsprint was less pronounced, and the pages remain quite legible.' Bradbury looked up summarily.

Lapslie had kept his gaze steadily on Reid throughout, watching keenly every nuance of his expression. He'd instructed Bradbury to make something of a production of reading out the findings, so that the impact of the package wrapping would hit Reid all the harder. Reid had started shaking his head lightly halfway through, becoming stronger as Bradbury finished.

'I told you – I know nothing about it. It's just a coincidence with the *Racing Post*,' he blustered. 'And like I said – it's probably someone planted it, like they did with Tulley.'

'You're the gambling man, Mr Reid.' This time it was Lapslie's turn to smile incredulously. '*Racing Post* used, and someone planting packages with *both* you and Tulley, with little connection between you except that one driveway job? You probably know the odds against that better than me.'

Over the following week, much of the rest of the supporting evidence trail fell into place. Jim Thompson's report on fibres came in two days after their last interview with Reid: with the package, they discovered fibres matching that of a donkey jacket owned by Reid and found at his aunt's house. Most tellingly in Thompson's report was the fact that a number of fibres were found inside the package, 'which strongly indicates that the person concerned was involved in wrapping that package,

the fibres couldn't simply have arrived there by handling the package or being close to it after the event.'

They also found a stack of *Racing Post*s at Reid's aunt's
house, where he'd circled favoured horses and past form
and obviously kept them as a guide. Out of a stack of
eighty-three newspapers, they found that six weeks were
missing, including the 7th May edition used to wrap
James Lewis's severed forearm. But most damning of all
were the few faint blood spots on the edition beneath that
missing week, on which – four days later – Thompson
received a DNA match to James Lewis's blood.

They had a final interview with Reid with Roland
Mattey present, and Reid's answers to this latter evidence became increasingly desperate and unconvincing.
He simply kept repeating that he knew nothing about
the package, would never have harmed young James: 'I
liked him ... we were friends ... I tell you, someone
must have planted it all.'

Even his solicitor appeared to find his excuses unconvincing. He looked down awkwardly and buried himself
in his notes as Reid's responses became more splutter-
ing and defensive.

At one stage Reid blurted out, 'Why aren't you out
there, Chief Inspector, looking for the man who has

planted all this stuff on me, set me up. This is *two* men now he's set up . . . and he's still out there roaming free.'

Lapslie just stared stonily at Reid, allowing himself a thin smile after a moment. 'Well, forgive me, but that might be because I feel the culprit is right before me now. But you will no doubt get your chance to plead your case before a judge and jury.'

The final element of the case had been ascertaining when Reid did the driveway work at Tulley's house. Reid and Tulley's accounts differed by a few weeks, so in the end they'd had to track down the rest of the work crew and talk to neighbours to tie down the exact time: the work crew had commenced the work four days after Ben Tovey had disappeared.

Lapslie went to the CPS with all the case files the same day. Eight days later he received their confirmation of prosecution.

Beernem, Belgium
May 2013

The stamp album arrived in the post at the Meerbecke home a week after young Justin's birthday, four days after articles about his elder brother's disappearance had appeared in the newspapers.

His eyes lit up as he opened it, but when a minute later his mother Marisha read the card that had come with it, she immediately phoned the police; then, a second after hanging up, she phoned her uncle, Eric Arles.

'And you're sure it's Luke's handwriting in the card?' Arles quizzed as she finished.

'Yes, it's his. No question. And a stamp album is exactly the sort of present Luke would have bought for Justin.'

After the call finished, Arles phoned and talked to Victor Mertens, the detective handling the case at Beernem. Arles had offered his help because, as Chief Inspector in nearby Ostend, his extra eye on the case could be invaluable. But he had to be careful not to pull rank on Mertens. Just remain a 'concerned advising party', and not try to take control – however much he might be tempted to do so. Luke was one of his favourite great-nephews, and he had vivid, happy memories of playing with the two boys on the beach at Denia, when he'd visited them on hot days.

Arles was pensive as he considered this new development. Tall and wiry, now just two years shy of his police retirement at fifty-five, he already had a slight stoop in his posture – possibly from too many years of leaning over to hear the evidence of those invariably smaller than him; to stay perfectly upright, he felt, might make him seem aloof and distant to them. So he stooped to show his interest and hopefully gain their trust. His growing bald patch ringed by sandy-grey hair was heavily tanned from keen weekend gardening.

At present there was no body, and this written card now suggested that Luke was still alive. He'd hopefully turn up within a few days, safe and well, and there'd be a simple explanation.

The first 'simple explanation' to strike Arles was that Luke would be down with his relatives in Spain. Luke had always loved it there and hadn't wanted to leave, and he wouldn't put it past his father to try to talk the boy into returning on a quick, clandestine trip back.

But when he'd tried Frank Meerbecke's old phone number in Spain, it was disconnected, and when he'd asked the local Denia police to visit Frank, they reported back later that he'd vacated the address six months ago and the neighbours had no idea where he was now.

That didn't surprise Arles. The divorce and custody battle had been bitter, and Frank was five months behind with maintenance payments, so he had good reason to lie low and not be found by his ex-wife.

Now, with the stamp album and card with Luke's handwriting sent four days ago, it seemed even more likely that he was with his father in Spain.

Eric Arles picked up the phone again. If the local Spanish police couldn't locate Frank Meerbecke, hopefully Interpol would have more luck.

Le Talbooth restaurant, Essex
August 2014

Lapslie had arranged lunch with Charlotte at Le Talbooth, one of their favourite restaurants near the coast.

They made a day out of it, one of those rare bank holiday Mondays when he wasn't on duty or Charlotte on call, and hopefully no fresh bodies would turn up – for either of them – which had happened on more than one occasion on past dates.

On the drive, he said that he needed to take a quick detour to check in with George in Clacton harbour to see how he was getting on with the work on his boat. But it had been partly engineered. Last time out on the boat with Charlotte, they'd got caught in a storm. So while George went through a quick summary of what he'd done so far, with Lapslie nodding eagerly – 'That's great . . . looking forward to taking her out' – he had half an eye on Charlotte for her reaction. He was concerned the storm experience might have given her cold feet.

No storm clouds in her expression – in fact, no firm indicators either way – so as they said their goodbyes to George and headed back along the quayside towards the car, he commented, 'Hopefully we'll have more luck next time out – won't get caught in a squall.'

'Squall? More like a force eight or nine. The sort of thing I'd only previously heard about on short-wave radio or from watching *The Perfect Storm*.' She smiled lop-sidedly. 'Besides, you seemed to be more concerned with how I'd cope with the storm than I was myself.'

'Well, it was a bad one – so you can't blame me for being concerned. Even I was starting to worry, and I've got a fair few sailing hours under my belt now.'

She nodded as they got into the car, but a few minutes into the drive her lopsided smile resurfaced. 'You know, at times like that you remind me of some of the fresh doctors and interns we get – eager to shield me from the more horrific injuries in case they upset my delicate female sensitivities. But even after a single month on an emergency ward, you've seen it all.'

'Yes, I'm sorry. I didn't mean to be patronizing.' He smiled tightly. 'So you're up for more sailing?'

'Of course. It would take more than a force eight or nine to put me off.' She shrugged. 'Besides, it was getting a bit boring just sitting in an idyllic, tranquil bay having strawberries and cream with champagne.'

It took a second for Lapslie to cotton on that she was joking, and she lightly punched his arm, smiling, as she looked across.

She gave him much the same light punch too halfway through lunch when he'd teased her with the stock response, 'Well, since the investigation is ongoing – obviously I can only say so much.'

'This isn't one of your press conferences now.'

'I know.' He shrugged as he took another bite of his saddle of venison. 'But that's pretty well it. We've had all the main interviews, and the CPS finally gave us the green light just the other day. So this lunch is to thank you for digging me out of the doldrums over the failed case with the last suspect and getting me back on track again.'

'Well, we couldn't have you moping between your house and local pub just in your carpet slippers for ever, could we?' She took a sip of wine. 'Besides, that was more Emma Bradbury's doing. If she hadn't alerted me to what was wrong, I might never have known.'

'Oh, I think you'd have guessed when I turned up on the next date in my slippers, and with the stains from last night's takeaway still on my shirt.' He joined her in a brief chuckle. 'Still – you rose to the challenge.' He raised his glass and clinked it against hers. 'So I wanted to thank you for that.'

'That's okay. Don't mention it.' Charlotte chewed on her sea bass with truffle linguine for a moment. 'Which brings me neatly back to my first question – do you think you've got the right man?'

'I think so.' Lapslie sighed. 'But I answered flippantly before, partly because I'm afraid of jinxing the case.'

'Do you think that's likely?'

Lapslie shrugged. 'Look what happened last time. And that also raises the question – what do *I* know? I thought I had the right man with Alistair Tulley too, and put his getting off purely down to his barrister Toby Sinclair's machinations and slippery tactics at trial.' Lapslie took a sip of wine. 'It wasn't until halfway through the evidence coming in against Harvey Reid that I realized we might have made a genuine mistake with Tulley, and I revised my earlier opinion.'

'So you're saying that, if it hadn't been for the fresh evidence against Reid, you might have still suspected Tulley?'

'Yes. I think that's fair to say.' Lapslie's attention was drawn by a raucous cheer at the far side of the restaurant from what looked like a birthday party. He had a quick impression of tattoos and visible bra straps – what passed for fashion statements these days. Six miles from Clacton, the Michelin-starred restaurant was far enough away to avoid the normal bucket-and-spade mob, but obviously some people had bothered to look up the local *Good Food Guide*. Lapslie grimaced. 'More poignantly, if it hadn't been for the earlier case collapsing and this fresh evidence coming in, Tulley no doubt would have gone down for it. We'd have convicted an innocent man.'

'I hadn't thought of it that way.' Charlotte forced an uneasy smile. 'But if at this stage you're past that juncture – and everything has fallen into place – what's the worry now?'

Lapslie had to think about that for a second. 'Nothing, I suppose.' He held a hand out. 'Except, perhaps, the concern that the same thing might happen again.'

She nodded in understanding, pulling a wry face. 'You should have more faith in yourself. And the case.'

'Yes, you're right. I should.'

And in the following months of trial preparation, he did.

Until a month before the trial, when he received the news that Harvey Reid's appointed trial barrister was none other than Toby Sinclair, and his confidence collapsed back into self-doubt again.

PART TWO

8

'Lapslie. Thank you for coming up at such short notice,' Chief Superintendent Rouse greeted him as Lapslie walked into his office. Rouse extended a hand towards the man who was sitting in one of the two chairs on the far side of his desk. 'I'd like to introduce you to Benedict Allsopp, recently transferred from the Met. You'll be working closely with him over the coming months.'

The man stood and held one hand out, though Rouse remained seated.

Early forties, with light-brown hair, and an inch shorter than himself, Lapslie noted, though quite stocky, as if he went to the gym regularly.

'Pleased to meet you,' Allsopp said.

'Yes,' Lapslie said, leaving it equivocal whether he too was pleased or was merely acknowledging Allsopp's pleasure. Until Rouse explained just how and why he'd be interacting with Allsopp, he didn't know how he felt.

Rouse gestured towards the end of his desk. 'We've been chatting more than I realized and there's only one biscuit left. You can have it, or I can get Susan to bring in more, if you like?'

Lapslie recalled that Rouse set a lot of store by mind-game choices: he'd often have two pens at the end of his desk for filling out and signing forms, and if you chose his personally engraved pen rather than the plain one, that apparently indicated you had little respect for other people's property. He wasn't sure which was the right answer in this case.

'It's okay. I've just had my usual elevenses of a crois-sant with almond butter. Just tea, thanks.'

Rouse's PA, Susan, had hovered by the open office door after showing Lapslie in. She went back into the adjoining office to prepare his tea.

'Yes, well,' Rouse said, as if still evaluating Lapslie's response. He looked across and adopted his best 'smooth-ing the way' smile. 'Benedict Allsopp has joined us as a DLO – District Liaison Officer – so both you and I will be dealing with him regularly over the coming months.'

Lapslie nodded. 'Forgive my ignorance, sir – but what exactly is that? And how will it affect us?'

Rouse tried to keep his patient smile from fraying at the edges. 'As the name implies, Benedict here will act as liaison between us and other departments, particularly where we might be having problems.' He opened out one hand. 'Or in specific cases which might be proving troublesome – such as this current case, with a second suspect in this linked child murder case.'

Allsopp interjected, 'I understand that's coming up quite soon? And once more against the notorious Toby Sinclair?'

'You know him?' Lapslie enquired.

'Well, know *of* him . . . he's built up something of a rep with the CPS. They've had more than their fair share of lost cases against him; they're licking their wounds.'

Rouse held out the same hand. 'I should explain. Benedict spent almost two years as liaison officer between the Met and the CPS. So he has a lot of experience in that area.'

'Yes, and Sinclair's a particularly slippery character,' Allsopp concurred. 'Not a nice piece of work.'

'You obviously know him well.' Lapslie smiled wryly,

nodding in acknowledgement as Susan put his tea down. He didn't usually like departmental change and having to deal with new characters – saw it in the same light as extra paperwork – but he was beginning to warm to Allsopp; or at least defrost a fraction. He took a sip of his tea. 'And have you just been brought in to deal with this case? I should feel honoured.'

Rouse grimaced. 'This, and others. We have a few other awkward cases with the CPS right now. The other part of Benedict's experience relates to internal liaison, offering a sounding-board between squad rooms and department heads. So he would also act as an extra set of eyes and ears on key matters between you and my office.'

'I see.' Lapslie nodded. He could imagine that any-thing which meant less work for Rouse, and provided more of a buffer between his office and the inspectors, would appeal to the Chief Superintendent. 'So who do I come to first with anything problematical – yourself or Benedict?'

'Go to Benedict first, then he'll streamline and add clarity where need be before presenting to me. It should greatly help the process rather than hinder it.'

'Yes, it should,' Lapslie remarked, leaving unsaid his doubts that this would happen in practice. His experience was that more heads examining a problem usually further complicated it. Or gave rise to more conflicting thoughts and opinions.

As if reading Lapslie's thoughts, Allsopp took a fresh breath. 'But let's get you on track first with Sinclair for this second bout with him. Because we haven't got long now – only a few weeks. So let's see what useful tips I can give you to win the day this time against the sly fox.'

Central Library, King's Cross, London
June 1998

Over the following weeks, librarian Christopher Wilmott found out a bit more about the 'bag lady' who visited the library every Tuesday to do research.

Her name was Betty McCauley, originally from Dumfries and living in Peterborough at the time of her son's disappearance twenty-four years ago, before moving to Chiswick, London, with her husband Ronnie shortly after. 'But hardly a day goes by that I don't think about him.'

Christopher gestured towards the newspapers spread before her and the microfiche screen. 'Or research what might have happened to him, by the looks of it.'

'Yes, I had some help from Ronnie at first.' Betty sighed. 'But he's been gone a good ten years now.'

Christopher nodded solemnly. 'I'm sorry to hear that.'

'Drink got him in the end, you see. First few years, we were both full of hope that David would be found, and the media circus partly kept that hope alive with fresh speculation now and then. That's what in fact brought us down to London, because the centre of it all was here, plus staying in Peterborough was tough after David had gone. Too many memories.' Her look became glazed for a second, as if many of those memories were already too distant or difficult to recall. 'But as it began to sink in that we weren't going to see David again, Ronnie hit the bottle. Only so long you can do that without it catching up with you.' Betty grimaced tautly. 'David was our only child, you see. So it hit us both hard, but Ronnie probably harder than me.'

Christopher nodded again. Researching for hours every week, twenty-four years after the event; it was difficult for him to imagine someone taking that loss harder. 'And have you been able to uncover much with your research? Found any clues as to what might have happened to your son?'

'Some clues, yes, but most of my research has been following ideas and theories. Also a lot of it is to do with those I feel might have been behind his disappearance.'

'What? You think you actually might know who was responsible?'

'Not *know*, exactly, but more have an idea.' Betty's eyes drifted across some of the newspapers. 'You see, that's why I was also looking in the Dumfries press. I think the people behind it were originally from there and the Ballantrae area, but are now here in London and elsewhere.'

'You say *people*.' Christopher's brow knitted. 'You think there was more than one person involved in his disappearance?'

'Oh, I think only one or two people abducted him. But there were others behind it, for sure – particularly those involved in the final ritual of eating him.'

Christopher blinked slowly, not sure if he'd heard correctly at first. But he didn't want to repeat the word to check; already there were a few people nearby who had probably overheard, no doubt wondering why a skilled reference librarian was wasting his time talking to a mad bag lady. He could partly understand it, and sympathize – how the loss of an only child, then your husband, could push you over the edge – but indulging whatever fantasies she now found herself clinging to by prolonging a drawn-out conversation was another matter.

Possibly Betty picked up on his awkwardness, observing him glancing at the people close by, because she quickly added with a tight smile, 'Not *all* of him, you understand. That would be ridiculous. But a small "taste of flesh" has been part of this clan's ritual for many years now.'

Chelmsford Crown Court, Essex
March 2015

'Did it never strike you, Chief Inspector, that what my client is suggesting – that the very same person who planted a package at Alistair Tulley's residence has now also done the same with my client at this barn – is in fact the most likely scenario. You missed this factor in the last case, and you're missing it again now.'

'Yes, of course we considered that. But the connection

between the two was seen as too fleeting and tenuous. After all, they were only in each other's presence for three days while Alistair Tulley's driveway was asphalted – too short a period for an outside party to observe and make a firm connection between the two.'

Toby Sinclair lifted one hand dramatically. 'Ah, but this could be the vital point you're missing, Chief Inspector. Think about the time period for a moment. Whoever set Alistair Tulley up by planting a package would have needed to observe his movements for a while – ascertain when his house might have been empty for them to sneak in and plant a package. And I under-stand from your investigation that my client's work crew turned up at the Tulley residence just four days after young Ben Tovey disappeared. Is that correct?'

'Yes, that's correct.' Lapslie swallowed back a lump in his throat, already uncomfortable at where this was heading.

'So, think about the timing for a moment, Chief Inspector. This person who, of necessity, would have been observing the Tulley residence for a while – would have been doing so at precisely the time that my client, Harvey Reid, would have been working there. Is that a reasonable assumption, Inspector?'

'Yes, I suppose it is,' Lapslie admitted grudgingly. 'But such a person could just as easily have observed Tulley's movements in advance, before Reid even showed up.'

'Yes, they could have, Chief Inspector. But we'd still be left with a fifty-fifty situation – which, as you and I both know from many past criminal investigations, is far too high a percentage to discount out of hand.' Sinclair swept one hand towards Reid. 'Especially when a man's possible incarceration for life is at stake.'

Lapslie mulled it over, pursing his mouth for a moment, as if tasting Sinclair's theory but finding it unpalatable. He recalled Allsopp's advice: *flatter him, he's not used to it. It will catch him off-guard.* 'I'm sure you know more about such percentage risks with criminal prosecutions than I do.'

Sinclair's brow knitted. 'Perhaps I do, Chief Inspector, but the point being made here is that—'

Then, while he's still off balance, let him down. 'But I'm sorry, I still find the suggestion too tenuous. And, indeed, following that same thread, the most likely person to plant a package at Tulley's was in fact Harvey Reid. He was there at the time and so had the greatest opportunity – far more than any random casual observer.' Lapslie looked towards the jury; Allsopp's tactics appeared to be working. They too looked off-balance, uncertain. 'Then we also have Reid's later contact with young James Lewis which, to many observers, appeared an unnaturally close relationship between a grown man and a boy. None of which is answered by your suggestion now.'

Sinclair started, paced away from his position facing the bench, then turned quickly back on himself. 'I can see how you might hold that view, Chief Inspector. After all, having prepared this case for the CPS, it's your job to support the prosecution. But consider this observer for a moment, and indeed whether they were so random and casual. Then roll it forward to take in this association with young James Lewis that you mention.' Sinclair continued pacing, a tight repetitive route of only a few paces back and forth, starting to flap his gown slightly. 'Our observer, watching Tulley's house with a view to planting a package there, spies Harvey Reid in the driveway, and even at that juncture notices something different about him.' Sinclair looked at Lapslie directly. 'You no doubt will have seen our report on just what that "difference" entails?'

'Yes, I have.'

Sinclair's eyes drifted to take in the jury and gallery. 'Well, for the benefit of the jury, that "difference", according to the files of three medical and psychiatric experts, is that Harvey Reid has a "learning difficulty" which has restricted his mental age. He suffered from what is known as "global syndrome" as a child, and that has carried forward into his adult life. All the experts on file agree on that, the only small area of disagreement is regarding the level of mental age, which ranges from ten to eleven for some, thirteen to fourteen for others. And remind us, if you will, Chief Inspector Lapslie, what was the age of James Lewis at the time my client first met him?'

Lapslie cleared his throat. 'He would have been twelve years old then as well. He died just two months short of his thirteenth birthday.'

'I see. Twelve.' Sinclair looked from Lapslie towards the jury again. 'Right slap-bang in the middle of the likely age projections of the various experts. So, you see, Harvey Reid would have viewed James Lewis simply as a friend – since, in terms of age, they'd have been on much the same wavelength, with nothing untoward about their friendship at all. Yet to any outside observers, unaware of my client's history and his medical reports, they might have viewed that association, that "friendship", as somewhat unnatural between a grown man and a boy. Including our so-called "casual observer" planning to plant a first package at Alistair Tulley's house.' Sinclair let that thought settle for a moment with the courtroom, then took a fresh breath.

'And as our casual observer watches Harvey Reid laying the driveway at Tulley's house, he picks up on that "difference" – perhaps demonstrated by his over-friendly reaction to a paperboy visiting the house or a Scout on 'Bob-a-job' week, or even simply boys that passed by on their bikes and skateboards. Reid pausing for a moment to smile and talk to the boys would have been enough to give our watcher the signal – in this case, unbeknown, the *wrong* signal. And having picked up on that, it's enough for him to follow Reid to another driveway job a few months later, where he sees his inter-action with young James Lewis – and he has both his next target and the ideal recipient on whom to plant the blame all in one. Except he doesn't appreciate, as just a casual observer, that indeed there's nothing sinister about Reid's reaction to young James. My client doesn't see the boy as a predator might, but purely as a "friend" on the same age wavelength.'

Lapslie had to give it to Sinclair; he built up a good case. Indeed, one of his first thoughts upon hearing that Sinclair would be acting as defence barrister – aside from his initial trepidation after their last run-in – was how on earth Sinclair would prevent blame being attached to his past client, Tulley, while avoiding implicating Reid – since the prosecution case was that Reid was responsible for *both*. So, conversely, if Sinclair shifted guilt from Reid, it then might automatically fall on Tulley, as the only other party involved. But cleverly Sinclair had built a case out of a third party being responsible for planting both packages, and had then used every conceivable argument to support it.

Sinclair had even managed to dovetail Reid's learning disability neatly into his 'casual observer' argument, though Lapslie realized that part of this was also a fall-back stance. From his pre-trial discussions with the CPS and prosecuting barrister Roderick Daylesford, they knew this would be raised at some stage. If Reid were convicted, then he'd likely get a lesser sentence due to that 'diminished responsibility'. But Sinclair had also craftily angled his questions to support the argument that Reid wasn't a child-predator or molester at all: he was simply friendly with boys of that age because they

were on the same mental wavelength. Again he refer-
enced Allsopp's pre-trial advice: *Whenever Sinclair might
try to blind the jury with science and a complex argument,
bring them back to basics with the hard-core fibre and DNA
evidence.*

'That might be worth considering,' Lapslie said, 'if it
weren't for the fibres found inside the package containing James Lewis's severed forearm.'

'Ah, Chief Inspector,' Sinclair held one hand up dramatically, 'again, you appear to be missing the obvious.
Having decided on planting the package, it wouldn't
take much to sprinkle inside a few fibres from one of
Reid's jackets.'

'And the blood-spots found on Reid's *Racing Post* at his
aunt's house, which matched young James's DNA?' Lapslie made no effort to temper the incredulous timbre in
his voice. 'What earthly explanation there?'

'The same, Chief Inspector Lapslie. The same.' Sinclair
kept his voice calm and assured. He held one hand out
towards the courtroom. 'After all, having decided upon
setting my client up for a fall, these also would be quite
basic, obvious embellishments to seal the case.'

Lapslie couldn't resist an equally incredulous leer.
'I'm sorry. But I don't buy any of it.'

'If you will persist in missing the obvious – even when it's right before you – then I can't help you, Chief Inspector Lapslie.' Sinclair smiled cynically. 'But thankfully, deliberation today isn't down to you. It rests with the jury.'

Lapslie joined Sinclair for a moment in looking in their direction. *Sinclair will try to side with the jury, make out he's their friend and is talking the same language. Don't be shy in voicing your belief that they'd be foolhardy to simply accept that.* 'Perhaps you're right. They might well accept a hotchpotch of tenuous assumptions, combined with some phantom, third-party evidence-planter, more easily than I can.'

Judge Morton looked sharply at Lapslie. 'The jury will disregard that last comment – clerk to note.' One of the few interruptions the judge had so far made to the flow of proceedings. 'And you should know better, Chief Inspector.'

'Yes, I'm sorry, Your Honour.'

Sinclair dismissed Lapslie from the stand then and called his next witness.

Lapslie ensured that no trace of his inner smile showed on his face until he'd left the courtroom. He knew of old that, although a judge might instruct a comment to be struck from the records, all too often the comment stayed in a jury's mind. And that muted chuckle from the public gallery plus a few on the jury bench had been unmistakable; he'd struck a chord, and some of the jury at least were thinking the same as him.

9

Berlare Lake, Belgium
July 2013

Eric Arles arrived at the lakeside four hours after the body had first been found. His name had come up on the national police alert list for notification of any bodies found in the region which could be that of a twelve-year-old boy.

It was a fifty-minute drive to get to the lake at Berlare. When he arrived two police divers were still trawling the shallow waters by the lakeside and the body itself was now on a camp bed-style stretcher and sealed in a clear plastic bag. Even at that first sight, as a detective nodded solemnly to him before unzipping the bag to allow a clearer view, Arles felt sure it was Luke, the knot in his stomach gripping tighter. He felt suddenly light-headed and queasy. If it hadn't been for his years of viewing autopsies and gruesome corpses, he was sure he'd have thrown up on the spot.

With the bag fully unzipped, there remained no doubt. Some bloating and decomposition from being almost two months in the muddy water, but still enough discerning features beyond that for him to see that it was Luke. He nodded in turn, with equal solemnity, and the zipper was pulled up again.

'Who found the body?' Arles enquired. 'Fishermen?'

'No, it was a couple in a rowing boat.' The detective pointed to one side of the divers. 'They were trying to tie up to that submerged branch there. One of their oars stirred up the muddy waters, and they saw the body.'

'Surprising, really, that it wasn't spotted before.'

'I think that might be partly due to the lower water levels now. As summer has progressed, the lake has dried up a bit. Submerged objects are more easily visible.'

'Yes,' Arles said blandly as he looked out across the lake. 'And I suppose, with summer, more people are coming out on to the lake.'

'That too. If it wasn't for this couple looking for a discreet spot amongst the reeds here to have a picnic in their boat, the body might not have been discovered for another two months.'

Arles nodded. 'Any guesses yet as to cause of death?'

'From the bruises on the neck, looks like strangulation; and from the angle of the head, looks like the neck has been broken too. We'll know more no doubt from the pathologist's report.'

'And the marks I saw on the body?'

'There's a heavy stomach gash and the right forearm is missing. Severed cleanly just below the elbow joint.'

'But you don't think they were the cause of death?'

The detective considered the body bag for a moment. 'From my basic knowledge of corpse reaction and pathology – no. There doesn't appear to have been heavy blood loss, so it looks like the stomach wound and the arm being severed occurred sometime after death. The strangulation appears to have come first. But, like I say, we'll know more from the autopsy.'

Arles looked out thoughtfully across the lake again. 'Any idea what might have caused such a limb-severing and the stomach wound?'

'Perhaps a small boat with a prop. That could have done it.' The detective nodded towards the divers. 'But they're still searching the immediate area, so perhaps they'll find something.'

'Perhaps they will,' Arles echoed, the emptiness he felt inside gripping him tighter. Already he was forging in his mind the words to break the tragic news to Marisha; and he wondered now why he hadn't thought about those words before – after all, he'd had two months. Or was it because he'd always clung to the hope of Luke being found alive. And if he'd started to form the words in his mind, it would have meant that he'd given up on that hope.

Rose and Crown public house, Essex
March 2015

The atmosphere in the pub was subdued. A lot of half-smiles and polite comments, but nothing substantial – nobody willing to venture too bold or detailed an opinion on which way the jury might call it.

Besides, prosecuting barrister Roderick Daylesford had pretty well laid out how he saw it running before they adjourned to the pub: 'Only a one- or two-hour deliberation and it will probably be a guilty verdict, the evidence against seen as too clear-cut and overwhelming. Three or four hours hints at some serious doubt. Anything over that and we might be in trouble. The defence might have raised sufficient doubt for it to swing against us.'

What in essence Daylesford was saying was that he felt he'd provided a sufficiently strong case to avoid a swift 'not guilty' verdict, but was unwilling to place any bets beyond that.

They were already approaching the three-and-a-half-hour mark, and over the past twenty minutes the frequency of anxious glances towards the main pub door had increased, expectant of Daylesford walking in to tell them the news.

They hadn't gone to the nearest pub to Chelmsford Crown Court, but instead to Daylesford's favourite in the area, the Rose and Crown, a quarter-mile from the courtroom.

As Emma Bradbury glanced again at her watch, Lapslie assured her, 'I'm confident it will be fine. I think Daylesford hit enough of the salient points in his summing-up. And Jim Thompson's testimony hit the mark too. I saw the reaction of the jury.'

'You think they followed it okay? It wasn't too complex for them.'

Lapslie shrugged. 'As with every case, that's the risk we take. I don't think Thompson could have laid it out any clearer or simpler. He did his bit – we *all* did.'

Lapslie smiled tightly and took another sip of orange juice, glancing towards Jim Thompson at the bar getting more drinks in with DC Kempsey. No doubt another lemonade shandy, an apple juice for Bradbury and a Coke for Kempsey.

Perhaps that had also partly led to the subdued atmosphere, their adherence to soft drinks. Although the observance of not drinking on duty had more or less officially ended when they'd finished giving their testimony, the last thing they wanted to do was reappear in the courtroom as a drunken rabble, punching the air, '*Yes!*' as a guilty verdict was delivered.

Jim Thompson had been one of the last to be called into the witness box, and had made a strong case for the fibres and the *Racing Post*-wrapping evidence, citing the odds of the combination at 'somewhere in the one-in-three-or-four-million range'.

Sinclair had attempted to sweep it aside with an elaborate arm flourish and a condescending tone. 'But as I suggested to your colleague, Chief Inspector Lapslie, the premeditated action of somebody planting that evidence would negate such odds, would it not?'

'I'm sorry. As a forensic examiner, I can only comment on the odds of the evidence found, nothing more. I'm sure there are odds too against "evidence-planting", which Chief Inspector Lapslie would no doubt have given you if you'd asked. Perhaps not the answer you were looking for, but he'd have answered nonetheless.'

Lapslie smiled now as Thompson returned to the table, in much the same way that he'd smiled in the courtroom when the comment had been made. He owed Jim Thompson a decent drink – perhaps a double shot of his favourite Hine Cognac – when the time was right.

'Thanks for that,' Lapslie said as Thompson set their drinks down.

'That's okay.' Thompson looked a bit nonplussed for a moment, not used to Lapslie being so polite. He forced a smile. 'It was my round anyway.'

'No, I meant for the way you handled Sinclair.'

Thompson shrugged. 'Well, I couldn't just let the supercilious prat ride roughshod over me, could I?'

'No, I suppose not.' Lapslie's return smile was more uncertain, reminded of his own past run-ins with

Sinclair. 'Though it took me a while to reach the same conclusion.'

Thompson nodded and looked as if he were about to add something, but at that moment Bradbury turned and looked towards the pub entrance. Thompson, Lapslie and Kempsey turned too.

Roderick Daylesford had just walked in.

His poker face gave little away.

The Bell public house, Essex
Three days later

The pub get-together was lively and raucous, the conversations animated, smiles easy – a celebratory atmosphere.

Emma Bradbury had set it all up. Lapslie thought he was meant to be going just for a quiet drink with Charlotte at his local pub, but when he walked in with Charlotte practically his whole squad was already there.

A loud cheer and raised glasses as they came through the door, then a succession of back pats and congratulations that at one point appeared to overwhelm Lapslie. Emma Bradbury directed the cheers like a conductor, from one side, watchful that too much noise might over-load his senses, then calming the cheers to a more subdued level as quickly as possible.

'Sorry about that, sir,' Emma commented as he broke through from the final flurry of congratulations. 'Couldn't resist it.' Then, noticing that he still seemed flushed, she enquired concernedly, 'Are you okay, sir?'

'I'll live – as soon as that strawberry cheesecake and creosote taste subsides.' He forced a cramped smile. 'Besides, the creosote grows on you after a while.'

Emma returned the smile meekly, unsure whether Lapslie was joking or not. 'I felt that *not* celebrating would have been equally wrong – given the history of the case and the problems it has caused you.'

'You're forgiven,' Lapslie said, deadpan. 'I'll buy you a strawberry cheesecake with creosote topping in thanks.'

Emma, more confident that he was joking, joined Charlotte in a brief chuckle.

Lapslie turned to Charlotte. 'You were in on it too?'

'Guilty as charged. My, your powers of deduction are on form today.'

Lapslie rode with it, tapping his nose. 'Ah, creosote sharpens the senses, you see.'

Smiles all round, more backslapping, congratulations.

'Well done, sir.'

'Tough going for a while, but you won through in the end.'

'Much deserved, if I may say. Nice to see you finally winning the day with that supercilious prick.'

The last comment came from Jim Thompson.

Lapslie raised an eyebrow. 'I take it you don't like him?'

Thompson smiled. 'Put it this way, I don't like people who instantly assume that everyone else is less intelligent, so spend most of their time talking down their noses at them.' Thompson took a sip of his drink. 'I suppose I've got one of the few jobs where I might be entitled to adopt that attitude with any certainty.'

'Why's that?'

'Because everyone in my unit is an assistant or rookie learning from me. Detectives such as yourself are reliant on my findings – and everyone else I come into contact with is dead.'

Lapslie nodded and smiled. He pointed to the drink in Thompson's hand. 'Is that your normal Guinness?'

'Yes.'

'Then I think there's something you need to go with that. Hine, isn't it?'

Thompson held a hand up in protest. 'I'm okay.'

'Listen, I promised you one last time. And it's the least I can do after how you handled Sinclair.' Lapslie in turn held a hand up, making it clear he wouldn't take no for an answer, and turned to the bar to order.

As the barman poured the brandy, Thompson enquired, 'When's sentencing?'

'End of next week. With Sinclair having raised the issue of "diminished responsibility" and Reid's "real" mental age, I daresay the judge wants to consider that carefully.' Lapslie paid the barman and passed the brandy to Thompson.

After the James Bulger case, mental age 'diminished responsibility' claims were rarely seen as grounds for a 'not guilty' verdict. If actual eleven- and twelve-year-old murderers could be sentenced and incarcerated, then an adult with that same mental age could not expect to be treated any differently; any mitigation would therefore normally be reflected in sentencing.

Lapslie took a sip of his beer and smiled tightly. 'But we've done our bit. Can't do any more.'

Thompson nodded in mute acceptance; they had enough problems striving for convictions, let alone hoping to influence sentencing. He took a sip of his brandy, a mellow smile rising as he swallowed. 'Ah, pure nectar. Thanks.'

'My pleasure.' Lapslie raised his own glass. 'And hopefully Sinclair is at this moment imbibing a glass of corked wine to reflect the sour grapes he's now experiencing.'

Thompson chuckled, and with a final murmur of thanks Lapslie politely broke away and mingled for a moment, enjoying more back pats, raised glasses and congratulations. And it struck him how drastically things can change, his gaze drifting for a moment to his favourite alcove where he'd sat despondently, alone and in his carpet slippers, after the collapse of the last trial when he'd faced Sinclair. He wondered whether Sinclair was sitting alone right now in a similar pub alcove some-where, sipping his glass of corked wine and nursing his bruised pride. Wishful thinking; Sinclair probably didn't give a jot about Harvey Reid's welfare. Reid was just another client to him. But the reflection gave him pause for thought for a moment, until his introspection was broken by Benedict Allsopp approaching.

'So, we won the day in the end.' Allsopp beamed.

'Yes, we did,' Lapslie said blandly. He hadn't made his

mind up yet about Allsopp, wasn't sure if he felt entirely comfortable sharing his moment of glory with him. Or maybe it was the fact that Allsopp was Rouse's new golden boy – the chief's 'go-between' – that was at the root of his hesitance.

'Hopefully the advice I gave you on handling Toby Sinclair came in useful.'

'Yes, I think it did. Particularly the bit about playing up to his vanity, flattering him. He looked like he'd been caught completely off-guard for a moment.'

'Ah, yes. That's the thing about Sinclair.' Allsopp sipped at his drink, soda with a slice of lemon. 'He's so used to being in combative mode that when someone sides with him, or flatters him, he's not sure how to take it.'

'My last comment casting aspersions on Sinclair got me into a bit of hot water with Judge Morton for a moment, but I think it—' Lapslie was distracted by his mobile ringing, the first bars of 'Knights in White Satin'. But he couldn't feel it vibrating, and when he reached inside his jacket and patted his side pockets, it wasn't there. Then he noticed it, a yard to one side, on the bar counter. Perhaps he'd left it there when he took his money out for the first round of drinks. But he was too late answering it, the caller had rung off; and when he checked his caller history, it was a withheld number.

'I'll leave you to it,' Allsopp said.

'Yes, sorry.' Lapslie looked up as he put his phone back in his pocket. 'And thanks for the advice on Sinclair.'

'No problem. Glad I could be of assistance.' Allsopp smiled primly as he noticed Emma Bradbury heading towards them. 'Looks like you're the man of the hour now.'

As Allsopp drifted off and mingled with the crowd, Emma Bradbury commented, 'Are you okay now, sir? Or are you still getting bursts of creosote?'

Lapslie forced a smile. 'No, that's mostly gone now. Just that Jim Thompson was asking about sentencing, and it got me thinking about Reid. I mean, did you catch his expression when the guilty verdict was read out? I know we're used to people displaying mock shock and horror and protesting their innocence – but this went beyond that. It looked like he truly believed he was innocent.'

'Or Sinclair assured him so strongly that he'd get him off, perhaps his shock and surprise was mostly due to that.'

'Yes, I suppose there is that factor.'

As Lapslie took a sip of his beer, Bradbury could see that he wasn't fully convinced, so she added, 'Or with his lower mental age, maybe he simply didn't grasp the seriousness of what he'd done in the same way as an adult might.'

'Now you're starting to sound like Sinclair. And if I seriously considered that, I might feel some genuine compassion for Reid. But then, when I remind myself of poor Ben Tovey and James Lewis's broken bodies and recall their parents at interview – how destroyed they were – that swiftly evaporates.' Lapslie took another slug of beer, his expression as quickly lifting from its momentary moroseness. 'Still, we got there in the end.'

'Yes, sir. We certainly did.'

For a moment they both rested on their laurels, enjoying the warmth and self-congratulatory atmosphere of their gathering in the bar. And while nothing was said between them in that pause, their expressions – a warm glow tinged with faint awe – said it all: moments of glory like this were few and far between in their work.

Office of the Medical Examiner, East Flanders, Belgium
July 2013

Eric Arles stayed for most of the autopsy on Luke. *Most*, because although he'd arrived on time, he'd agreed with

Medical Examiner Jules Maes that he'd wait out the first twenty minutes of the autopsy – while Maes made his initial incisions, removal, weighing and inspection of organs – then would join Maes for his summary deliberations and to clarify any points which arose.

It wasn't a question of him having an aversion to autopsies, though he'd felt decidedly queasy during the first half-dozen he'd attended when first joining the Antwerp murder squad – and there were many, he knew, who still felt that way – it was more for practicality's sake. He thought that Maes might work more efficiently during the initial stages without him looking on intently – especially given the fact that he was a relative – plus there wouldn't be any pertinent questions to ask until Maes had made his initial examination.

Relative. He wondered whether, subconsciously, Luke being family – one of his favourite nephews – had also partly guided his decision to take a back seat during the initial stages. Seeing young Luke's chest cavity being cut open and his organs removed and coolly examined – juxtaposed with images of him kicking a ball in the park, on the beach at Denia, or playing with a remote-control aircraft that he'd been given one Christmas – might have been too much for him to take. Even after being battle-hardened from witnessing countless autopsies over the years.

He looked up as Maes' assistant peered through the small glass screen that separated the annexe from the autopsy room. She nodded and beckoned with a latex-gloved hand.

Arles was already latex-suited and booted and made little comment for the first few minutes as Jules Maes ran through a quick summary of his findings: liver, kidney, heart and lungs, all major organs within acceptable range for a twelve-year-old boy. 'And no signs of water ingestion in the lungs. So drowning would not appear to have been the cause of death.'

'What would be your deduction as to cause of death?'

Maes pursed his mouth slightly and moved around to the side of Luke's corpse on the slab, pointing to his neck. 'You see here heavy bruising on the base of the neck as it traverses into the shoulder, on this left side.'

Arles nodded. He'd kept the image of Luke's butchered body purposely on the periphery of his vision, but now he was forced to look at it directly. 'Are you saying that he was probably strangled?'

'Yes, but not fully. Only sufficient to cut off his airway and render him unconscious.' Maes took a fresh breath.

'Then I think, shortly after, his head was yanked sharply to one side and his neck snapped.'

Arles nodded morosely. 'So that marking on the base and side of his neck is where you think he was strangled, and the neck's angle is due to it being broken?'

'Yes, I believe so. But the depth of the bruising running down to the shoulder blade indicates that he was perhaps moving and struggling before his killer got a proper grip on his neck. Otherwise, the bruising would just have been to the side of the neck, not lower down like this.'

Another curt, morose nod from Arles, the unbidden image hitting him of Luke struggling against his killer in those final moments.

Perhaps noting his countenance, Maes added, 'I don't think he suffered much. It would have been quite quick.' Maes grimaced tautly. 'If it's any consolation.'

Quite quick . . . any consolation. Arles wondered if Maes would have used the same terms with a detective on an everyday case. Obviously, Maes had been informed in advance that he was related to Luke. Probably Mertens in explaining why a Chief Inspector from Ostend wished to be present for the autopsy.

'And your estimate for time of death?'

Maes considered for a second. 'Well, certainly decomposition is consistent with a body that's been immersed in fresh water for almost two months. And from what I understand, the boy disappeared about that time?'

'Yes, that's the case.' Arles waved one hand. 'But it's the "about that time" which I'd like to dig down further into. In your estimation, would Luke have been killed a day after abduction, or two or three days after?'

Maes mulled over the question for a moment. 'Difficult to say with any accuracy at this late juncture. The only thing which can be assessed with reasonable certainty – from blood lividity and how other fluids have settled in the major organs – is that the body was not moved for at least eight to ten hours after death.'

'I see.' Arles nodded thoughtfully.

Maes appeared to be struck by an afterthought. 'The only other indicator might be what foodstuff remnants we find in the stomach and gut, and the level of digestion. But that would also require you finding out from the mother what Luke might have eaten in the last twelve hours before he disappeared – if you were able to get that information?'

'Yes, yes. I'll ask her about that.' *One possible indicator*, Arles considered; if, indeed, Marisha could remember with the shock of it all. She was still numb, in a trance-like state half the time, and on regular Amytal prescribed by her doctor. He studied Luke's corpse intently for the first time since walking into the room as he came to the final element which had nagged away at him. 'And the stomach wound and severed arm. Do they appear to have been done before the body was put in the water, or after – perhaps by a boat propeller or suchlike?'

Maes looked down for a second. This part was going to be more difficult. 'The stomach wound appears to have been done for a reason – to gain access. When I examined fully, I discovered that a part of Luke's liver was missing.'

Arles cringed, brow knitting at the oddity. 'A *part*?'

'Yes, quite strange. So we're certainly not talking about organ-harvesting,' Maes added swiftly, as if that would somehow make the revelation not so unsettling. 'But both the partial organ removal and the limb severing were done sometime before the body was placed in the water – so that precludes it being done by a boat propeller, which I believe was an early suggestion. The lack of major blood loss plus overall lividity also supports that.'

Arles gestured towards the limb and the stomach wound. 'And the likely implement used?'

'A scalpel, surgical saw or very sharp, weighted knife. They're very clean, clinical cuts.'

'And you say *sometime* before, Doctor. Again, any indication of a more exact time frame? One day ... three days?'

Maes shrugged. 'Again, that can't be determined precisely. From lividity of blood and body fluids, all that can be said with any certainty is that the limb and liver portion were removed at least eight to ten hours after death.'

'Not *before* death?'

'No. As said, I think there was some effort made not to cause unnecessary pain and distress to the victim before death. Some care was taken.' Maes grimaced awkwardly. 'If that's an appropriate term for a killer who then coolly and methodically removes limbs and organs from his victim.'

10

Gabriel's Wharf, London
December 2013

Tom Barton was a pie and pints man.

He'd have pie and a pint at lunchtime at various pubs close to his office, now narrowed down to half a dozen which he felt were the best – but when he wanted a real 'pie gourmet' treat he'd go to Gabriel's Wharf on the river at Southwark. It was over a mile from his office, so he went there at most once a month, saving his visits for special occasions or when he wasn't dining alone to show off their tremendous pie range to guests.

'I'd recommend the pigeon pie or the venison,' he said to Josie across the table.

'Right.' Josie scanned down the men. 'I see they also do pasties, a 'gourmet treat' from my neck of the woods.'

'Ah, coals to Newcastle,' Barton waved one hand dramatically. 'You don't want to be having pasties at one of the best pie places in London. Plenty of opportunity to have that when you're back in Plymouth.'

'True.' Josie kept scanning down the menu.

'Anyway, time to think about what you'll be having while we're waiting.' Barton went on to explain that they'd come to Gabriel's Wharf today because there was someone he wanted her to meet who he thought would help progress her story. 'She's been making noise about a cannibalistic 'clan' being behind a series of murders for a little while now, but nobody's really been listening.' He gave a strained smile, then looked towards the bar. 'Cider, lager or ginger beer?'

'Uh, ginger beer.' She smiled and nodded. She'd been with Tom Barton three months now and so he pretty well knew her usual drinks. In that time, they'd been to various local pubs close to the newspaper office, but this was her first time at Gabriel's Wharf – so she perhaps should have guessed that Barton saw it as something of a special occasion, and that meant they'd be meeting someone else. It was just that he hadn't mentioned anything in advance.

She'd hopped between different YMCAs for six days before finally getting up the guts to contact Barton. By then the bruises from her accident and showdown with

Swan-Tattoo had mostly subsided, but Barton was still sympathetic and, most importantly, a keen listener, becoming quickly enlivened by her account.

Yes, it was very much Barton's type of story. Barton ran a small alternative press and blog site called *TNT* . . . *all the explosive news that's unfit to print*. He'd told her over their first pie and pint together that it stood for 'Tattle-Nuclear-Tale', but that became quickly forgotten after the first year of publication. Founded not long after *Viz*, 'Because that more than anything inspired me that you could get away with just about fucking anything in the magazine business,' Barton told her. The journal went online with the advent of the internet, and now trod a line somewhere between *Private Eye* and WikiLeaks.

'The establishment and big business hate me,' Barton admitted. 'And if they didn't, I'd start to worry that I was doing something wrong.'

Brought up on the wrong side of Manchester, in Salford, and a politics and economics graduate of Manchester University, Barton had been in London now almost twenty years.

Barton had put Josie on a retainer to work the story, with a bit of filling in with subediting other articles to help make ends meet. He'd also found her some cheap accommodation with a lovely 'mother hen-style' landlady, Doreen, in nearby Elephant and Castle. 'Doreen's is a sort of "safe house" too for those writing controversial stories. Nobody will know you're there. And if anyone comes asking for you, Doreen will take that fag-end perpetually hanging from her lips and stub it out on their face.'

Josie liked Tom Barton. He had a ready, self-effacing sense of humour, and she had the feeling that he was doing far more for her than he needed to. Either that, or her story had really grabbed him. Barton admitted he was intrigued by a couple of big names on her list, but the story needed 'rounding off' and more backup substance before he could run with it.

'That's probably the only thing Kevin Lanham at the *Post* got right. Something set in the UK and more recent would provide the cherry on the cake. That's no doubt what enticed you into the set-up.'

But after weeks of digging, she could find nothing in the UK that could possibly be tagged to John Farren's group. The only thing she uncovered was a recent child disappearance and murder in Belgium. The disappearance had been months ago, but then the boy's body had been found in a lake during the summer. She'd told Barton about it straight away.

'The date of disappearance is spot-on, 16th May, and with the body found, initial reports said only that there'd been a "limb-disfigurement". I had to phone the police directly before they admitted, yes, it was the right forearm that had been severed. So right now we know something about that investigation most others don't.'

Barton had admitted to her that, where possible, he liked to have the jump on the rest of the press. Even though most of his work was with stories they wouldn't dream of touching. 'Yes, there is that.' Barton had smiled wanly, perhaps in acknowledgement of that edge. 'Give me a couple of days to think about it.'

Tom Barton was now returning from the bar with their drinks. He set them down on the table, then took an envelope out of his side pocket.

'Oh, before I forget.' He slid the envelope across the table.

'What is it?'

But Barton just nodded to the envelope with a smile, which hinted at some nice surprise: tickets to watch Coldplay or an executive box at Plymouth Argyle?

It was a return flight to Ostend-Bruges International Airport for the following week.

She beamed, leaned across the table and gave him a hug. 'Thanks.'

'No problem. The more gaps we can fill in on all this, the—' Barton broke off as, over Josie's shoulder, he spotted their guest approaching. He pulled back, holding out one hand. 'Josie, here's someone I'd like you to meet.'

'Pleased to meet you.' Josie smiled and dutifully shook hands with a straggly-grey-haired woman in her seventies.

'Betty. Betty McCauley,' Barton said. 'Who'll hopefully be able to fill in even more of the picture for us.'

Chelmsford Police Headquarters, Essex
April 2015

Emma Bradbury noticed those thoughtful, slightly lost moments grip Lapslie over the following two weeks, particularly in the days immediately after Harvey Reid's sentencing.

But it wasn't until she had an appropriate moment one morning while going through pending case files with Lapslie in preparation for his forthcoming holiday break that she ventured, 'Still concerned about the Reid case, sir? Think the judge might have got the sentencing wrong?'

'No. I don't think he could have done more under the circumstances. But even with a recommended fourteen-year tariff, there'll no doubt still be an appeal from Sinclair.'

'And that concerns you?'

'Not unduly so – because I think the chances of success are slim. Though a heavier sentence might indeed have increased the chances of a successful appeal.'

Daylesford had laid out the sentencing options after the guilty verdict: a mandatory adult life sentence would definitely be appealed on the grounds of Reid's diminished responsibility, given his mental age, and would likely be successful: 'The Bulger case was initially a ten-year sentence. But then there are the additional factors that Reid is an actual adult, his mental age is a year or two above that of the Bulger murderers, and he's been found guilty of two murders – indeed, with some degree of cunning and planning, with the planting of evidence at Alistair Tulley's home. The sentencing would normally reflect that and therefore be higher than the Bulger case.'

Lapslie continued, 'So I think the judge more or less got it right with the recommended tariff for an eighteen-year-old murderer.'

'So a sort of halfway house?'

'Yes, I suppose that's one way of putting it.' Lapslie went back to perusing the final pages of a folder in front of him before looking up again. 'But we'll still no doubt see Sinclair trying his luck with an appeal, given that Reid's supposed mental age is a few years below eighteen.'

'But as you said before, sir, we've done all we can – got a conviction. Even if Sinclair is successful, the most he'll achieve is a reduction to ten years. Reid will still do serious time.'

'Yes, of course. Perhaps I'm worrying about nothing.'

Bradbury could sense some lingering concern still on Lapslie's mind as he looked down again at another file and flicked quickly through. Either he was reluctant to share whatever was troubling him, or perhaps he hadn't even got clear in his own mind what it was. He slid two files across to her side of the desk.

'That's the Westbury and Benton files. I think those are the only likely ones to come up and need attention while I'm away.'

'When is it you head off?'

'Friday is my last day here. Then it's off with Charlotte to catch the Eurostar and a stopover that night in Mont-Saint-Michel, before heading down the coast the next day to La Rochelle. George will have left with the boat the day before, so he should already be there by then.'

'If you don't mind me saying, sir – you need the break.'

'Your concern for my welfare is noted.' He managed a lopsided smile. 'I wasn't aware the frayed edges were showing.'

'Sorry. No reflection on your competence intended.' She looked down for a moment at the files he'd handed her as she searched for the right words. 'It's just that, well, some cases get to us more than we're sometimes willing to admit. And I think that James Lewis's murder, given your background with Sinclair, is one such case.'

'I daresay you're right.' Lapslie sighed. 'Hopefully the week away, aside from some well-earned R & R, will give me a chance to clear my thoughts.'

Kombuis restaurant, Ostend
January 2014

They met at Kombuis restaurant in Ostend. It was a Thursday night and the restaurant was heaving, locals already getting in the mood for the upcoming weekend.

It seemed strange talking about death in a setting so full of *life*, Josie thought. But it had been Eric Arles' choice of venue for them to meet up – obviously keen to show off a local restaurant renowned for the best *moules frites* in Ostend.

She was a bit apprehensive upon learning that Eric Arles, apart from being a local police chief, was also related to the victim; that Luke Meerbecke had been his favourite nephew. She supposed that explained why a police chief from Ostend had become involved with a case from Beernem almost forty miles away, with the body finally found in a lake near Brussels.

But given that personal involvement, she realized she'd have to soften many of the more macabre elements she might have more openly shared with an unrelated police officer.

'And you're certain that the right forearm missing from Luke's body was severed purposely?' Josie enquired. 'It was a clean break?'

They were almost twenty minutes into their meeting, the introductions and preambles out of the way, their food ordered, before Josie asked the crucial question. After all, if the forearm had been severed accidentally by a passing boat, then there would be no possible connection to her past cases. She'd gone for *moules frites* too, and the central platter of mussels put in front of them four minutes ago, piled high and interwoven with salad and onions, was impressive.

Arles was a tall man, and Josie had noticed him waving to and acknowledging a few people as they'd walked in. He was obviously a well-known local figure.

'Yes, our medical examiner was pretty sure,' Arles said, dabbing at his mouth after his fifth mussel. He held a hand out. 'A clean break wasn't so much a factor. A propeller might have achieved that too. It was the lack of major loss of blood before the body was buried in the lake that determined the cut was made beforehand.'

'Buried?'

'Yes. The body was initially weighted down. A passing boat or fishing line loosened those ties. Plus the mud and silt at the bottom of the lake was harder than usual.' Arles eased out a slow breath, obviously pained by the recall. 'I don't think it was their intention that the body be discovered.'

Josie nodded. On all fours with the other cases. Suspect disappearances were numerous, but discovering actual bodies with that telltale forearm severing were few and far between.

'And no limb found nearby in the lake?'

'No. Although that might have been more difficult to discover in such a large lake.' Arles was thoughtful for a moment as he chewed another mouthful of food. 'You mentioned some other past cases which might tie into this case now with Luke. When and where did those take place, if I might ask?'

'The first main case which set off my investigation was quite some while ago. In fact, going back to 1944 and the last year of the Second World War in the south-west of England.'

Arles' eyebrows rose, and she went on to explain that the case had only come to light recently due to a human-interest story on a dying veteran. Only as she mentioned some possible later cases did his quizzical expression relax.

'Though I say "possible" because only the dates of the boys' disappearances matched, no bodies have ever been found. The last firm case we had with a body found with right forearm severed was in fact in Gdansk, Poland, in 1977.'

'So none particularly recent, and not all of the cases in England?'

'No, true.' Josie was unsure what point Arles was making. 'As indeed with this case now, it would appear.'

'Well, that explains one thing,' Arles said. 'Usually the first to contact me over such things are other police departments making connections to current cases they're handling. The cases you mention would have been off their books long ago.'

Josie nodded. So now the point was clearer: only a journalist would bother herself with such long-dead cases.

But another thought appeared to hit Arles then, bothering him. 'However, with the cases you mention, we certainly aren't looking at the same killer being responsible for them all. So what possible connection do you see between these murders?'

Josie liked mussels, as any Plymouth-raised girl should, but after the eighth or ninth they became tiresome and more difficult to chew and swallow. Now she found herself swallowing without any mussel sliding down to constrict her throat. Arles was probing, edging in.

'We're still putting all the pieces together, trying to work out the connection.'

Arles lifted his napkin and dabbed at his mouth after another mouthful of mussel and two fries. 'But what are your main theories?'

'We have a few, but it's probably too early really to speculate.'

'The same family, perhaps?' Arles pressed. Met with silence from Josie, he added, 'That would be quite an extended family, given the time span and the number of countries involved.'

'Yes, it would.' Josie swallowed again. *Too close for comfort.* Another prod from Arles and she'd be into Betty's centuries-old-clan-flesh-sampling territory, which she wanted to avoid, especially given his family ties to Luke. 'Which is exactly why we don't want to say too much until we've finished our investigation and joined up all those dots. We're well aware of the unlikelihood of that scenario.'

Ile de Ré, France
April 2015

Four days later, the case was still on Lapslie's mind. He'd hoped that whatever was troubling him would fade as he got deeper into the holiday and relaxed more. But it had almost the reverse effect: as his thoughts relaxed, he started to get a clearer picture of exactly what was niggling him about the case, and on day four the final component parts fell into place. He let them settle and did a quick part-by-part review, in case he'd missed something vital.

Charlotte's voice drifted up from the galley. 'Sausages, bacon and eggs up in just ten minutes.'

'Okay. Great. Fried bread, too?'

'No, toast. We don't want to make it a complete cholesterol overload.'

Lapslie could hear the smile in Charlotte's voice, and smiled to himself as he looked out across the small harbour. They were moored fifty yards from the quayside at La Flotte, one of the most picturesque villages and harbours on the Ile de Ré. The whitewashed buildings reminded him of the Greek islands or Ibiza, and they'd spent the previous afternoon meandering through its narrow cobbled lanes, where he'd bought Charlotte a brightly coloured sarong she'd taken a fancy to.

She'd held it up worriedly at first. 'You don't think it makes me look too much like an ageing hippy?'

'Nothing sa'wrong with that.' He forced an apologetic smile at the pun. 'No, seriously. It suits you.'

They'd decided to dine that night at a seafood restaurant by the harbour, which looked appealing, then they'd spent that night in the harbour and were planning to set sail mid-morning – after he'd had his 'full English'.

Four days and they were completely into the French lifestyle: French bread, brie, pâté, seafood, and practically every meat in a rich and delicious cream sauce. The only break had been that, after three days of croissants, Lapslie had a sudden yearning for a 'full English' – though he'd still swill it down with a strong coffee or two.

Charlotte came up beaming proudly, a plate in each hand. 'There you are. Fit for a king.'

Lapslie nodded his thanks as he took his plate. Thankfully, sausage, bacon and eggs was one of those smells and tastes that didn't engender another smell or taste. It remained true to its own – which Lapslie was grateful for. He didn't somehow think the smell of asphalt would have gone with it.

He'd been good at hiding his lingering concerns from Charlotte, not wishing to dampen the holiday mood. Besides, if she'd caught him looking sullen and thoughtful for a moment and asked what was troubling him, he wouldn't have been able to answer directly, because he hadn't been able to pinpoint exactly what it was – until that morning. So now he was eager to bounce his thoughts off someone, put them to the acid test of a second opinion; and right now Emma Bradbury was 300 miles away.

'You know this recent case of mine with young James Lewis and Harvey Reid?' He rolled straight on after a swift nod from Charlotte; it was almost a redundant question, given how much it had consumed his life, on and off, in recent months. 'There was one small element which troubled me.'

'Which was?'

'You'll recall that it was argued Harvey Reid had diminished responsibility, that he was operating well below his mental age – indeed, somewhere between a twelve- and fifteen-year-old, depending on the psychiatrist or social worker consulted.'

'Yes, I recall you explaining how it became an important part of Sinclair's defence of Reid, and finally no doubt led to a reduced sentence.'

'Exactly.'

That had been practically Lapslie's last word on the subject before the holiday, telling her about Reid's sentencing, as if to say: *that's it, case wrapped and sentenced. We're free to go now.*

'But what suddenly struck me was that you have someone who on the one hand has obvious learning difficulties, yet on the other hand is duplicitous enough to plant evidence to set someone else up.'

'But I thought the evidence which finally convicted him – James Lewis's limb – was found right in the middle of the barn where he stayed, on and off, through the summer.'

'Yes, that part rings true with someone of limited mental capacity; the limb was left carelessly in the barn where Reid slept and also wrapped in his own *Racing Post* copies. It was more the limb found at Alistair Tulley's fourteen months beforehand I was thinking of. That part required some planning and forethought, which seems out of character with what we know of Reid.'

It had been recalling Roderick Daylesford's words in summing up, pre-sentencing – *indeed, with some degree of cunning and planning, with the planting of evidence at Alistair Tulley's home* – which had finally helped his thoughts to gel.

Charlotte's brow knitted. 'What? Are you thinking that Sinclair should have picked up on that, perhaps made more of it?'

'Very much so.' Lapslie cut a fresh bit of sausage and dipped it in his egg. 'At first when I ran through everything in my mind, I thought perhaps he might have painted himself into a corner with this "third-party planting" claim. But focusing more on Reid's mental capacity, well, that indeed might preclude him from being crafty and inventive enough to try to frame Tulley. Therefore, it had to be someone else – ergo, a third party – so why didn't he jump on that more, to support his claim?'

'Yes, good point.' Charlotte nodded thoughtfully as she chewed and swallowed a bit of toast with Boursin. She was still on a partly French-inspired breakfast. 'Are you thinking that if Reid himself wasn't capable he might have had an accomplice? The "third party" raised?'

'No, not for Reid. But hold that thought for a moment and look back at Tulley.' Lapslie's eyes drifted for a moment across the tranquil bay as he focused his thoughts. 'We know, for instance, that Tulley was inside when the second murder took place, so it couldn't possibly have been him – so in that respect an accomplice starts to make more sense.'

Charlotte held up a hand. 'But Tulley was cleared, in the end, of that first murder. So there would have been no need for his accomplice to commit a second murder in order to point the finger at someone else.'

'Ah, yes. And that sticking-point blocked my clarity on the topic at first. But at that stage they couldn't have known that Tulley would be cleared; in fact, the odds might have looked weighted towards him being found guilty. And if he was found guilty, a killing with an identical MO would have provided the perfect grounds on which to launch an appeal: *the murderer is still out there, we told you that you'd got the wrong man and evidence had been planted first time around.*'

'Why didn't they just wait until the verdict had been given?'

'Because that might then have appeared too engineered. A guilty verdict, and suddenly there's another on-all-fours murder. And if James Lewis's murder had taken place *after* Tulley had been cleared, he might well have been rearrested for that one – everyone immediately thinking they'd got it wrong first time around.

Also, I think there's another reason the murder took place when it did.'

Charlotte arched a brow. 'Oh, why's that?'

'Habitual behaviour pattern. Don't forget the two murders took place at practically the same time, a year apart. And people with impaired mental capabilities are often kept to strict regimes, which they then get used to applying to themselves. Step outside of that and they get upset.'

Charlotte nodded thoughtfully. 'But this evidence-planting tack could easily have backfired on Tulley. Because if we think in terms of Tulley having an accomplice, he could then have been implicated in planting the evidence on Reid to clear himself.'

'Exactly. And I think that's why Sinclair stepped gingerly around it and didn't make more of it, because it could then have been turned around to implicate his past client.' Lapslie took a fresh breath. 'Indeed, it was that factor that initially surprised me when I heard Sinclair was taking the case: a possible conflict of interest between his clients, with the guilt of one exonerating the other. But then, as we got further into the proceedings, I discovered that Sinclair had very craftily focused in on the theory of a third-party evidence-planter, common to both suspects. So any conflict was gone – indeed, they both shared a common cause.'

'Quite ingenuous, then.'

'Yes. Which is what we've come to expect from Sinclair.'

Charlotte shrugged. 'So why wasn't that tack successful with a jury this time?'

Lapslie shrugged in turn. 'I don't think it would have bothered Sinclair one way or the other if Reid was cleared – he'd got what he already wanted with Tulley. But I think he knew at heart that a third-party evidence-planter might be accepted in one case, but *two*? That was stretching it a bit – plus the DNA and *Racing Post* evidence and the fact that Reid was doing Tulley's driveway at the time of young Ben Tovey's murder. *Opportunity* rears its head.'

Charlotte sipped at her coffee as her thoughts settled. Then, as the realization hit her, 'My goodness! Are you suggesting that Sinclair might have been involved in some way with this evidence-planting, or indeed knew about it?'

'Very much so. I don't see how else he'd have known to steer a clear path through it all to present his case.'

Charlotte nodded slowly. 'But how would you ever get to know or prove that theory? Not the sort of thing that you'd find out through the Bar Council.'

Lapslie sighed. 'No, it isn't. But villains often end up knowing the fighting weight of solicitors and barristers: who will or won't be willing to pull a fast one or turn a blind eye.'

Charlotte raised a challenging brow. 'And I daresay you know a few of those villains.'

'Yes, unfortunately, more than I care to think about. But often that too ends up something of a closed shop – coppers are the last people they talk openly to.' As he pondered on the one or two reliable snitches he knew, he was reminded about Emma Bradbury's relationship with Dom McGinley. He sipped at his coffee as he briefly surveyed the bay again, his eyes narrowing. 'Though hopefully we'll hit on someone willing to open up.'

Elephant and Castle, south London
January 2014

Perhaps if Tom Barton hadn't already been awake, he wouldn't have heard the faint noise from downstairs. Light steps, something being moved?

He wasn't totally sure. Could be his dog, Wilson, an Alsatian–Labrador cross, moving around or lapping at his water bowl in the kitchen. But this sounded more towards the lounge area, and different from Wilson moving around – unless the dog had bumped into a dining chair or some furniture. Unlikely. Didn't they use Labradors as guide dogs?

He'd heard Wilson barking ten minutes ago, which is what had woken him, but the barking had stopped after a minute or so – otherwise he'd have got up to investigate. But listening out, there had been nothing since, and he was just on the edge of dozing off again when he heard the faint sound from downstairs.

He sighed and swung his legs out of bed. He'd better go down and check it out.

Barton wasn't a security freak, but he was cautious nonetheless; necessary, given his line of work and some of the controversial subjects TNT covered. A few years back, he'd had a permanent bodyguard for almost eighteen months, supplied by HM's security services, following an exposé article on two radical imams.

But now, for the past year, it had just been his security cameras and his trusty Second World War Browning service revolver. Barton was an avid collector of antique guns and rifles, and let that fact be known through TNT and other press and TV interviews – not only to deter madcap imams but also local thieves. The Browning was one of the few working examples of his collection, and he kept it regularly oiled and loaded in his bedside drawer.

Barton checked the monitor screen in his bedroom, switching between the front door, hallway and back kitchen-door views. Nothing untoward on any of them. He put on his dressing gown, took the gun from his bedside drawer and headed downstairs.

Towards the bottom of the stairs, he called out tentatively, 'Wilson?'

No answer, which struck him as strange. Wilson might have slept through that small sound, if identifying it as non-intrusive or non-threatening. But he'd have bounded up, tail wagging, when his owner was barely halfway down the stairs. Let alone all the way down and calling out his name.

He tried again as he approached the kitchen door, 'Wilson?'

His apprehension rose, nerves tightening as he slowly swung the door wide. Wilson was laid out prone on the floor only two yards on the other side, just out of view of the back-door camera.

Barton's heart clenched. He knew immediately from its awkward position that the dog wasn't asleep, and he knelt and quickly felt the pulse in Wilson's neck. Thank God! Faint pumping, light breathing. He was still alive!

Perhaps Wilson was ill, had stumbled into some furniture before finally keeling over. Possibly that was what the earlier barking and later noise had been about. All he could think of.

The door from the kitchen to the dining room and lounge was only two inches ajar. He couldn't get a clear view of the room beyond. And, listening more intently now, he also couldn't hear any more sounds.

He straightened up, his Browning leading the way as he went cautiously towards the door, pushing it slowly open with his left hand, gun in his right. The view that he was presented with in the faint glow filtering through from the outside streetlights perplexed him at first: what looked like a rope noose suspended from the central ceiling-lamp rose hook, with a dining chair directly beneath.

He switched on the lounge lights, not sure if he was seeing right amongst the shadows – and as the light hit, causing him to squint, his gun hand and arm were clenched tight. A strong, paralysing grip – he couldn't even squeeze the trigger, let alone swing the gun towards his attacker.

The gun was shaken loose from his hand, clattering to the floor. At the same time a larger man came at him from the other side, the two of them shifting him quickly towards the chair and lifting him on to it.

Barton knew immediately what was about to happen, and writhed and bucked. But to no avail, the two of them had him in a vice-like grip – the larger man on his own holding him easily as his colleague put the noose around his neck and tightened it.

Then the chair was kicked away.

Barton's hands went frantically to the rope around his neck, but they were pulled back behind him and held firm. His vision blurred as the room swayed around him, his breath gasping.

His only saving grace as the life ebbed from him – still thinking like an investigative journalist to the end – was that if they intended to make this look like a suicide, they probably wouldn't kill Wilson. They'd spare his dog.

11

King's Cross, London
October 2008

They arranged to meet in a café two hundred yards from King's Cross station, Angelo's. Within their first few minutes of sitting down, Betty McCauley explained that the reason she'd recommended it was that it was one of the few cafés in the area that wouldn't shoo vagrants away.

'They're quite happy to let you sit over a cup of tea for an hour or so, particularly in the winter.'

The smartly dressed young man she was meeting looked briefly around the café and noticed half a dozen others amongst the thirty or so in the café who could be vagrants or bag ladies like Betty.

'So, they finally decided to send someone out to meet me,' Betty said. 'Take me seriously at last.'

'Yes, they did. And that privilege has fallen to me,' the

young man said, smiling graciously. He'd purposely used the word 'privilege' to add some weight and import- ance to the meeting. His department was the closest Scotland Yard had to an *X-Files*-style operation, and after nine years of meeting notes and letters from Betty with no more than polite standard 'holding' responses – *Thank you for your additional information. We will certainly look into how this might assist in throwing further light on this case and will keep you informed of any new develop- ments . . .* – it would be easy to assume that they weren't taking her 'additional information' that seriously. But then, with a recent case which had crossed his desk and the last letter from Betty, that stance had changed.

'So was it my mention of the connection between Dimock and Sinclair which caught your interest, or the previous boys who went missing on a similar date to my David's disappearance?'

'Both were contributory factors.' He took the first sip of his latte and smiled understandingly. Betty was hav- ing a luxury hot chocolate with cream and cinnamon topping and a slice of lemon cheesecake. Probably a rare treat and a change from her normal tea because Scotland Yard were paying. 'But before we get into that, best we start at the beginning. Some of your past letters and comments have been handled by my colleagues before my arrival, so I want to make sure I am fully up to speed.'

'The beginning?' Betty arched a brow sharply and took a sip of her hot chocolate.

'Yes, if that's okay. Not a problem, is it?'

'No, no problem. Just that the true start of this story goes back some while before David's disappearance in 1974. Some five hundred years before, in fact – to Scotland, in May 1496. On the Ballantrae Coast in Ayrshire, if I can take you back for a moment to those horrendous events . . .'

James IV sat proudly on his grey mare as he surveyed the scene ahead. A faint mist still clung to the hills by the coastline, even though they'd left it until late morning to move in. A growing band of highwaymen had been laying siege to travellers in the area, many of them never to be seen again. The local sheriffs and magistrates should have taken care of the problem years ago, but after two searches along the coastline with nothing uncovered – and with the number of disappearances causing such alarm that stories had now spread from nearby Dumfries to as far as Edinburgh – more drastic intervention was required.

Crowned at only fifteen, and now twenty-three years of age, James IV was still a young king. While no doubt many of the tales had been embellished and become more gruesome and alarming en route from the Ayrshire coast to Edinburgh, James nevertheless saw an opportunity to improve his standing and popularity by taking personal action and laying the fears of locals and travellers finally to rest.

He took with him a sizeable division of 350 men, led by his right-hand field general, Travis, and a pack of thirty blood-hounds. But for the first hour, with nothing uncovered, and some of the bloodhounds spreading in different directions along the fields and coastline clifftops, he too feared his gang of men might not uncover anything. Then, as the mist started finally clearing, five or six of the bloodhounds appeared to pick up a scent in the same direction, and the rest of the pack quickly followed. At that moment Travis rode towards him through the last wisps of coastline mist.

'Sire. It appears they've found something. The men are fol-lowing the bloodhounds' lead, and some caves are now visible ahead.'

'Are these caves accessible from this direction along the coast?'

'It appears so, sire.'

James broke his horse into a steady trot in the direction of the bloodhounds. 'Then we should follow with all due haste.' Just before encouraging his horse into a full gallop, he added, 'But leave forty or so of your men in the fields at the back of the caves, just in case there are other entrances and possible escape routes.'

Travis nodded and urged his horse into a heavy gallop, riding ahead to give the instruction.

As if a portent of what lay beyond, a last patch of mist clung to the mouth of the main cave. James and his men heard the sound of baying bloodhounds and some grunts, shouts and shrieks from the struggle within. The tide was mostly out, so there was barely a foot of water as they made their way in.

And as the final mist cleared and the king's eyes adjusted to the dim light, the sight presented to him made him catch his breath for a moment: half-butchered torsos hung from the walls of the cave, visible body parts were hanging out of barrels, while a collection of men, women and children of varying ages – grimy and in rags, and some smeared with blood – sneered and hissed at him as they were held back by his men. The scene was given an even more ominous, hellish atmosphere by the glow of a fire on which a cauldron brewed, the red glow flickering on the cave walls and the bloodied corpses.

James picked out an elderly man with straggly grey hair and gnarled hands; perhaps he was their leader.

'What is your name?'

Only a guttural grunt came in return, the old man shaking off one of the soldiers who were holding him, to wave an arm in protest.

James started to count the numbers in the cave, but lost track at over thirty. Some of them were still moving around and others remained indistinct in the background.

'Do we know how many we have here?'

'Forty-two or -three,' Travis answered.

James nodded solemnly. 'And do we have them all?'

'I believe so . . .'

But one of the soldiers behind who had recently ridden up to join them half-raised his pike staff, appeared more uncertain. 'If I may, sire. We might be a little hasty in reaching that conclusion.' Under his king's withering gaze, he went on to explain that a nearby farmer had approached them shortly after they'd taken up position at the back of the caves, saying that he'd seen a number of people running across his fields ten or fifteen minutes beforehand. 'Men, women and children, grimy and in rags, like these ones here.'

James was lost in thought for a moment. The baying of the hounds had certainly been evident for a while, so might have forewarned them. 'How many people?'

'At least a dozen. Maybe as many as eighteen or twenty.'

'James's men tracked down two or three of those escapees from what was known locally as the Bennane Caves, but no more than that.' Betty took a quick sip of her hot chocolate. 'Though they wanted, of course, to keep that as quiet as possible. Having just quelled one lot of horror stories, the last thing they wanted was to give rise to a new set. And whether only ten or fifteen slipped through the net that day, their descendants now number in the hundreds.'

'And it's these "descendants" that you think are connected to these current disappearances and murders today?'

'Yes, without a doubt. They've gone on to infiltrate every facet of public life, both here and abroad.' Betty shrugged. 'Yes, some of them are just waiters or manual workers, but then we have barristers like Toby Sinclair and MPs like Gerald Caulfield. I've made a list of the most likely ones.' Betty fished a folder out of one of her two shopping bags. He noticed that both bags were full of nothing but folders and papers. She opened the folder as she slid it across the table, tapping at the list on top, a sly smile rising. 'You could even have some of them in Scotland Yard. Who knows, you could be one of them.'

'Well, I haven't eaten you yet, so I think you're safe for

now.' He patted his stomach. 'Besides, got to leave room for a slice of cheesecake. It looks quite appetizing.'

He thought he could get away with the jibe on the back of her teasing, and it might also help ease the cloying mood after her gory descriptions. But as her mouth hung open for a second, he thought he might have read it wrong.

Then she burst out laughing and punched his arm lightly. 'You're all right, you are.'

He beamed a tight accord in return. Praise from vagrants. An internal promotion couldn't be that far away, he thought wryly. But his focus quickly settled on the names of Gavin Dimock and Toby Sinclair in the list. Dimock was the main suspect in a recent child disappearance, and Sinclair was one of three barristers slated to represent him.

'And these are all people you suspect are descended from these Bennane Caves escapees?'

'Yes, it took me years to put together. But those I contacted in the Ayrshire and Dumfries region were particularly helpful. To them, you see, this tale of Sawney Bean and his gang is part of their local folklore – as important as Robin Hood is to the English. So I got a lot of help in marrying up local rumours and new names appearing on historical registers between Dumfries, Edinburgh and Glasgow, and their descendants since. That's not all of them, mind you, only sixty-three names there, whereas I think they're in their hundreds now, a number of them abroad. And some of those names I might have got wrong. But it's a start.'

He nodded. *A start?* A somewhat lightweight term for Betty McCauley's years of research. He leafed through some of the newspaper clippings.

'And these clippings link to names in the list, give some guide as to how it's been compiled?'

'Yes. If you look at the fourth one down, about Sinclair, in that article he talks about his family clan being traced back to the "Court of James IV". But no Sinclair can be found in those close to James IV, so I think this is a sly play on words by Sinclair, as in "almost caught by James IV".'

He grimaced tautly. He could just imagine his chief rolling his eyes if he ran that one by him. But it was the Gavin Dimock and Toby Sinclair connection which had brought him out to see Betty today. That, and past disappearances of young teens who had gone missing in the same month as her own son.

'You mentioned also in your letters about specific limb-severing and a particular time of year?'

'Yes. But that ties into what Sawney Bean and his clan did to their victims before killing and eating them, and how they in turn were killed when James IV caught up with them.' She took a bigger slug of her hot chocolate, as if more sustenance were needed for this part of the story. 'You see, when they first caught their victims they shackled them and then cut off their right forearms and cauterized the stump in an open fire. They'd then roast that limb on the fire and eat it while their hapless victims looked on and considered their fate to come. Other limbs were then cut off and cauterized as needed, before they finally killed and butchered their victims.

'When King James finally caught them, public outrage called for an extreme punishment, so that's what was done to them – well, the male members of the Bean clan at least. Each had their right forearm cut off and cauterized, and they were then shackled again to watch and wait while it was done to the rest of their clan. Then their remaining limbs were cut off and they were left to slowly bleed to death. Finally, a big fire was built – all of this in front of an eager crowd by Leith Castle – and the women thrown on it and burned as witches, then the children thrown on after them, including infants and babies.'

'Punishment to fit the crime,' he said with a resigned sigh, as if that might help assuage the brutality and somehow explain the five-hundred-year gap in the evolution of retribution and justice since. 'And how many did this highway-robbing clan of cannibals start out as?'

'Maybe only eight or ten. Sawney Bean, a younger brother, two cousins and their respective womenfolk. Though local folklore has it that they also captured a number of women and kept them just for procreation. But for the most part their numbers grew through incest, reaching almost seventy over a twenty-five-year span. And the number of victims was rumoured to be five hundred to a thousand over that period.'

'And since – due to those who possibly escaped?'

Betty dug into her shopping bags for another file and dumped it on the table between them, opening it and sifting through. 'More difficult to pinpoint, obviously, but we have one child found dead with its right forearm missing in 1748. Another in 1821, one more in 1874 . . .'

'So, more spread out – and all some while ago.'

'Yes, but of course they've become more careful since.

Make sure the bodies are buried where they can't be found, especially today. Criminal record-sharing these days would too easily link these deaths.' Betty leafed through the clippings more frantically. 'But still we have one here in Berlin in 1937, an eleven-year-old with the same disfigurement ... another in Russia in 1956 ...'

He reached a calming hand across the table, touched her arm. 'It's okay, I'm not doubting you. It's just that I have to answer to others, and they might be more questioning.' He looked again at the clippings she'd spread out. 'All of these child murders are around the same time of year?'

'Yes. Early to late May.'

'And why is that significant?'

'Because that's when the clan was caught and most of them killed. A specific date can't be pinpointed, it was simply entered in records for that period as "between Easter and the summer solstice".'

He nodded, gesturing towards the files. 'So you see these more recent disappearances and murders as some form of homage and remembrance of that original event?'

'Yes.'

He'd noticed a fervour in Betty's eyes as she'd related everything. Possibly the drama and gore of the tale, possibly the fact that someone was at last taking notice of her and so she finally had a shot at justice and retribution for her lost son, after all these years.

It had obviously been a real labour of love for her over the years, some might term it an obsession, and he felt slightly guilty now that some in his department had labelled her 'mad Betty' due to the notes and letters she'd send in every other month.

But with only a couple of matched names and a few coinciding dates to link these cases to a 500-year-old tale, it would still be seen as tenuous by colleagues. Until such time as either there were bodies uncovered with the same severing of the right forearm and the same date, or the likes of Dimock and Sinclair came more to the forefront. There was also the prevailing thought amongst colleagues, which he had no ready answer for, that Betty, in desperately searching for answers to her son's disappearance, had latched on to this local Ayrshire story simply because she was originally from that region and so the tale meant something to her, had more resonance. He didn't want to suggest that to her directly, so he couched it as best he could in a tame question.

'Much of this indeed might end up holding substance.' He gestured towards the files. 'And we'll certainly be looking harder and deeper at both Dimock and Sinclair. But what I don't understand is why you think this five-hundred-year-old clan with links worldwide might be responsible for your son's disappearance. We've never even found a body, let alone the limb-severing you describe here.'

Betty patted the file, a gleam in her eye as she leaned across. 'That's the thing. The link is right here. The farmer who reported to King James's men seeing people escaping and running across his fields – his name is Joshua McCauley.'

Elephant and Castle, south London
January 2014

Josie started to tap one finger impatiently on the table. Almost ten minutes now she'd been waiting.

She'd gone into the police station at the Elephant and Castle, the nearest to Tom Barton's home, and said that she had some vital information about Barton's recently reported suicide.

A female desk sergeant made no comment and didn't ask any questions beyond asking Josie's name and relationship to Tom Barton.

'Just a work colleague. I worked for Tom for a while.'

Then she was shown to an interview room down a side corridor, one of four or five in the same stretch, Josie noted.

A small room, no more than eight-foot-square, with a table and two chairs on each side. The door had a foot-wide glass panel stretching most of its length. If they'd opted for a small pillbox-style window, it might have felt like a holding cell, Josie thought. A couple of people passing had looked in at her.

Then finally, two minutes after her finger-tapping had started, an officer walked in. He introduced himself as Detective Sergeant George Strudwick, heading the Barton case, and spent the first few minutes covering the details she'd already given to the desk sergeant.

'. . . and is this the address you're at now?'

'No, it's not.' Josie had given her original Plymouth address. 'I've been in London for a while now.'

'I was going to say – you're a long way from home.'
Strudwick forced a smile. 'And where are you staying
now, while you're in London?'

Josie looked at Strudwick's pen poised over his pad.
She had no intention of disclosing her current address.
The whole idea of Barton setting up her safe house with
Doreen was that nobody knew her whereabouts, and
that included the police.

'I'm staying with friends right now. But I plan to be
moving soon.'

'Okay. But where can we contact you meanwhile, if we
have a need to?'

'I can be reached on my mobile, and I regularly check
my emails too.' Josie gave Strudwick her mobile number
and email address.

Was it her imagination, or was Strudwick disappointed that she hadn't given a current address? Or
perhaps he just found it unusual.

Strudwick took a fresh tack. 'I understand you have
some information regarding Mr Barton's reported
suicide.'

'Yes. I don't believe it was suicide. I suspect he might
have been murdered.' No point in beating around the
bush.

Strudwick appeared to be off kilter for only a moment. 'And what might lead you to believe that?'

'Well, first of all he wasn't the type to commit suicide. Also, we were in the middle of a big story that he'd have been keen to see through to the end.'

Strudwick nodded, then briefly consulted a file to one side. 'As for Tom Barton not being the "type", his sister informed us that he suffered from depression four or five years back. Were you aware of that?'

'No, I wasn't.' Though perhaps Swan-Tattoo and his crew had been aware of that, so knew that suicide wouldn't appear too odd. Then she recalled another event Tom had mentioned from five years back. 'Although that would have been just after Tom's divorce, so perhaps that was a factor. I certainly found him very upbeat during the time I was with him.'

'And how long was that?'

'Nearly five months.'

'Five months? So you might concede that you didn't know Mr Barton as well as, say, his sister.'

Josie met Strudwick's gaze steadily. 'I can only comment as to how I found him, not regarding what went before.'

Strudwick nodded, sought refuge for a moment by looking back at pages in his file. 'Now, as for possible murder. What makes you suspect that?'

'It links to the big story I mentioned we were working on.' Josie sat forward keenly. At last they were getting to the nub of it. 'The people involved would have done anything to avoid exposure.'

Strudwick shrugged. 'But I understand that was the nature of Barton's publication, *TNT*. So by that token, you could name any number of people that he had stories aimed at.'

'Not like this.' She didn't want to get into the ramifications of the investigation, knew from experience that this would just engender doubt, be considered a 'claim too far' – but she needed enough to support her case. 'Our investigation involved a number of children disappearing over the years, and some high-profile figures were implicated, including politicians.'

Strudwick nodded in acceptance after a second. Hopefully she'd struck a chord; rumours about paedophile cases involving politicians had been rife over the past few years.

Strudwick held a hand out. 'Even if that were the case, we have the issue of Barton's dog. He would have barked or intervened in the case of a murder, would as a result have been harmed or perhaps also killed. Yet he was discovered alive and well.'

Josie's mind darted around for possibilities. 'Perhaps they locked the dog in another room at the time.'

'There would still have been signs of an initial struggled or scratching at a door. Nothing of the kind was noticed.'

'Or perhaps it was drugged or somehow knocked out.'

'I think we're stretching things a bit now,' Strudwick said, with an incredulous smirk rising.

'Are we? We're talking about a very inventive group of men here. I was set up with a false story, abducted by them and barely got away with my life. That's what brought me into contact with Tom Barton in the first place.' But as soon as she'd blurted it out, she realized from Strudwick's reaction that she'd made a mistake.

'I see.' Strudwick was thoughtful for a second. 'And did you report this abduction and attempt on your life to the police?'

'No, I didn't,' Josie said, her stomach sinking with the admission, realizing her last chance of building a credible case was probably gone. And it would just make matters worse if she added that Barton had advised her not to. Raising the issue of possible mistrust of the police was probably not the best card to play while sitting in a police interview room. She started to feel uncomfortable, felt she'd made a mistake coming to this police station now to report her fears.

'Any particular reason for that?' Strudwick asked.

'Since the false story might have been set up through a leading newspaper office, we weren't sure how far the tentacles of this organization spread.' This was the closest she felt she could go without spelling it out directly. Strudwick was hopefully astute enough to join up the dots, though from the dawning realization on his face, it took a moment to do so.

Strudwick looked around; another officer was knocking on the glass pane of the door. Strudwick wasn't sure at first if he was coming in, but as the officer made a beckoning motion, Strudwick went over and opened the door. They stood in a huddle by the half-open door for a moment – Josie wasn't able to hear their conversation – then Strudwick looked back at her.

'Sorry. Something's cropped up, I'm afraid. I won't be a minute.'

And then she was on her own again, resuming her finger-tapping on the tabletop as another minute passed and there was still no sign of Strudwick. She shouldn't have come here in the first place, should have trusted Barton's word that there was only one police department he'd trust with something of this magnitude. But she simply hadn't been sure that this other department would have details of Barton's suicide.

And what was so urgent that Strudwick felt he'd had to break off from their interview? Then it struck her: maybe they were trying to trace her current whereabouts from the few details she'd given, and the officer knocking on the door had an update on that. *Or perhaps it was simply a delaying tactic to allow Swan-Tattoo and his crew to get into place for when she left the police station.*

Her throat felt suddenly dry, the room constrained, claustrophobic. She was overwhelmed with the urge to get away, *escape*.

And after twenty seconds of more finger-tapping, with still no Strudwick returning, she edged towards the door, opened it and looked out: nobody in sight, except some people in a general office visible through a similar part-glazed door at the end of the corridor. She was sure that if she chose her moment and was quick, she could make it out without being seen by anyone.

She waited until the person closest to that door was turned away, partially blocking the view of the corridor for those beyond, then slipped out, picking up her pace rapidly. Four more paces and she'd be at the door at the far end where she'd entered, then maybe only five or six more paces to make it across the entrance vestibule and out.

She took a fresh breath of resolve as she opened the end door and kept her gaze straight ahead, hopeful that the desk sergeant to her side didn't think anything untoward, perhaps assuming her interview had ended. But thankfully somebody else was at the desk holding her attention.

And then she was out and walking briskly away. No sign of Swan-Tattoo or any police pursuing her; and as she let out a final breath of relief, she wondered whether she might have built up her fears too much, been too hasty in leaving.

Better to be safe than sorry. Nothing was being achieved by staying, in any case, and she could always call later to see if Strudwick might have had a change of heart and was ready to launch a murder investigation.

12

'So, no emergencies while I was away?' Lapslie enquired.

'No, nothing to speak of, sir. The CPS called to say that a preliminary hearing date has been scheduled for the Reid appeal. Just over a month from now, and they expect it to run a half-day at most.'

'Okay. I'll note it in my desk diary.'

Bradbury smiled primly. 'Already done, sir.'

Lapslie nodded. Ever-efficient Bradbury.

'Anything else, sir?'

'Yes, there was, actually.' He hadn't wanted to make it the first subject aired, even though it had been predominantly on his mind since the possibility had been raised. But some of that depended on Emma's current situation with Dom McGinley, her ex-villain boyfriend for the past four years, so he needed to tread carefully.

For obvious reasons, Lapslie had strongly advised against the relationship, before finally giving up the ghost. He gave his best paternally concerned grimace. 'I wondered, are you still seeing Dom?'

'Yes, I am. Why?'

'No problems now?' Lapslie would get to the why in a minute, when he saw how the ground lay on other fronts; in particular, a situation not long ago when Emma feared Dom was becoming suspicious of her seeing another man (which indeed she had been at the time).

'No. That's all settled down now.'

'So you've stopped seeing the other guy?' The slight pause and flicker of concern that crossed Emma's face in that instant made Lapslie fear the worst. 'For goodness' sake, Emma. I made it clear to you before – that isn't the wisest of moves with a man like Dom. He could end up taking a chisel to your face, or worse.'

'I haven't seen the other guy in months.'

'How many months?'

'Three or four.'

Lapslie paused, absorbed in thought for a moment. 'But you're planning to – is that what you're saying?'

Another pause, with a conflict of emotions crossing Emma Bradbury's face.

'I don't know,' she said. This wasn't the sort of conversation she wanted to be having with her boss. She saw his point, but it was too intrusive. She wanted to keep her private life separate from her work – but when you were hitched up with an ex-villain, that was more difficult to do. She'd explained it before, in her own mind and to Lapslie, her theory of 'opposites attract', and how their own work was very similar to that of a villain's – just the other side of the same coin. They had more in common with villains than perhaps they were willing to admit.

'But if now, with you having stopped seeing this other guy – a schoolteacher, if I recall correctly? – everything's settled down with Dom. Why risk that?'

She shrugged, deflecting his question with another, 'I don't know.' Then added, 'And he's a college lecturer, actually. Genetic engineering.' Bradbury pondered that, while Lapslie might understand that first part of the equation, how was she to take it to the next stage of explaining that both men satisfied different needs in her?

Dom was hard-edged, manly, direct, and she liked that about him. While his soft-edged side was formal and predictable, with buying flowers or taking her out for meals, his protective nature was equally predictable for a villain: if anyone was threatening her, he'd warn them off or put a bullet in their kneecaps. She felt safe with Dom, as long as – as her boss rightly pointed out – she didn't two-time him.

But with Peter, the lecturer, his soft-edged side was something else entirely: sharing passages in books or philosophical debates covering a whole range of subjects – travel, lifestyle, ethnic diversity, ecology, fashion trends – that she simply didn't get with Dom. He answered a more thoughtful, feminine side in her. She recalled when she was younger being attracted to guys with long hair who were 'artier', perhaps for the same reason. But now it was hard to find guys with long hair who weren't either bums or ageing hippies. And she didn't realize that this had been an underlying need of hers over those years – until she met Peter. So now she was caught between satisfying those needs and possibly upsetting Dom – losing that harder, protective side which she also needed; and also, as her boss bluntly put it, possibly getting a chisel in her face.

'I haven't got any plans right now to see this other guy, if that's what you're worried about.'

'It's not me who needs to worry, Emma.'

'Yes. You've made that very clear.'

Lapslie sighed. 'So what you're saying is that you might see this other guy at some stage, but not right now?'

Emma Bradbury didn't answer, just stared steadily back, which Lapslie supposed was an answer in itself. Then after a second, she said, 'Sir. You've obviously asked about Dom for a reason. What might that be?'

'Yes, yes . . . I did.' Lapslie was caught off-guard by her directness, a clear indication that she thought he'd gone too far. But he stopped short of an apology. 'There's something I'd like you to ask Dom – about our barrister friend Sinclair.'

Bradbury shrugged. 'Why would Dom know much about him? They move in totally different circles.'

'They do. Very much so. But villains tend to know the fighting weight of many barristers. Which ones are best to defend armed robbery or murder cases, which are best with fraud or extortion . . . that type of detail. After all, a villain's entire fate often depends on whether they choose the right solicitor and barrister.'

'And what was it you specifically wanted to know about Sinclair? After all, we know from his first run-in with you over Tulley that he's no slouch when it comes to murder cases.'

Lapslie smiled crookedly at the sideswipe, and perhaps

he deserved no less after giving Emma a tough time over Dom. 'Yes, we know he's strong with murder cases, but is he also a barrister who can be tainted?'

'In what way?'

Lapslie glanced down. He'd hoped to be able to delay airing his concerns fully until he'd ascertained whether Bradbury felt Dom might be able to help; but he couldn't see a clear way of short-circuiting that now. He took a fresh breath as he explained his concerns about the Reid case, very much as he had done mid-holiday with Charlotte. 'So what I'm keen to find out is whether Sinclair has a reputation for involvement with cases where evidence might have been covered up or tampered with? Or even in some cases planted?'

'I see.' Bradbury nodded, then fell silent for a moment. 'And was this what was troubling you before you went on holiday?'

'Yes. But I didn't have my thoughts on it fully clear then. Now I have.'

'Are we talking about perverting the course of justice here?'

Lapslie met Bradbury's sharp look; the acknowledge-ment was clear between them that this was a career-ender for any barrister if uncovered. It would have to be handled with kid gloves, and he tempered his answer accordingly. 'Yes, we are. But not overtly. Sinclair could never admit that he was directly involved in any of that, or had any knowledge of such actions – otherwise he'd have been struck off years ago. So, if anything, it would be a silent conspiracy, and might only show up in the number of cases Sinclair had where suspect evidence might have been an issue. But something might have also filtered through on the criminal grapevine that, if you wanted a barrister who might turn a blind eye to all of that, Sinclair is your man.'

'I see.' Bradbury nodded thoughtfully. 'And you haven't shared this suspicion with anyone else, aside from Charlotte and myself?'

'Of course not.' Lapslie could see that, thankfully, Bradbury had the lie of the land clear too: this wasn't something they'd wish to come back and bite them, especially when dealing with a character like Sinclair. He smiled slyly. 'Why do you think I'm going about this the unconventional, out-of-department route by asking you about Dom?'

She mirrored his smile, though more uncertainly. 'Rouse would go apoplectic if he got wind of it. Apart from the dangers of going against Sinclair with something so potentially explosive, there's also the fact that it would mean yet another failed case on the books if Reid was cleared.'

'Yes, I'm aware of that.'

A connected afterthought hit Bradbury. 'Right now you're in Rouse's good books, having salvaged your reputation after the first disastrous case with Ben Tovey. Are you sure you want to unpick that and go back into the doldrums again? While, in a perverse way, also handing Sinclair another victory with the Reid case.'

'I think the term you're searching for is *pyrrhic* victory.' Lapslie smiled tightly, took a fresh breath. 'But regardless of what Rouse's internal case-victory score sheet might say, if my theory is proved right, Sinclair has won yet again – because he's got what he wanted with Reid. And as for my own victory in this, I'm not sure I'd feel comfortable with that, knowing that an innocent man has been jailed.'

'I understand.' Bradbury nodded solemnly. 'I'll find out if Dom might have heard anything.'

'Thanks. I'll check my contacts too. I've got a few snitches always keen for a bit of extra beer money.'

*

Over the next few days, Lapslie had two more conversations on the subject with Emma Bradbury and another with Rebecca Graves – the one officer they both felt could be trusted not to let the topic slip outside of their circle. Ostensibly, Lapslie liked to feel he could trust all of his team not to talk out of turn, but it was more a question of who might be more lax and prone to gossip, and so could inadvertently let the subject slip. Bradbury had reminded him that, two years ago, Graves had apparently had a harassment issue with another officer. 'Apparently', because they'd first got wind of it through someone else in the team, yet when they'd asked Graves directly about it, she'd refused to say anything and possibly implicate a fellow officer: 'The talk that went around the squad room was that she'd "take the information to the grave" with her. So it's unlikely that she'd spill the beans over this either, sir.'

As the thoughts and comments they'd bounced around coalesced, he started making a core question list:

- Timing: Just pure chance that Ben Tovey and James Lewis were murdered at almost the same time a year apart, or planned or significant in some way?

- Sinclair as the barrister in both cases: did Harvey Reid's solicitor approach him, or did Sinclair make the first move?
- If input from Dom McGinley or snitches indicates some past form with Sinclair, then what past cases have given rise to that? Any similar past cases involving attacks on children?

Then he started making his calls. His first was to Gerald Coates, Alistair Tulley's solicitor. He spun the story that some bright spark at the CPS had raised the issue of just how and why the same barrister was used in both the Tulley and Reid cases, 'And so I'm trying to find out so that I can close the file internally.'

'I'm afraid I don't have any idea, either,' Coates commented.

'I see.' Lapslie took a fresh breath. Chamomile and rose hip. No smell or taste indicator that Coates was lying or covering up. 'But possibly a good starting point in joining up the dots is how you first came upon Toby Sinclair. Was he one of your usual roster of barristers, or did the recommendation come from elsewhere?'

'Elsewhere, in this case. Indeed, from Tulley himself – he said that Sinclair had been recommended by a friend as a strong barrister with "unusual and challenging" murder cases.'

'Did he give details as to who that "friend" might be?'

'No, he didn't – though I must admit, we didn't particularly ask. This case was always going to be a stretch for our regular barristers, so when we had a briefing with Sinclair and he seemed to tick all the right boxes, we didn't ask questions beyond that.'

'And did Harvey Reid's solicitor, Roland Mattey, contact you about Sinclair?'

'No, he didn't.' Then, after a second's deeper contemplation, 'Though that might be, as I said, because he wasn't one of our usual roster of barristers. Though I daresay Mattey might have contacted Sinclair directly.'

'Yes, I daresay.'

After finishing up with Coates, that was Lapslie's next call. Roland Mattey was in a meeting, and so he didn't get to speak to him until after lunch. Mattey was more circumspect, so Lapslie had to dress it up a bit.

'I think the issue has only come up with this CPS pen-pusher because of the possible issue of a conflict of interest between the two clients, Tulley and Reid.'

Mattey sighed. 'Yes, indeed, Chief Inspector. And that's exactly why no such contact with Sinclair would have been initiated by my office.'

'So, you're saying that you weren't first to contact Sinclair – he or another party contacted you initially?'

'You're quite a quick learner, Chief Inspector.'

'I try my best,' Lapslie said, deadpan, but inwardly he was smiling. No doubt Mattey was still miffed after their last run-in, especially with having lost the case. But he'd managed to get Mattey to open up, obviously keen to exonerate himself from any misstep or wrongdoing.

'In this case it was Sinclair himself who tackled straight away the issue of a possible conflict of interest – by stating that, actually, in this case he felt there was a common interest. He proposed that the same evidence-planter with the Tulley case had been at play again with Reid. Obviously, I was intrigued by this angle and felt it had a strong chance of convincing the jury, and then Sinclair's dazzling form with the past Tulley case pretty much guided the rest of it. Quite simply, given that background, I'd have been a fool not to advise my client to go with Sinclair.'

Lapslie sensed a plea in Roland Mattey's voice, as if convincing himself as much as Lapslie that he'd made the right decision by ignoring that initial possible conflict of interest. Lapslie, though, couldn't resist a further prod. 'And do you still feel you made the right decision?'

'Yes, I do. Very much so.' A suddenly more defensive tone. 'Toby Sinclair pushed strongly in court the case he presented to me and Reid – that of a third-party evidence-planter – it's simply that events ran against him on the day.' Mattey took a fresh breath. 'But there'll be an appeal – which both I and Sinclair feel assured will be eminently more successful, and we'll find justice finally for Harvey Reid.'

Justice for Harvey Reid. Roland Mattey's words struck a chord with Lapslie. The very same thing that was at the root of his quest now – their only common bond – but he couldn't share anything on that front with Mattey, nor indeed anyone else outside the tight circle of Charlotte, Emma Bradbury and Rebecca Graves. But as he finished with Mattey and looked again at the third core issue on his pad, he suddenly realized there was one connected point he'd missed with Gerald Coates. However, when he called back, this time Coates was in a meeting and it was almost an hour before he finally got to speak to him.

'Sorry to trouble you again. One thing I forgot to ask this morning: you'll recall the trial was initially set for late April. But then, out of the blue, came an unforeseen delay – which then pushed the date back by seven weeks. Do you recall whether that came about through your offices, or Toby Sinclair's? Or was it ordered by the judge and the court sessions arranger?'

'That was from Sinclair's end. A timing conflict with another case which had overrun, and also one bit of evidence he wasn't happy with and wanted to look at in depth again.'

'I daresay that didn't please Tulley too much; with him not having bail, and being held in prison for those extra seven weeks.'

'I daresay not.' Coates's tone lifted. 'Though I'm sure if that last bit of evidence examination led to him finally being cleared, he'd have been able to look on the bright side of it.'

'Yes, there is that,' Lapslie agreed.

He tapped one finger thoughtfully on his notepad after hanging up. So Sinclair had not only done most of the running, he'd also engineered that final seven-week delay in the Tulley case. Crucial, because if Tulley had already been released when James Lewis's murder took place, he'd have been the first suspect. Which brought Lapslie's focus back more acutely on to the related point: had James Lewis's murder initially been planned earlier – to take place exactly a year after Ben Tovey's – thus coinciding with a date that was somehow preset, preordained?

Emma Bradbury had trouble getting to sleep that night. And when she did finally drift off, her sleep was fitful, interspersed with dreams.

Dom was gently stroking her throat, but on the third or fourth stroke, it became bolder, stronger, his hand wrapping around her neck and starting to grip her more tightly by the throat.

It was a replay of a night a while back when she and Dom were making love and he gently stroked her throat midway through, as he sometimes did, her breath coming shorter, almost mirroring an orgasm – but then the grip started to become tighter and tighter, and she felt her breathing almost totally restricted – before Dom finally released his grip.

At the time, she'd been midway through her on-off affair with the college tutor, Peter, and she worried that Dom might have suspected something and this was his subtle way – albeit unsubtle to her and most people – of warning her off.

This time, though, the pressure on her neck in the dream was more constant, tight and restrictive, but without actually choking her; and the menacing part came through the leer on Dom's face as he stroked and pressed – which then as quickly changed to Tulley then Harvey Reid – before returning to Dom again.

She woke up with a start, eyes flickering to bring herself back to the reality of the darkened bedroom. She'd obviously disturbed Dom, because she felt him turn towards her and reach one hand out towards her back, gently stroking. But as the hand snaked up to softly caress her neck, she brushed it away, sitting up sharply in bed.

She took a sip from the glass of water she always left by her bedside, and could sense Dom's eyes on her back.

'Are you okay?'

'Yeah, fine.' She realized that her action of brushing his hand away had probably seemed brusque. She couldn't relate the dream to Dom, didn't even fully understand it herself. Was it guilt, because she still thought about Peter and had plans to see him again? 'Just a bit of a tight throat, that's all. I'm sensitive to being touched there when it's like that.'

She coughed to back that up, took another sip of water and padded to the bathroom. She stayed on the toilet a moment more than she needed, getting her thoughts settled, and when she walked back into the bedroom Dom's eyes were closed. Whether he was actually asleep or feigning it, she was pleased that she didn't have to offer any further explanation right then; that might have kept her awake for a while afterwards.

But the subject was obviously still on Dom's mind the next morning, because he raised it over breakfast.

'You feeling better now?' he asked over a freshly filled cup of coffee.

'Yes, fine now. It comes and goes.' She took a sip of her own coffee, grimaced. 'Maybe I'm just a bit wound up over this current case.'

Dom nodded, thoughtful. 'I have noticed you working quite a few late nights with Lapslie on it.'

Emma shrugged. 'I always have those, regardless of the case.'

'Yes, I know.' Dom's stare was level and appraising across the table. 'But more than normal.'

'It's a difficult case,' she said. But as Dom's gaze remained steady, as if that answer wasn't quite enough, she looked down, took a bite of her pain au raisin pastry.

Were Dom's comments code for *I don't know whether you're still seeing another guy or not, so I'm just going to lump it all together with extra hours with Lapslie*? It was true that on many of the past evenings when she'd sneaked time off to see Peter, her excuse had been extra hours working a case with Lapslie. And now that it was a real excuse, it was coming back to bite her.

Or maybe Dom was just venting his frustration over her extra hours worked, regardless of who or what was responsible. The complaint of many a copper's partner or spouse. Dom was resentful of the extra hours she worked with Lapslie purely because it stole home-time away from him; and she'd exacerbated that by adding on some extra hours for the time away with Peter. So, in a way, the two were merged in her own mind as much as Dom's.

But she saw now an opportunity to perhaps soften that resentment by involving Dom more in the case and those extra hours it was demanding. She recalled the topic Lapslie had raised the other day about the 'inside SP' on Sinclair; now was probably the ideal time to broach it because Dom had raised the issue first.

'Though there is one area you might be able to help with on this current case. Something Lapslie in fact mentioned just the other day.'

'Oh, what's that?'

Guarded surprise, but she could tell that Dom's interest had been piqued. She took another sip of coffee to get her thoughts clear, then she started to explain what Lapslie hoped to find out on the villains' network about Toby Sinclair.

13

Scotland Yard, London
January 2014

'I was sorry too to hear about Tom Barton's death. I only read about it a couple of days back in the newspapers.'

'So nothing reached you internally about it?'

'No. But then it wouldn't with a suicide. If it had been elevated to a murder case, then it would no doubt have filtered through to my department. But from what you say, that looks unlikely to happen – unless I push things from my end.'

Josie nodded. They'd gone to a Caffè Nero a couple of blocks from Scotland Yard, one where they could tuck themselves away in a back-booth table and have reasonable privacy. Alongside a telephone number, Tom Barton had written the man's name down simply as 'Scobe', a nickname apparently given him by Betty McCauley: 'So he's already up to speed on this story from Betty, and I've been feeding him bits and pieces too. But if for any reason I'm not around, or I'm unavailable, contact him directly. He's probably one of the few people at the Yard you can trust with this story.'

But reflecting now on Barton's comments when he'd handed her the scrap of paper, it made Josie wonder whether subconsciously Barton was concerned something might happen to him; or at least was taking precautions if it did.

'How long were you with Tom?' Scobe asked.

'Barely five months. But we became very close in that time.' She wondered whether part of that 'closeness' had come out of sheer desperation: the knife-edge set of circumstances which had brought her to Tom Barton's door, and what she saw as her last hope. And now perhaps, too, she saw Scobe as a replacement 'last hope'.

'Do you think Betty knows about his death yet?'

'I don't know. She hasn't contacted me about it.'

Scobe lapsed into thought for a moment. 'But then she often gets so absorbed in trawling back through old news stories that she doesn't pay attention to current news – at least for a few days.'

'It's okay. I'll phone her, break the news to her.' Josie

grimaced awkwardly. 'Probably better coming from me, given my association with Tom.'

Oddly, Betty had been the one to introduce Tom to Scobe. Tom knew of the department – one of the few he trusted at the Yard – but these had been his first dealings with Scobe directly. Though when Tom had brought Josie up to speed on the connection, he explained that he'd quickly added his weight to Betty's contact with them: 'It appears that she'd been contacting them for years, and this character Scobe was the first one to sit up and take any notice. I didn't want that focus to dissipate, so I was keen to add my support to her tale. And of course what you've now brought to the table furthers that support.'

Josie had spent the first ten minutes with Scobe venting her concerns about the suicide, very much as she had done at the Elephant and Castle police station the day before. Part of that account appeared to trouble Scobe, and he now went back to it.

'And the people you escaped from before contacting Tom – you think they might be the same people who staged his suicide?'

'Yes, I think so. There wasn't anything else nearly as controversial and incendiary that he was working on.'

'So this would be the man with the swan tattoo, and any possible accomplices?'

'Yes, I . . . uh.' Josie faltered, her brow knitting. 'But I don't recall mentioning him to you.'

'No, but Tom did.' Scobe smiled tightly. 'You might not have mentioned him or the incident directly to the police, but Tom wanted to make sure it was on the system somewhere and getting tracked.' Scobe shrugged. 'In case it linked or matched in with something else we have on file.'

'And did you manage to link it to anything?'

'There was a possible match through the MOD to someone, but we've found only a few tenuous links to this particular group. And he certainly doesn't seem to be actually part of that clan.'

'Oh, I see.' After the brief glimmer of hope, Josie felt disappointed.

It obviously showed on her face, because Scobe was quick to offer his reassurance. 'I don't think that would necessarily point away from his involvement. Not everyone working on their behalf is going to have the same ethos or directly be part of this extended clan, particularly for some of their "dirty work". Some "mercenaries", if you will—'

Scobe broke off for a moment as a waitress came close to clear the table next to them. He took a fresh breath as she moved away. 'And if this was, as you claim, a staged suicide, what do you think might have led them to take action at this stage? After all, you'd been working this investigation with Tom for some months before that.'

Josie took a sip of coffee, applied her thoughts for a moment. 'Tom was concerned that while there were a number of historic cases, we had none that were current.' She held a palm out. 'Sure, there were a number of suspect disappearances in early to mid-May in the UK, but none where a body had been found with the right forearm severed. So I started digging and found something in Belgium just last year, with the body only discovered two months later because it had been submerged in a lake. Tom got me to go over and investigate, and I'd put the full story on his desk just a week before his death.'

'You think he intended finally to run with the story, and that's what set everything in motion?'

'I think so.' Josie shrugged. 'I can't think of anything else that would tie in timewise.'

'You don't think he was still holding out for a more recent UK-based case?'

'Well, if he was, he didn't mention it to me.' But from the way Scobe had asked, she sensed he had something specific in mind. 'Why do you ask?'

Scobe sighed. 'Perhaps I have to admit to some guilt on that front. I'd told Tom previously that I could only push things so far internally with my department with merely historic cases to go on. And cases abroad carried limited weight because they should primarily be investigated by the police in the countries concerned, or by Interpol.'

Josie felt exasperated. 'Are you saying that these foreign-based cases, including this more recent case of a young boy murdered in Belgium, don't help at all?'

'No, I'm not. Because each piece of the puzzle helps, lends overall weight to my efforts. It's just that with a more recent UK-based case, I could ensure it had prime-time attention within my department, devote more resources. That would without doubt be the cherry on the cake.'

Chelmsford, Essex
April 2015

'What do you think?' Dom looked across the dining table hopefully.

Emma took another mouthful and nodded her approval. 'It's good. Good. You've got hidden talents I didn't know about.'

'I thought I'd give it a try, you know – something more exotic. Beef bourguignon. Bit of a mouthful.' Dom smiled.' But hopefully not because I haven't cooked the beef enough. I can see why Dumper always called it "Beef Bugger-on". Tender enough?'

'Yes, perfect. Almost melt in the mouth.' She didn't want to dampen Dom's spirits by saying it tasted just like his mum's trusted boiled beef and carrots, just with some wine splashed in and courgettes replacing the carrots. Dom had taken to cooking more the past couple of years, particularly when she'd been working late, but at first his repertoire had been restricted and mainly inherited from his mum's old recipes.

Dom took a sip of wine, waving his glass for a second. 'Oh, talking about Dumper, unfortunately this barrister Sinclair didn't ring any bells with him, and Horseradish Tom and Jesus weren't much use either.'

'Oh, right. I didn't know you'd started any digging on that front.'

The rogues' gallery of Dom's circle of friends; Dom had given her the background on their nicknames long ago. 'Dumper' was a getaway driver, but had gained his name from dumping getaway cars in unusual places; 'Horseradish' because he always had a hot tip on horse races, and 'Jesus' because he was Jewish and had been a carpenter for a few years before becoming a 'fence'. Michael was his real name.

'Well, you did ask – and I don't like to let the grass grow and all that.' Dom took another quick swig of wine. 'But I did hit a bit more luck with a name passed on from Horseradish – Gary Tic-tac.'

'Tic-tac?' One nickname she couldn't recall from Dom's usual roster.

'Yeah. Gary Baxter. Bit of a blast from the past, so you probably wouldn't remember him. Haven't seen him myself for a while – but that's mainly because he's been inside for a stretch.'

'I see.' Emma seemed to vaguely recall a story about an old blagging partner of Dom's always having a packet of mints on him and being handy with offering them around. Could that be the same Gary? 'But he's out of prison now?'

'Yeah, but just the past year or so.' Dom took another mouthful of food, was thoughtful for a second. 'But sounds like he'd have still been inside if it wasn't for this Sinclair character. He originally got sent down for eight years as an accomplice in an armed robbery, and this guy Sinclair was handling his appeal.'

Emma noticed a fresh gleam in Dom's eyes as he spoke, a spark that she hadn't seen there for a while. Was it just talking to all his old villain buddies, or talking about them, that had enlivened him? Or was it suddenly being involved in one of her cases, when so often he'd be detached and only a passive listener?

'And Sinclair got his sentence reduced?'

'Yeah, and then some. But it was the way he did it that was impressive.' Dom leaned forwards. 'And there was far more to the story than might first appear on the surface.'

Private sports club, Reading
January 2014

'So do you think it went well?' Toby Sinclair asked. 'Smoothly?'

'Yes, I think so,' Mandrake said. 'It'll have looked like suicide, as instructed.'

'That's good. Good.' Sinclair took the first sip of his tea. Like all good barristers, he never asked a question without first having a good idea of the answer. So he'd waited four days for this meeting, so that he could gauge from the initial press and police reactions that Tom Barton's death had been determined as 'suicide'.

Sinclair knew that Mandrake wasn't his real name, just a moniker gained from his early days with the SAS in Afghanistan. One night one of their regiment had been killed, so he'd gone out with a unit of twelve in the dead of night to enact their usual ten-to-one policy. He'd been personally responsible for four of those kills, with one of them killed so deftly and silently that none of the five Taliban sleeping close by had been disturbed. A fellow SAS man had described him moving silently and gracefully, 'like a swan', and the moniker had been born. When investigations started into the army's conduct in Afghanistan and Iraq, the MOD shifted him from the front line to a desk job in Colchester. But he'd quickly become bored.

Only five-foot-six, and prematurely balding at the age of thirty-one, apart from his strong muscle tone he was far from an imposing figure. But aside from his ability to kill silently and gracefully, Mandrake's nondescript appearance made him ideal for surveillance work.

They were meeting now tucked away in a quiet corner of the café at a Reading sports club. Nobody was within earshot; the closest people were three tables away, with most in the room watching the tennis game on a large screen at the far end. Mandrake had arrived there two hours beforehand for his regular gruelling gym and weights session, while Sinclair had indulged in just half an hour in the gym and fifteen minutes in the sauna.

Mandrake smiled crookedly. 'Would have been simpler just to put a bullet through his head and save one for the dog too.'

'Yes. But for that I could have hired any goon from the backstreets of Deptford or White City. It's your expertise that I'm paying for.'

'Ah, yes. My expertise.' Mandrake sipped at a San Pellegrino.

'Which wasn't quite so apparent with the girl.' As Mandrake stared icily across, without a flinch or pause in sipping his water, Sinclair wished he hadn't said it. Mandrake had little sense of irony or humour, and his professional acumen was a particularly sensitive area. The barrister forced a smile, waved a hand to one side. 'No matter. What news on that front?'

'It appears she's gone to ground. No sign of her.

Wouldn't be surprised if she hightails it back to Plymouth.'

'Well, she never reported her initial abduction and chase to the police. So I daresay she was already on thin ground as to who she felt she could trust. Hopefully Barton's "suicide" will have been the final straw.'

Mandrake shrugged. 'If it isn't, I'd have no qualms about getting rid of her.'

'I'm sure you wouldn't.' Sinclair looked back levelly. No doubt dispatching the girl would be seen by Mandrake also as a way of making good on her escaping from him that night. 'One suicide, okay. But two closely linked together would look highly suspicious. And, as explained before, we only take ultimate sanctions against people when absolutely necessary.'

Mandrake stared back impassively, and Sinclair knew from past experience that it was hard to explain such subtleties to Mandrake.

At one of their first meetings, Mandrake had commented, 'So your little group has a "thing" about kids. Means nothing to me either way, this is just a job to me.'

'It's not a "thing", as you term it. There's no pleasure in it, and we insist that they're unconscious first so that they suffer no pain.' As he'd sought to explain, he realized that uncharacteristically he was losing his usual calm demeanour. How to explain to someone outside of your clan that your ancestors had been hunted down like animals and killed in the most brutal way possible? And that this simple blood-rite, which paled in comparison, was the only thing to stand as testament to that memory, keeping that ethos and their spirits alive.

The fact that they had managed to do so for over five hundred years stood as testament also to their ingenuity and enduring spirit, which Sinclair took a certain pride in. He revered the Machiavellian skills required to continue such a clandestine activity undetected over so many years, rather than the blood-rite itself. But Sinclair knew that it was often difficult for outsiders to understand that core ethos, which is why they only dealt with a handful of them at any given time. In Mandrake's case, his 'specialist kill' skills were rare.

In the end, the only way he'd been able to explain it to Mandrake was to relate it to those special skills. 'You know how your SAS unit had a strong history and tradition of operating stealthily and silently, and killing in the same manner where necessary? It was an important part of what made them who they were. And then you became part of that ethos and tradition, and proud of it, so you wished to continue it to the best of your ability – no matter what the cost.'

He'd seen a final glimmer of recognition in Mandrake's eyes at the mention of regimental tradition, as he knew he would, lending both a glory and acceptance to Mandrake's many kills over the years.

And he used some of that now as he started to wrap up his meeting with Mandrake. 'No different from your days with the army. You only kill those necessary to achieve an aim or objective. Never anyone superfluous, or for personal gain or gratification.'

Old Windmill public house, Essex
April 2015

'Okay. What was it you were about to tell me about Sinclair?' Lapslie said, forcing a taut smile. 'Before we got so rudely interrupted.'

Emma Bradbury had been about to share with him what she'd been able to find out from Dom about Sinclair, when Benedict Allsopp had knocked on Lapslie's office door and peeked his head in. Lapslie had decided that it was getting too risky to talk about the case at the station, so had decided to meet at an out-of-town pub two miles away at lunchtime, arranging also for Rebecca Graves to meet them there. Lapslie had started their meeting by laying down the ground rules of future meetings where they'd discuss the Sinclair case.

'Too many prying eyes and ears back at the station for something as delicate as this. As we all know, if Rouse got wind of it, he'd clip our wings in no time. So in future anything to discuss about the case will be at the Old Windmill here, and the other place will be ...' Lapslie thought for a moment. 'The café in the Springfield Garden Centre, just off the A12.'

Bradbury nodded. Both locations were relatively quiet, which suited not only holding private meetings but also Lapslie's condition. Plus the fact that neither were regular haunts of others on the force, so it was unlikely they'd bump into colleagues there.

'From hereon in, these will be known simply as "Place One", the pub here, and "Place Two", the garden centre café. So even if, by chance, anyone overhears that we're meeting up, they won't know where.'

Keeping any information away from Benedict Allsopp had become as important as keeping it from Rouse, with Allsopp being so close to the Chief Superintendent. Despite Allsopp's help with the Sinclair case, he hadn't become popular with the squad. One of the most vocal on the subject was DC Derek Bain, who'd joined the squad only three months ago. He complained about Allsopp forever snooping around, like some 'phantom time-and-efficiency man'. Benedict quickly became 'Been-a-Dick' when Bain related stories, and Allsopp got changed to 'Balls-Up'. That generally raised a few laughs in the squad room, quickly muted when Allsopp would appear on one of his regular sorties. Perhaps part of Bain's resentment was that they both covered some of the same ground; both were good liaison men with outside departments. And the fact that Allsopp was Rouse's new golden boy fuelled a resentment that was then shared with the rest of the squad.

Bradbury started to share her discussion with Dom.

'He didn't know much directly about Sinclair, so this information – the "SP", as Dom terms it – came from a mate of his, Gary Baxter, sent down for eight years as accomplice to an armed robbery, with Sinclair handling his appeal.' Bradbury took a quick sip of her drink, an orange juice, before continuing. 'A crucial part of the initial conviction was due to shells from a shotgun registered to Baxter being found lodged in the bank roof – nobody was actually shot; these were fired solely in warning. Eyewitnesses putting him on the scene were non-existent – everyone was wearing ski masks – and Baxter claimed the shotgun had been stolen in a robbery at his farmhouse five months beforehand. He'd reported the robbery, but not the missing shotgun, so this was made a meal of by the prosecution, and the jury convicted him.'

'As they well might, given that set of circumstances.' Lapslie nodded slowly. 'So how did Sinclair hope to turn that situation around?'

'He got Baxter to admit why he hadn't included the shotgun in that initial theft report – because he'd in fact sawn the end off, so thought he'd get into trouble for that. Sinclair made the point with Baxter that the sentence for sawing-off would be far less than accomplice to armed robbery, adding, "And don't worry, I'll get around the *Ladd* v. *Marshall* objections the prosecution will no doubt raise."'

'And Sinclair won the day at appeal with that new tack?'

'Yes, he did. Got Baxter a one-year suspended over sawing-off and cleared of the armed robbery conviction. Sinclair apparently built a strong case out of Baxter having no past links with the crew involved in the robbery, and the fact that they obviously kept quiet about his alleged involvement, otherwise they'd implicate themselves in his farmhouse robbery too.'

'Impressive.' Lapslie took a fresh breath, 'And what reasons did he offer, if any, for sawing down the shotgun in the first place?'

'Baxter's farmhouse is fairly remote, and he'd had a suspected break-in just months before the bigger break-in, so he'd sawn the shotgun down for more effective protection. Not to shoot anyone – more to warn them off.'

'And was that true?'

'The smaller break-in, yes, but Baxter had confided in Sinclair that it was to warn off some guy who'd been heavy-handed with his nineteen-year-old daughter and almost raped her. Sinclair didn't think that would go down too well with a judge and jury, so suggested linking it as a protective action to the last, smaller break-in.'

Lapslie nodded thoughtfully as he sat back. 'So not averse to bending the truth if he thought it might get the right result.'

'Yes, it would appear so.' Bradbury reflected that getting the information from Dom had in a strange, unexpected way helped remedy a growing problem area in her relationship with him: it made him feel more involved in something concerning her and Lapslie, rather than being kept on the outside of that circle, which was normally the case. She looked across the table as she took another sip of her drink.

'There was something else, though, that Baxter thought was worth sharing. On one of Sinclair's visits to Belmarsh Prison to prepare his appeal, at one point another prisoner passed them, closely escorted by two guards. Sinclair apparently raised a brow, commenting, "High security risk, eh?", and Baxter put him straight that it was a "nonce", and the guards had to be with him for his own protection whenever he came out of isolation and into the general prison population: "The other prisoners would 'ave him at the first opportunity."'

'Yes, pretty much standard in most prisons – keeping child-molesters separate for their own safety,' Lapslie agreed. But from the glint in Bradbury's eye, he suspected there was a sting in the tail of this story. 'And what was Sinclair's reaction to that?'

'Sinclair apparently pulled a sour-lemon disgusted face at the mention of the word "nonce", commenting that it wasn't his cup of tea, either. "I'm afraid that I could never with a clear conscience represent a man like that." '

'Odd to say the least,' Lapslie commented after a moment. On the face of it Sinclair's stance was completely at odds with his defence of both Alistair Tulley and Harvey Reid. But he wanted to let his thoughts settle more on the topic, so he meanwhile turned the conversation to what might have been uncovered on past similar cases.

Rebecca Graves spoke first; she'd taken the lead on that front, with Bradbury more preoccupied researching Sinclair's past form. 'Nothing identical at all going back over the past twelve years. I can go further back, if you like?'

'Was that just local – Essex and surrounding counties? Or did you go national?'

'National. Well, England and Wales.'

Lapslie nodded after a second. 'Yes, okay. Dig further. Go back another ten or fifteen years, and include Scotland and Ireland as well.' Lapslie was contemplative as Graves made a note in her pad. 'You say not *identical*. Were there any vaguely similar cases?'

'Only one. But the similarity might be so tenuous that it's probably worth disregarding.'

'I think I'll be the best judge of that.' Lapslie smiled patiently. 'So, tell me.'

Emma Bradbury fired Rebecca a quick apologetic look, as if to say: *take no notice. I told you he could be like this now and then.* She'd some while back explained to Rebecca that Lapslie's medication made him testy at times: *with the social graces of Attila the Hun.*

Rebecca Graves held a palm out. 'Well, it's the case of that young African-Caribbean boy fished out of the Thames a while back.'

'And when exactly was that?' Lapslie sought to clarify.

'Nine years ago now. Badly decomposed when the body finally washed up, torso almost cut in half; it appears, from a boat propeller. But there was some confusion at autopsy, in that some internal organs and the right forearm were also missing, which appeared to have been from a cleaner cut. So an African or Haitian-connected ritual killing was at first suspected – though nothing in the end was proven.'

The 'tribal ritual' sparked the connection in Lapslie's mind. 'Yes, I seem to remember something about the case. And what date do we have for the murder occurring?'

Graves consulted her notes for a moment. 'The body was discovered in the Thames on 8th October. And pathologists estimate it had been in the water between three-and-a-half and four months.'

'And what date was the boy reported missing?'

'Sometime between the 10th and 11th of June. The boy's school were the first to report him missing rather than his family.'

Lapslie did a quick calculation. Even if the boy had been killed on the first day of his disappearance, it was still twenty days beyond the likely date that Ben Tovey had been killed, and Tovey's murder had been several weeks before that of James Lewis. So some 'anniversary killing' link between the boys was looking less likely – if this Nigerian boy was linked at all.

As if reading his thoughts, Bradbury commented, 'Even if this boy found in the Thames is somehow connected to some annual serial-killer event, we have all the missing years in between to consider. There's a seven-year gap between his murder and that of Ben Tovey, and no murders in the three years before that to the twelve-year mark – without even going back another ten or fifteen.'

'Yes, there is that,' Lapslie agreed emptily, sighing.

'Doesn't look like any of our past theories are coming up trumps today. No likely links to past murders, and Alistair Tulley and Harvey Reid looking like the last people on earth that Sinclair would wish to defend.'

Bradbury nodded pensively. 'Unless of course he truly believed they were both innocent.'

'Yes.' Lapslie stared vacantly ahead for a moment. People milling about and getting served at the bar passed by his vision unseen before the connected thought struck him. 'You realize of course what that might mean?'

Bradbury arched a brow. 'What's that, sir?'

'It means that, if Alistair Tulley was our killer, after all – or someone else still loose out there, if Sinclair is to be believed – then he might well kill again. And with both murders so far being local, the likelihood is that it will be on this patch too.'

14

'I'm sorry I wasn't able to make it to your little pub celebration the other week,' Chief Superintendent Rouse
said, with a tight smile somewhere between formal and
apologetic. 'Prior engagement that night, I'm afraid.'

'That's okay. I understand.' Lapslie was sure his brow
had raised initially at the comment, but hopefully he'd
eased his expression before it was noticed. He could
hardly remember Rouse joining his staff for any outside
celebrations. The last get-together Lapslie could recall
Rouse attending, on that occasion at a local restaurant,
had been for a retiring, long-serving duty sergeant – the
closest Chelmsford HQ got to a *Dixon of Dock Green*
character – and no doubt that had only been because the
hierarchy and Essex Police Commissioners had advised
him that it would have looked bad if he hadn't attended.

'More rested now?' Rouse enquired.

'Uh . . . yes. Thanks.' It took Lapslie a second to realize what Rouse was referring to. Twelve days back from his holidays, and everything was in full swing again, the break already seeming a distant dream.

'That's good. That's good.' Rouse's eyes stayed on Lapslie for a second, as if evaluating whether he appeared as rested as he claimed. Then he half-stood, holding one palm out. 'Ah, I took the liberty of getting Susan to bring you in a cup of tea. I've already had mine, you see.'

Lapslie nodded as he glanced at the cup and saucer by Rouse's right hand, which Susan dutifully cleared away as she put Lapslie's cup down. 'Thank you. Very kind of you,' though his comment was directed as much at Susan, Rouse's PA. He half-turned and smiled at her.

If Rouse had asked him whether he wanted tea, he'd have said no, eager to get away and back to the comfort of his own office. Away from Rouse's searching gaze across the desk. He could sense that Rouse was digging for something. Rouse hardly ever invited him to his office just out of politeness or to say sorry for missing a pub get-together. Something specific was on Rouse's mind.

Rouse's hands, interlaced on the desktop in front of him – a guarding stance – opened out briefly. 'It's good that Benedict Allsopp's advice was able to help you win the day in court this time with Sinclair.'

'Yes, it was.' Lapslie nodded, took a sip of his tea. 'I was the first to thank him at our little pub celebration.'

'Yes, and much deserved, I might add, after that first run-in with Sinclair at the Tulley trail.'

'Indeed.' Lapslie had added his last comment in case Rouse thought he might not have been grateful for Allsopp's advice on Sinclair. Or could Allsopp have forgotten he'd thanked him and made a comment? He took another sip of tea; the sooner he was out of Rouse's way, the better. He could sense Rouse circling around to something.

'Although we can't by any means give all the credit to Allsopp's advice. Much of your success at trial was due to you having a far more solid case this time against Harvey Reid. For which the credit falls to you and your team.'

And there it was, thought Lapslie. Had Rouse somehow heard he wasn't fully settled in his own mind with the Reid conviction? Or was it just a suspicion based on his thoughtful huddles with Bradbury, or perhaps not being as joyous in the wake of the conviction as he should be. But then, with his synaesthesia, he was hardly in 'happy as Larry' mode at the best of times.

'Yes, I suppose so,' he answered ambiguously, leaving it unclear whether he was unsettled about the conviction, or just being coy about taking the credit for it. He took another hasty sip of tea.

There was a moment's silence, somewhat unsettling with only the sound of his tea-sipping, and then Rouse took a fresh breath.

'Benedict also mentioned that you hadn't really come to him with much since returning from holiday after the trial.'

So was that what might have led to the suspicion? Purely his quietness and lack of contact with Allsopp, leading them to think that he might be dissatisfied with the conviction or was up to something?

Lapslie's brow knitted. 'But surely that would be a good thing, sir. Little or no contact would usually mean little or no problems.' Lapslie held out a hand. 'At least, nothing worth troubling Benedict Allsopp with, or yourself for that matter.'

'So nothing worrying you about the Reid case? Or anything else which you would like to share?'

'No, sir. Nothing I can think of.' Lapslie swallowed

imperceptibly, forced a smile. 'Perhaps just post-holiday blues. Wishing I was still out there sailing.'

Rouse stared at him evenly for a moment, as if gauging his sincerity, before nodding. 'That's good, then.' He smiled tightly. 'But you'll let Benedict know if there is anything troubling you. However small.'

'Yes. I certainly will, sir.' Lapslie took another sip of tea.

'That's encouraging to know. I like to see accord between my officers.' Another strained smile. 'And I'm glad we've had this little chat.'

'Yes.' It took a second for Lapslie to realize that the meeting was over and he was being dismissed. He still had an inch of tea in the bottom of his cup, but it would be excruciating to sit there finishing it under Rouse's intense gaze. So, with a curt but polite, 'Thank you, sir,' he stood up and left.

Camden Market, London
June 2014

Josie's mobile buzzed in her pocket. She took it out. It was a text from Scobe: *You know what I mentioned last time about 'cherry on the cake'? Well, I think we might have found it. Meet me at Bar Cuba in Camden Market at 6 p.m. Betty will be there as well.*

Josie arrived on time and spotted Scobe and Betty at the far end of the bar.

'Betty's only just arrived,' Scobe said as Josie approached. 'And as I was just saying to her, it looks like we could have a breakthrough at last with a recent case here in England—' He broke off as a waiter hovered to one side. 'Betty and I have already ordered. What would you like?'

'Just a beer. A San Miguel would be fine.' Josie leaned across and gave Betty a quick hug in greeting, then looked back at Scobe. 'And when did this come up?'

'The murder was in early May of last year, but the case is just coming to trial now. There have been a number of procedural delays – not least the difficulty of tracking down and interviewing members of the travelling community, who are reluctant to cooperate with the police at the best of times.'

Josie nodded. 'The Ben Tovey murder. But I don't recall there being any oddities with body parts removed with that case.'

'No. The police and prosecutors purposely kept that under wraps,' Scobe said. 'Because, as you'll see as the trial progresses, that becomes a crucial part of the evidence. So they didn't want any prior influence on the jury. And as is standard with many murder cases, they filter out bogus claims by withholding such details.' Scobe took a fresh breath. 'But the main reason for my contact at this juncture is that the illustrious Toby Sinclair, no less, has stepped up to the plate to defend the suspect accused.'

Josie and Betty exchanged a look. Toby Sinclair was one of the high-profile, well-connected names that had cropped up on both of their lists.

'And where was the boy's body found?' Betty asked. Unlike Josie, she wasn't fully aware of the case.

Scobe answered. 'In Essex. One of Essex's best, a certain Chief Inspector Lapslie, is leading the investigation. He won't be an easy touch for Sinclair.'

Josie noticed a slightly distant look in Betty's eyes as the information sank in. Perhaps she'd been seeking retribution for so long that it seemed unreal it was finally within reach.

From Josie's last meeting with Betty, she knew that Betty suspected her family name of McCauley had been linked to the farmer who'd alerted King James's men outside the Bennane Caves; then, seeing that she and her husband were originally from Ayrshire, they'd purposely targeted their son David. But then after years of knocking on Scotland Yard's door, the main reason for the police holding back had been the lack of other recent cases where the bodies of young boys had been found with their forearms severed. Josie had mentioned the case last year in Belgium and that had provided a glimmer of light; and now there was this case in England to throw a stronger spotlight.

Scobe grimaced tautly. 'That's not the only thing. The accused Sinclair is defending turns out to be a cousin of Gavin Dimock's on his mother's side.'

Josie nodded. Gavin Dimock had been the main suspect in a young teen's disappearance in Darlington six years ago, but no body had ever been found. Then subsequently a strong alibi had materialized for Dimock. But Josie knew from her last conversation with Betty that she'd never been convinced about Dimock's innocence.

'Thanks, Scobe. I knew you'd get there in the end,' Betty said.

Josie noticed an affection between Betty and Scobe that went beyond a purely professional association. At their last meeting, Scobe had explained that when he'd first met Betty, she'd been sleeping rough.

It had seemed wrong to him that such harsh circumstances had forced her on to the streets, not least because
it involved a general failure of the police and justice system, and so he'd sought to change that. He'd contacted
social services not long after their first meeting, and
after a few months of paperwork – and pulling some
strings to jump the housing queue – he'd got Betty into
an assisted-housing unit in Camden Town. Betty was
one of only four women in a large three-storey town-
house. 'Assisted' simply meant that a carer would be on
duty to cook, clean, do their laundry and administer
medication where necessary. In Betty's case that was
simply Metformin for mild diabetes diagnosed by her
GP, and daily aspirin to thin the blood.

'Lively here, isn't it?' Betty remarked, looking towards
one of the barmen drying glasses while swaying to 'Oye
Como Va'.

Bar Cuba in Camden Market was walking distance
from Betty's new home, and Scobe thought she'd appreciate the atmosphere.

'I recall you mentioning taking up salsa with your
husband and that you were partial to a bit of rum, so I
thought this was the closest to hit the mark.' He looked
up as the waiter approached with their drinks. 'Ah, here

we are. Your San Miguel, Josie . . . and Betty, your rum punch, Cuba-style.'

'Thank you. Looks marvellous.' She smiled and took a first sip, though her expression sank into a mild frown after a second. 'I didn't know that you were allowed.'

Scobe glanced at his watch. 'Signed off duty over an hour ago. And despite what you might have heard, many coppers I know drink like fish when they're off duty. Perhaps compensates for the rigours of the job, the horror stories and the failures.' He too became more thoughtful after the first few sips. 'I never asked you before, but where did my nickname "Scobe" come from?'

Betty smiled, and for a second the smudge where her lipstick had smeared her teeth could be seen. Though she was smartly dressed and took far more trouble with her appearance these days, they were reminded that Betty was now in her late seventies.

'Because you're from Scotland Yard, and before you introduced me to Josie here,' – Betty smiled and clinked glasses with Josie – 'you were the only one to dig and search hard on my behalf.'

In turn, Josie grimaced. She'd never troubled to ask about the nickname, from either Betty or Scobe directly. But an afterthought about Sinclair troubled her. 'The only thing is – if Sinclair is involved, no doubt he has a game-plan in mind already.'

'No doubt. But it's the first real breakthrough we've seen in a while.' Scobe raised his glass. 'So let's hope we finally see some light.'

The Essex countryside
April 2015

Emma Bradbury wove the Volvo S80 though the late-afternoon traffic. An hour short of rush hour, but still catching the tail-end of the afternoon school pick-up.

The last thing they wanted to do was run over one school kid while desperately chasing a lead which might save another, so although the siren was put on at intervals to clear the traffic ahead, Bradbury was more cautious when passing schools.

'Sorry, sir,' Bradbury said as she put on the siren again to warn the last few out-of-uniform stragglers crossing from a comprehensive school they'd just passed, then sped quickly up to sixty again.

The alert had come in just fifteen minutes ago: a young boy matching the description of twelve-year-old Steven Worley, reported missing the day before. The place where young Steven had been sighted was just three miles from where Ben Tovey's body had been found.

Lapslie had finally been able to distil some clarity from the last two local murders and possible connections with past cases. Aside from the Nigerian boy fished from the Thames, Rebecca Graves had hit upon only one other possible case. Almost exact date-period match, but no missing limbs. The only oddity had been a question raised at autopsy that an 'area of stomach flesh might be missing'. But decomposition by that stage was so severe that it had been impossible to determine whether it had been eaten away by maggots or cut away at the time of death.

The forensic examiner had summarized in his report that an open wound to the stomach might have led to more maggot infestation and resultant decomposition being heavier in that area. Again, open to interpretation.

Lapslie grimaced as they rounded a bend and had to slow down for a queue of traffic ahead. 'What's this? Roadworks?'

'No. Our local boys in blue have picked this as a good spot for on–off vehicular checks. There's a small lay-by ahead, and they pull in a fair few with defective tyres, no MOT, or goods vehicles overloaded.'

'We can't afford the wait.' Lapslie nodded ahead.

'If you're sure, sir,' Bradbury said, already swinging out as she put on the siren.

Lapslie's grimace tightened as they sped past the traffic. The taste wasn't too bad at first: sour apples with an acid tinge. It was only if the siren stayed on for too long that it would start to have more of an unpleasant ammonia edge.

A couple of streets flashing by to their left he recognized, and realized that they led to the fields where young Ben Tovey had been found, almost two years ago now. The murder that had started the whole case.

'Almost clear now,' Bradbury announced as they swung past a large trailer and the last few cars in the queue, one of the uniformed police by the roadside giving them a half-wave in acknowledgement. As they got clear of the traffic, Bradbury turned off their siren, but kept their speed up at 65 mph.

The police radio crackled.

'*Echo 524. Caught sight of the green van on Bell Hill in Danbury, and aimed to simply keep it under observation until your arrival, as instructed. But as we approached, it started pulling away and is now heading east along Maldon Road.*'

Bradbury checked her satnav. 'That's just half a mile away now, sir.'

Lapslie picked up the radio mike. 'Okay. Stay in pursuit. But try to remain discreet, a good distance back, no siren – though of course without losing the van. We'll be with you shortly.'

'*Understood. Roger.*'

Bradbury crept up to seventy, slowed for the next turn, then put her foot flat down again. After straightening out from one more careening turn, she announced, 'I think that's them there ahead, sir.'

Four hundred yards ahead Lapslie could make out the squad car, then two hundred yards beyond a green van. At that moment their radio crackled again.

'*I think unfortunately they've spotted us. They're speeding up.*'

If Lapslie hadn't known through the announcement, he'd have seen it from the gap growing between the green van and the squad car. He snatched at the radio mike again.

'Keep on them, but no siren. We're close behind you now. We'll overtake you shortly, and as we do we'll put on our siren. You follow suit with yours then too, so they know that the game is up.'

'*Okay.*'

Bradbury took the Volvo up to eighty ... and was touching ninety as the squad car loomed ahead. Ninety-two ... ninety-five as they passed it.

Lapslie reckoned the squad car and the green van were both touching eighty. The siren came on, sending a burst of acid-apple to his sinuses and the back of his throat, the squad car chiming in seconds after.

The green van swayed a fraction, the driver perhaps shocked by the sirens or checking his mirror; then, within seconds, they were alongside him.

Bradbury wasted no time in edging in front, then started steadily slowing. With the squad car now directly alongside the van, effectively blocking him in, they cut swiftly to sixty, forty ... twenty, and coasted to a halt.

Lapslie leapt out before they'd hardly stopped, his badge held out. He noticed the young boy in the passenger seat look startled more than relieved. Lapslie pulled the passenger door open as Bradbury and one of the squad car officers on the other side grabbed the driver and pulled him out.

'Are you Steven Worley of Woodhill Road, Sandon?' Lapslie enquired.

The boy nodded tentatively. 'Yes.'

Lapslie felt a wave of relief hit him, washing back the acid-apple taste. They'd got to this one in time.

'And has this man abducted you?'

'No.' The boy's brow knitted curiously. 'He's my father.'

Springfield Garden Centre, Essex
Four days later

Lapslie sipped at his tea and looked through palm fronds towards the greenery and flowers beyond, while Emma Bradbury finished summarizing from her notes.

'... Fourth time now he's done this, apparently. Turns up out of the blue outside arranged visitation times, says he'll only be a few hours with Steven – then keeps the boy overnight, and on one occasion kept him two days away from his mother.'

'What are his normal visitation times?'

'One weekend once a month.'

Lapslie took another sip and nodded. 'And what excuses does he give for keeping the boy for an extra day or so?'

'Oh, according to Steven's mother, Claire,' Bradbury consulted her notes briefly, 'he's quite crafty. Would phone late afternoon and say they got held up, then again late at night he'd ring and say they couldn't make it back, they were too far away or Steven was too tired and already asleep. Or the father, Len, had had a beer and so didn't want to take the risk of driving.'

'And so he'd spin it out another day.' Lapslie sat back and sighed. 'So this time she decided to teach him a lesson?'

'Yes. She warned him last time that, if it happened again, she'd phone the police or the social services.'

'You warned her no doubt of the possible conse-quences of wasting police time.'

'Yes, very much so. She was apologetic – but says she was frustrated. Social services had talked about arrang-ing another family court date to get a judge to warn Len and rein him in, but she could see that taking months. Claire felt the short, sharp shock of almost getting arrested would be the only thing to snap him out of it.'

'Yes, well, it certainly did that,' Lapslie commented, thoughtful for a moment as he gazed aimlessly at the few people visible browsing in the garden centre beyond the ring of palms encircling the café area. Midweek, Springfield Garden Centre – their 'Place Two' meeting point three miles from Chelmsford – wasn't very busy.

'And any indicators from cases in the date range we discussed the other day?' Lapslie looked towards DC Graves.

It took her a moment to realize the conversation had swung around to her. So far she hadn't been involved.

'Uh, no, sir. Only a 3 per cent increase on the month either side. But then September was 8 per cent higher. But with a baseline of only seventeen murders in twenty-five years, it doesn't really tell us much.'

Lapslie nodded. He'd asked Rebecca Graves to look into the general stats over the years to see if there might be a spike in murders of young boys in the two-week period in May when Ben Tovey and James Lewis had been murdered. That at least might give some sort of base statistic outside of the missing-limb factor.

'Another thing, sir,' Bradbury offered. 'If Steven Worley the other day had turned out to be a murder victim, it would have been about two weeks short of the time frame in which Ben Tovey was abducted and murdered, in any case.'

'Two weeks?' Lapslie aired his thoughts out loud to nobody in particular, then focused again on Bradbury and Graves. 'Or we'd simply have had to widen that time frame.'

'Yes, sir,' Bradbury agreed. 'But in doing so it would have made the date period less specific. Less of a factor.'

Lapslie took another sip of his tea. 'Or raise the question that if the date period was somehow significant – why did it have such a wide variance?'

The man in the light-green Lacoste aertex shirt was almost invisible as he perused the shrubs and geraniums ten yards from the café area.

Besides, he'd glanced their way directly only once, and briefly; they wouldn't have picked up anything from that, but having fixed them in the periphery of his vision, he was able to gauge the general mood and flow of the conversation and would know if they started to leave or move his way.

As he noticed Emma Bradbury get up and go back to the serving counter for something, he decided he'd seen enough and left.

Three miles down the road from the garden centre, he pulled over to the roadside to make the call.

No answer.

He left a message.

*

Toby Sinclair felt his mobile phone vibrate in his pocket halfway through his afternoon court session.

An hour and twenty minutes later, he heard the message and returned the call two hundred yards from Winchester Crown Court, getting back into his car.

'You have some news?'

Mandrake related what he'd seen in the garden centre. 'Fourth such meeting they've had in as many weeks between there and a local pub. Looks like Lapslie is starting to dig around.'

'Always the same group of three?'

'Yes. Just the three of them. Very cosy.'

'Perhaps it's a specific case which involves just those three.'

'That might hold water if it wasn't for the fact that each time they meet it's somewhere well away from the office or any regular Chelmsford police haunts. It looks like they don't want to be seen by *anyone*.'

Sinclair contemplated this new development for a moment. He'd hoped that the double-game he'd played against Lapslie would have seen the issue buried. Lapslie would have felt he'd finally won the day against him – due revenge for the failed Tulley case – and there would be so much interdepartmental back-patting over the subsequent successful case against Harvey Reid that Lapslie wouldn't have seen beyond that. Obviously, he'd underestimated Lapslie.

Sinclair took a fresh breath. 'So they're keeping it tight within that little circle?'

'Yes. Oh, except four days ago when an alert was raised for a boy gone missing not far away from where Ben Tovey was found. Amounted to nothing in the end.'

'As we could have told them it wouldn't have.' Sinclair's tone was mocking, as if he hardly had the patience for this tiresome turn of events. 'Still, an alert like that would have come in on a general feed, so they wouldn't have been able to keep that tight. So that element doesn't tell us much.'

'They're obviously keen to avoid someone with this. Do you think that might be Rouse or Allsopp?'

Sinclair pondered for a second. 'I think more likely Rouse. The Reid conviction was a big feather in Rouse's departmental cap after the fiasco with Tovey and Tulley, which is what we banked on. So he'd be keen not to unsettle that. But, no doubt, that golden boy Allsopp might feed any concerns expressed by Lapslie straight back to Rouse.'

'From how tight they're keeping this, it looks as if there are a number of others in their department they don't feel they can trust.'

'Looks like it. A question of 'Loose talk costs lives' and all that.'

'What was that?' Mandrake questioned.

'Just an expression.' Sinclair sighed. 'Before your time.'

15

Chelmsford Police Headquarters, Essex
May 2015

Two weeks? It preyed on Lapslie's mind after the last meeting. Two weeks until the anniversary of Ben Tovey's abduction and murder.

So he found himself often on edge, dreading the moment bad news might come in, anxious and finger-tapping his way through every missing young teenager alert in the area. There were eleven in that period, nine of them cleared up within a couple of hours, one four hours and the last six hours before the boy was finally located at a friend's house.

Lapslie had been about to extend the local alert to a wider Home Counties PB for the last one when the boy's mother phoned back to say that he'd been found safe and sound.

Lapslie's nerves eased, and he commented to Bradbury in the squad room as he helped himself to tea from the automatic dispenser, 'Is it my imagination, or are there more alerts for missing youngsters in the area than normal?'

'Your imagination, sir. I don't think the number of alerts is any more than normal.' She smiled tightly. 'I think what hasn't helped is that you asked to be advised of every missing young teen notification the moment it came in.'

'So you're saying it's my fault?'

Another tight smile. 'I didn't say that, sir.'

He retired to his office and sipped at his tea. It was strange. Along with the relief each time a child was reported safe and sound, he also felt a twinge of disappointment – which left him with a strong vanilla-pod aftertaste. Because it meant with each one, his theory about Harvey Reid might be wrong; with the last court case they'd nailed the right person after all.

Then he realized that he had another two weeks of the same to be totally sure. They'd had two weeks leading up to the pivotal date, now they had another two weeks on the other side before 'date significance' faded completely. He wasn't sure his nerves could take it, wasn't sure what he wanted anymore.

There were slightly more missing-person alerts for twelve-to-fourteen-year-olds in the following two weeks, fifteen in total, with one boy missing almost twelve hours before he was finally located, by which time a wider police bulletin had been out for five hours, and Lapslie had already gone out with Bradbury to trawl the last areas where the boy had been seen – a skate park and some nearby shops.

That was day nine of the second two weeks; the five days remaining after that, with four minor alerts, seemed inconsequential in comparison.

They'd had two meetings outside of the office during that time, both of them at the garden centre café – but nothing new or enlightening had been uncovered by Bradbury or Graves.

Any other comments or updates had only warranted a moment's conversation here and there, not full-blown meetings – so they grabbed those moments when they could at the station.

But Lapslie feared they might have risked exposure when he was in the midst of a brief conversation with Bradbury and Graves in the corridor, and Benedict

Allsopp spotted them as he came out of a room at the far end. Allsopp approached as they were finishing up and Bradbury and Graves headed back into the general office.

'Seems you're having a fair few meetings with Bradbury and Graves, these days,' Allsopp commented.

'Well, Emma Bradbury is my personal assistant.'

'Yes, of course.' Allsopp took a fresh breath. 'Just that I wondered, with Rebecca Graves involved too, whether it might be a special case you're working on.'

Lapslie met Allsopp's gaze evenly for a second, wondering whether he knew or suspected anything about their outside meetings. Perhaps Allsopp had picked up on the fact that they often left together or were all out of the office at the same time.

'Nothing particularly special. Just something that's cropped up with the Rutherford case,' Lapslie lied, picking a past case from memory. 'We all worked together on that a few years ago.'

'I see.' Allsopp arched a brow. 'Anything I might be able to help with?'

'No, it's okay. Thanks. Before your time.'

'The Tulley case with Sinclair was before my time as well, but I was able to offer some very worthwhile advice there.'

'Yes, you were.' *And we all know why that might be. That's in part why all this is happening now.* He forced a smile to deflect Allsopp possibly reading his thoughts. 'And very much appreciated. But the Rutherford case is almost wrapped up now. Only a few more loose ends to sort out.'

Allsopp held his gaze a second longer, before nodding. 'That's good to hear. But let me know if there's anything I can help with.'

'Certainly will,' Lapslie said, as with a final perfunctory nod Allsopp continued along the corridor. But his eyes stayed on Allsopp's back for a second before he turned back into the main squad room, reflecting that they would have to be more careful in future or make sure to wrap everything up quickly.

Essex/Kent coastline
Last weekend in May

'Doldrums?' Charlotte quizzed.

'Yes, sailing term. It's nice when it's flat and calm like this. But not when there's little or no wind – otherwise you can't make any headway.'

'Is that why you put the motor on for the last stretch?'

Lapslie nodded, surveying the flat sea with hardly a ripple running up to the chalk cliffs of Botany Bay half a mile away and the Thames Estuary beyond. 'And we'll have to put it on again heading back unless we get a bit of late afternoon lift in the wind.'

It had started out a fine, sunny day with a light wind and so they'd taken the boat out from Clacton harbour at first light and sailed down the coast. With their hectic schedules, getting slots where the weather was ideal and they were both free was something of a juggling act, so Lapslie thought it might be one of their few chances of going out on the boat this season.

He recalled happy memories of their short break on the Ile de Ré, and a few lazy summers spent sailing around the Isle of Wight, though now it was just a packed ploughman's lunch and a cheap bottle of Chardonnay rather than champagne and strawberries. And while the view of the white chalk cliffs backing Botany Bay was stunning, a mile further out two oil tankers waited their turn for passage through the English Channel.

Lapslie took another slug of beer, grimacing as it went down. 'Pretty good description too of where this case is right now – doldrums. No movement, no wind behind it.'

'But shouldn't that, in a way, please you? If there have

been no other twelve-to-thirteen-year-olds murdered in the area, then it starts to look more likely that, with Harvey Reid, you got the right man.'

'Yes, I suppose there is that way of looking at it.' Lapslie took another quick slug, looking out across the still waters for a moment. 'But I think you know why I wasn't completely comfortable with that.'

'Yes, I know.' They'd covered that ground in detail before, and Charlotte had observed it absorbing him more and more over the past few months as he bounced different hypotheses around in his head. 'So now you're split between the victory of knowing your last case was proven right, and you finally won the day over Sinclair, and the failure that your gut instincts with Reid might be proven wrong?'

Lapslie snapped out of his contemplation after a second. 'Yes, that pretty well sums it up. But it doesn't make it any the easier to deal with. And I'm sorry if at times I've used you as a sounding board on these trips out. When we should be relaxing more.'

Charlotte expressed her sympathy with Lapslie's forced smile after a second. 'Except that sometimes sharing the problem, getting the weight off, can be the key to relaxing more.'

Their conversation became lighter, more general, soon after that, and they did start to relax and enjoy the day more, Charlotte talking about how nearby Broadstairs was one of her favourite English seaside resorts.

'Picture-postcard, half-moon-shaped sandy bay, small fishing harbour to one side just where it should be. And the town full of antique and curio shops, rather than the usual seaside junk and games arcades of nearby Margate. I can see why Dickens bought a seaside house here.' She munched on some French bread with cheese and pickle that Lapslie had just prepared for her. 'Have you been to the Dickens museum there?'

'No, I'm afraid not. Only been to Broadstairs a few times, and most of those as a kid. Probably too young to appreciate Dickens then.'

They ate in silence for a moment, Lapslie noticing by the boat's movement and the regularity of wave-ripples lapping against its side that the wind was picking up slightly. Then Charlotte started on some stories from the hospital, perhaps to even the balance with his own work-related talk, but keeping them light-hearted to maintain the mood.

'. . . so this old codger had been on the ward nearly two weeks by this time and all the consultants were baffled as to what was ailing him. Some rare tropical stomach bug was the first thing explored, but he hadn't been abroad in two years. The only constant was the diarrhoea, which showed no sign of abating. His main visitor was his young son, who would bring him reading material. No grapes – they were on a banned food list until we'd worked out what was the problem – so just magazines and books. And knowing that the old boy particularly liked Second World War thrillers – Len Deighton, Alistair MacLean and the like – he discovers that he hasn't read Ken Follett yet. So one day he brings him *Eye of the Needle*.'

Lapslie nodded. 'Yes, good book. One of his first, if I recall.'

Charlotte smiled. 'Yes. But with the old boy's daily watery bowel movements now wearing him down, he takes one look at the cover and comments, "Is this your attempt at ironic humour?"'

Lapslie laughed. 'Well, good to see that the old boy's sense of humour hadn't been worn down.' He took a bite of his own French bread with cheese and swilled it down with some beer. 'What was ailing him in the end . . . ? Did your lot manage to work that out?'

'Seeds,' Charlotte said. 'Nothing more than seeds. It's a sort of extension of irritable bowel syndrome where the stomach lining becomes sensitive to seeds. So most fruit and some vegetables – anything which might contain a seed to self-propagate – was out.'

'What, lifetime ban?'

'No, few months at most. With the right medication, it usually settles down.'

Lapslie grimaced pleasantly as he scanned the sea and the horizon, reminded of why he liked Charlotte's company so much. A few hours ago, setting sail, he'd still been tense with work-related problems weighing him down. Now, after some light-hearted banter and anecdotes from Charlotte, he was completely relaxed, his problems forgotten. Well, at least faded – as hazy and distant as the French coastline, which he could just make out on the horizon.

The wind flurries had picked up a notch, but Lapslie reckoned it would still take them a good two hours to make it back to Clacton harbour, so they set sail after forty minutes.

'Don't want to use the motor, if I can avoid it,' Lapslie explained as they felt the first of the wind catch in the sails.

The wind, though, almost died completely for a couple of intervals, so it took them two hours and twenty minutes to make it back. It was almost dusk by the time that Charlotte drove them away from the harbour in her car. She'd picked Lapslie up on the way, and the arrangement was that she'd drop him off and then head home.

But ten minutes into the drive, she commented, 'I can stay over, if you like. But I warn you, I've got a 7 a.m. start tomorrow – so that means I'll have to head off at five and might disturb you.'

'That's okay. I've got some paperwork to do before I go in myself, so that won't be far off my own planned wake-up time.' He smiled gently towards her. 'So I'd like it if you could stay over.'

'Okay. Just that you probably need your beauty sleep more than me.' She returned his smile briefly with the tease, but then it faded as she spied the tailback of traffic ahead. She slowed and finally came to a stop.

It looked like a good quarter-mile tailback ahead leading up to some roadworks with traffic lights. She shook her head. 'Ever more popular these days. Weekend roadworks so that they don't disrupt the working-week traffic. It never occurs to them that we might want to pursue our leisure activities on time as well.'

'Thoughtless bastards,' Lapslie joshed, which raised a smile from Charlotte. 'Or maybe they think that sitting in traffic jams is just an extension of that leisure, so it . . .'

Lapslie's voice trailed off as he was suddenly hit with a thought: sitting in a similar jam, a month back, before Emma Bradbury put her siren on to swing past it; looking pensively to one side as he realized that the field where Ben Tovey's body had been found was only half a mile away.

Picking up on his suddenly more serious, contemplative mood, Charlotte prompted, 'What is it?'

Lapslie ran the scenario through in his mind once more, in case there was something he'd missed. 'I think I might have just found the key to this case which has so far been eluding me.'

PART THREE

PART THREE

16

Scobe realized he'd been guilty of avoiding both Josie and Betty for a while. The collapse of the case against Alistair Tulley had hit them hard, and the prosecution of Harvey Reid for James Lewis, a second murder in the same area – which Scobe had gone to great lengths to explain was an almost identical MO in terms of the boy's age and severed forearm, despite the June-date timing – had done little to lift their spirits.

Betty was adamant that it wasn't Reid, it was Tulley, Dimock or some other party connected to Sinclair. 'And Sinclair has put this poor man Reid in the frame to divert attention away from them.'

Whereas Josie was more in 'I told you so' mode. She'd warned prior to the Tulley case that no doubt Sinclair had a plan in mind, 'And now we're seeing the full scope of that plan.'

So he'd avoided them both because he simply didn't think he had anything worthwhile to tell them. Until such time as he discovered that Inspector Lapslie was thinking exactly the same way as them; that in Harvey Reid they might well have prosecuted the wrong man, and as a result he was starting to dig deeper into Toby Sinclair's background.

'So what led our Inspector Lapslie to think that Reid might be innocent?' Betty asked.

'I think it was mainly Reid's challenged situation with his reduced mental age.'

'What? Because he's a bit of a simpleton?'

'Yes.' Scobe smiled tightly, noting Josie to his side coughing to mask a guffaw. 'Except we don't use expressions like that in today's politically correct age. Anyway, due to Reid's "situation", Lapslie simply doesn't think he'd be able to orchestrate an elaborate frame-up of Tulley for the first murder, as was suggested at trial.'

'It's unusual also to get two murders in the same area, especially with both bodies being found,' Josie commented. 'Years waiting for a teen body with a limb severed to be found in the UK, and suddenly we get two in a row, one year after the next.'

'Yes, true. But I don't know if Inspector Lapslie is aware of that factor yet. With his main focus obviously on the murders on his patch, he's only recently started trawling for other similar cases outside his area.'

Josie nodded, and Scobe caught the residual doubt in her eyes before she glanced abstractedly across the bar. He knew that the let-down over the Tulley case had been harder for her than Betty. After the long years of waiting, Betty had built up a stronger resilience and patience; it was just one more disappointment and wait amongst the many she'd experienced over the years.

Whereas Josie had been at a total loose end. She'd gone back to a local Plymouth newspaper at the end of 2014, but had confided in Scobe in a phone call not long after that she simply didn't feel safe there. 'I got a call about a lead on a local story, but when I discovered that the meeting place was a remote warehouse, I bottled out. Told my editor I simply couldn't go. I feared it was another set-up – and a local paper doesn't have the resources to send a second reporter along for backup.'

Seven weeks later she called Scobe again to tell him that she'd turned up on Doris's doorstep, having rejoined *TNT* under its new editor, Dennis Ashby, who'd taken over and revived the journal and blog a month after Tom Barton's death.

'But there's to be no mention of the Swan-Tattoo–Sinclair case between us. I'm just chief bottle-washer and working other cases now.'

All those months of living a shadow life couldn't have been easy, Scobe reflected. Maybe the music and atmosphere would lift their spirits.

They'd gone to Bar Cuba again, at Betty's request. She liked the salsa music, but admitted last time with a mischievous grin that she also found the waiters 'easy on the eye.'

For a moment he'd got a glimpse of a young Betty at salsa clubs with her husband while both in their prime – their son David just a toddler with his whole life ahead of him.

But now that image was many moons and rough street-nights ago, and hard to correlate with the Betty before him. She'd boasted as she walked in that it had been too early for her carer to help her with her make-up, so she'd done it herself. She'd managed to keep the lipstick off her teeth, he noted, but she'd arched the liner over one eye far too sharply, giving it a vaguely 'Mr Spock' appearance.

Josie was having coffee today. She looked at Scobe above its rim, struck with a thought. 'This angle of pursuit by Inspector Lapslie – is this something generally shared within his department?'

'As we know from past bitter experience, if it's too open a line of pursuit, Sinclair appears to have ways and means of shutting it down, or at least interfering.' Scobe chose his words carefully. 'But put it this way, Lapslie has good support within his unit – even if it isn't all official and on the surface – some of which he isn't even aware of.'

'I see.' Josie noticed a gleam in Scobe's eyes as he'd said the last. The message was clear: this was about as much assurance and clarity as he was able to give.

But much of it appeared to go over Betty's head. She obviously wanted more clear-cut assurance.

'And do you think this Lapslie fellow will be successful?' she asked.

'I don't know,' Scobe said cautiously. Having built them both up over the Tulley case, only for them to be half-destroyed by the let-down, he didn't want a repeat of that. 'As we both know, Toby Sinclair is a slippery fox – so we can but hope.'

Yes, *hope*.' Betty looked vacantly across the bar for a moment. 'My only enduring companion for many years now.'

Old Windmill public house, Essex

'You'll notice a new addition with us today, DC Derek Bain,' Lapslie said, looking towards Emma Bradbury and Rebecca Graves.

They'd chosen 'Place 1', the Old Windmill pub alcove. From the quizzical looks shot at Bain on first sight, Lapslie thought he'd better cover the subject first. 'I've introduced DC Bain to our small group for two reasons: first, we'll need the extra manpower with what I foresee we'll now have to cover. Second, he's one of our best liaison officers for contact with Interpol.' The looks became more quizzical, and Lapslie held one hand up. 'The rationale for that will become clear as we progress.'

'But I thought security was a prime concern, sir,' Bradbury said.

Her disappointment was clear. Derek Bain was considered a 'lad' by some fellow officers, invariably male –

who liked his offbeat sense of humour – and a loud-mouth by others, usually squad females.

'I thought DC Bain might be ideal because there's clearly no love lost between him and Benedict Allsopp. And I think Allsopp is an increasing concern, not least because I think he already suspects something from our little meetings.' Lapslie went on to share his conversation with Allsopp when he'd been approached in the corridor the other week. 'So we're going to have to be doubly care-ful now, and try to wrap things up as quickly as possible. Another good reason for the extra manpower.'

Bradbury nodded slowly; a reluctant acceptance. Lap-slie wondered whether he might have made a mistake choosing Bain as the extra man; after all, that had been based mainly on Bain's name-games, taunting Allsopp.

'Anyway, let's get to it.' Lapslie took a fresh breath. 'For me, there's always been something missing from this case. Some vital component that we've overlooked. So far, we have two murders with almost identical MOs in the same area and we've proceeded against two sepa-rate suspects, later narrowed down to one suspect for both murders. With the concern that, in Harvey Reid, we might have nailed the wrong man, we've looked out for similar attacks on young males around the same approximate dates in the Essex area – particularly during the last few tense weeks.' He nodded at Rebecca Graves. 'While at the same time keeping half an eye on national cases with a similar MO. Nothing so far on either front. But I think there's a simple reason for that.'

'What's that, sir?' Bradbury prompted after a moment, noting the half-smile rise on Lapslie's lips as he savoured his *coup de grâce* comment.

'Because I don't think Ben Tovey's murderers ever intended his body to be discovered.'

Bradbury's brow knitted. 'But it was left by a hedgerow in an open field. Hardly any attempt made to cover it up.'

'In fact, if we're looking at a series of killings, I don't think it has been the intention for *any* of the bodies to be discovered,' Lapslie continued fluidly. 'Which largely explains why we've so far had no joy in finding murders with similar MOs.'

Rebecca Graves half-raised one hand. 'Except possibly for the Nigerian boy fished out of the Thames nine years ago.'

'Yes, that one's a possibility. But weighed down and

dumped in the Thames, it obviously wasn't the intention that the body be easily discovered.'

Emma Bradbury looked even more perplexed. 'If that was their intention – *none* of the bodies to be discovered – then the last two cases go directly against that. Because James Lewis's body was also found in an open field. One body left in the open might simply be put down to carelessness, but *two* would be remarkably sloppy.'

Lapslie nodded, 'Exactly so. Which is why, as you say, the first one was simply careless – under forced circumstances, I believe. But then the second murder just over a year later had to be a practically identical MO to put Harvey Reid in the frame. So that second murder was a pre-planned sloppiness, if you will.'

Bradbury's expression was still quizzical, and the other two didn't look any more enlightened, Lapslie observed. He'd have to guide them the rest of the way; after all, it had taken him a while to get there himself.

'The connection didn't hit me until stuck in a traffic jam this weekend gone.' Lapslie went on to explain about hitting a similar traffic jam with Emma Bradbury a few weeks back while in pursuit of missing boy Steven

Worley. 'And as I looked to one side, I realized the field where Ben Tovey had been dumped was less than half a mile away. And Detective Bradbury informed me that it was a regular on-and-off vehicle checkpoint. So first thing this morning, I checked with the highways division and they confirmed that they used that stretch of road as a checkpoint at most twice a month; sometimes two months would go by with no activity. And, yes, there had been a checkpoint set up the day before Ben Tovey's body was found.'

Bradbury's expression eased as the penny dropped. 'So, they're on their way to dump the body where it can't be found – but then see the checkpoint ahead, and panic.'

'Exactly.' Lapslie grimaced. 'They're on their way to a lake or quarry, or to prepare a deep grave – but when they see the police ahead checking vehicles, they take one of the first side turn-offs and dump the body in a hurry in the field at the end.' Lapslie watched the dawning acceptance amongst the small group for a moment before adding, 'Probably late in the day too – which is why the body wasn't discovered until the next day. Highways division say they ran the checkpoint until 8 p.m. that night.'

Bradbury nodded slowly. 'Explains why we've so far not been able to find any young teen murders with a similar MO. The rest are buried out of sight – never to be found again.'

'What's more,' Lapslie concurred, 'these last two murders have thrown us even further off track. Made us look solely in the area of similar murders – bodies in the open with limbs and organs removed.'

'Murders like that would hit the headlines in any case,' Derek Bain offered. 'But with specific details, like limb and organ removal, often kept under wraps by the investigative team so they can weed out hoax claims and more easily identify the real killer.'

'Yes, we covered that in a previous meeting.' Lapslie smiled patiently. 'Partly my fault for not bringing you completely up to speed beforehand. Because of the lack of murders over the years of young teens, we've ended up by default also tracking missing persons.'

Bradbury added, 'Which is why we think our killer has been aiming in the twelve-to-fourteen age range. Below that, disappearances are far less common.'

'And above, they're bigger and can fight back,' Lapslie said. 'Not so easily abducted. Both Ben Tovey and James

Lewis were small and slight for their ages. So that's been another factor to consider.'

'And nothing so far?' Bain confirmed.

'A few slim possibilities, such as the Nigerian boy. But nothing firm so far.' Lapslie nodded towards Rebecca Graves. 'And each time DC Graves has hit upon a possible match in age or date range, she's asked if there were any unusual details which might not have appeared officially on the crime sheet – which would then have prompted them to mention missing limbs or other oddities.'

Emma Bradbury had sunk into contemplation. She looked up after a moment, gesturing towards Bain. 'You mentioned using DC Bain to check with Interpol. Why is that suddenly a factor?'

'Nothing to do with this new angle now,' Lapslie said. 'Just something that's been building up in my mind on the case as it's progressed. Even in the twelve-to-fourteen age range, long-term disappearances are still fairly unusual. At most a handful a year. If we're looking at a specific three-to-four-week date range, the chances of a match are slimmer still. I looked back through all of the past case records dug up by yourself and Rebecca, and could find only five possible matches in the past twenty-five years outside of these last two murders. Which then made me think: what if there were other disappearances and murders beyond British shores?'

Bradbury shrugged. 'But then we come back round again to two murders not only within British shores, but in the very same area – which would go directly against that theory.'

'Well, first of all, I now suspect that second murder was a deliberate copycat killing to frame Reid. But let's think deeper about it for a bit: there might have been an added advantage as well.' Met with a continuing non-plussed expression from Bradbury, a faint smile teased Lapslie's lips. 'What better way to stop us looking over a wider arena than to have two murders within a five-mile radius.'

Bradbury's rising smile matched Lapslie's for a second before she shook her head. 'I take your point, sir. But don't you think you might be giving the killers too much credit?'

'I don't think so. You seem to have forgotten we're dealing with the likes of Toby Sinclair here. And if they've fitted up Harvey Reid so completely – then why not also use it as the perfect diversion.' Lapslie observed Bradbury mentally grappling her way around to accepting his suggestion; but still she appeared to hold some reserve. He shrugged. 'Though, of course, if I'm wrong we have indeed been giving Toby Sinclair and any killers he might be in league with far too much credit. And that means, with Harvey Reid, we nailed the right man after all.'

17

Harbour dockyard, Clacton-on-Sea, Essex

'Third section down on the left,' George said, pointing.

It took Lapslie a moment for his eyes to adjust to the light before making his way down. George's dockside 'shed' was in fact an old fisherman's boathouse: a thirty-foot-by-fifteen unit with an A-frame roof with high wooden cross-beams. George boasted he could get anything up to an eighteen-foot sailboat in there for maintenance without using dry dock: 'And speedboats are no problem at all.'

Lapslie could in fact make out a fourteen-foot Dory towards the back in a state of semi-repair. But it was the shelving units along one side that claimed his attention. He was searching George's Aladdin's cave of boat spares, which was the main reason he kept the shed. Lapslie had complained about some loose play on the main mast, and George had suggested it might need a new base-plate and spacers.

'I've got some in my shed from a Mazury a couple of years newer than yours, but in very good condition – come down and have a look.'

Lapslie had chosen a free morning a couple of days after his last meeting with Bradbury, Graves and Bain; he half-expected there to be a lull while they got to grips with trawling for information following his freshly suggested angle. He peered at the shelves in the half-light as he got to the third row down.

It was bright sunlight outside, but the 'shed' had only two small windows along its length, now heavily masked by years of dust and cobwebs. If fresh visitors to the 'shed' didn't know that George was a retired Royal Navy man on a tight budget, they'd have guessed it by the single light-bulb fitting that threw some light and clarity in the gloom.

'There it is,' George said cheerily, pointing. 'Mast base-plate, spacers and taper unit. The taper on yours might not be so much of a problem, but it comes as a set so you might as well have the lot done while we're at it.'

Lapslie nodded. 'And this lot fitted will do the job? Take up the bit of loose play in the mast?'

'Certainly should do. Yours has slackened over the years, and while this is only two years newer it went in for breaker spares some while ago – so it's hardly seen any wear.'

'And will it set me back much?'

'This lot here will cost you only a drink, whereas through the chandlers it would cost ten times as much – and we'd wait two weeks for them to get the parts in.' George shrugged. 'As for the work fitting, a few hours at most. Chandlers would charge you two-fifty to three hundred. So shall we call it a ton?'

'A ton ... done!' Lapslie did a captain's salute and smiled. He knew that selling off spare boat parts and a bit of fitting and maintenance was the only pin money George could rake in, and so was glad to put the work his way. 'When would you have it done by?'

'I'll do it over this weekend, so by Monday or Tuesday at the latest. Because next weekend I'm off seeing my old mates at Portsmouth. Probably head off Thursday to get in the extra day.'

'That's fine. I'm not planning to head out with her this weekend in any case. And after all, we've done several trips with her like this.'

George nodded. 'You've got your spare key still if you decide to go out the weekend I'm away and need anything?'

'Yes.' George had given him a spare key to the 'shed' in case he needed anything while George wasn't around: extra lifejackets, mooring ropes, sail ties or flares. Lapslie peeled a note from his wallet, and a second later his mobile started vibrating in his pocket. 'There's twenty for the parts, so buy a couple of drinks for your mates as well next weekend. I'd better get this—' He broke off and took out his mobile.

It was a text message from Rebecca Graves: *Think I've hit on something with one of the five time-linked disappearances. I'm in the station right now, but can meet you outside if you think it best.*

Moulsham café, Chelmsford, Essex

'And this was the disappearance case from eight years ago?' Lapslie confirmed after the first few minutes of Rebecca Graves relating what she'd discovered.

'Yes, sir. The Timothy Wright case. Disappeared seven years ago, never to be seen again. Presumed dead, but no body found so it can't be proved one way or the other what happened to him.'

'Just like the other three.' Lapslie nodded sagely as he took his first sip of tea.

They were in a greasy spoon café three blocks from Chelmsford HQ. Not the first choice for those taking a break from the station, or even the second – so unlikely they'd be seen.

There hadn't been the time to arrange a formal meeting in the pub or garden centre, but still Lapslie had taken the precaution of making sure they left separately. Bradbury said she wanted to stay ten minutes to check on something, and Derek Bain couldn't immediately be located, so they'd sent him a text to join them when he could.

But even with those precautions, walking out of the station five minutes after Rebecca Graves, Lapslie had the sensation of someone looking at him, the smell and taste of mulching grass assaulting him, and as he glanced back he saw Benedict Allsopp looking out of his second-floor window towards him. Allsopp looked hastily away, as if something else had drawn his attention in his office. Still, Lapslie hoped that Allsopp didn't pick up on them all leaving within minutes of each other and put two and two together.

Bradbury was up at the counter grabbing a coffee, and Lapslie gave her a nod of acknowledgement as she made her way over with it. He looked back towards Rebecca Graves.

'Remind me again, what were the details of those other three disappearances?'

DC Graves checked her notes briefly. 'Steven Proctor, 8th May, 1996 . . . Kyle Standen, 19th May, 2001 . . . then this one with Timothy Wright, 12th May, 2008. And the last one was Daniel Clough . . .' Graves flicked back in her notes. 'I'm sorry, I don't seem to have the exact date for that one—'

'Two thousand and twelve,' Bradbury interjected, 'if I recall rightly. And that would have been a similar period. All the disappearances occurred within a twenty-day or so timespan in May.'

'As with Ben Tovey. Although I think James Lewis was deliberately abducted outside that time frame to exonerate Tulley.' Lapslie nodded, letting the information settle for a moment.

Bradbury smiled tightly. 'Which was no doubt why you asked us to focus on that time frame each year.'

Lapslie picked up on the inference. 'Yes, of course. But what other disappearances do we have in that same age range for the months either side? That is, if you happened to check.'

Another tight smile. 'Already covered, sir. The number of disappearances for the months each side, April and June, are far fewer. Only two for both months combined in all of twenty years.'

'I see.' Lapslie took another sip of his tea. 'So of these five date-matched disappearances, what makes the Timothy Wright case special?'

Rebecca Graves looked briefly at Bradbury before answering. She'd already shared the information with her before leaving the station, so wasn't sure for a moment whether Bradbury wished to impart it. 'Because that's the only one of the cases where they had a suspect at one point and started preparing a file for the CPS.'

'Started?' Lapslie held a hand out. 'What stopped them?'

'The suspect, Gavin Dimock, was apparently seen by an eyewitness with young Timothy Wright the afternoon of his disappearance on a Darlington street only three miles from his home.' Graves took a fresh breath. 'What stopped the case progressing was that Gavin Dimock came up with a firm alibi.'

Lapslie gestured with the same hand. 'Which was?'

Bradbury took over. 'That he was visiting a relative over two hundred miles away. A first cousin who in fact lives only seven miles from here.'

Lapslie could tell from Bradbury's 'cat's got the cream' smile that there was a significance beyond this being the only one of the five cases with a possible suspect. 'Somebody known to us?' he pressed.

'Yes, very much so,' Bradbury said pointedly. 'Gavin Dimock's first cousin on his mother's side is none other than Alistair Tulley. He supplied the main alibi, and Dimock also produced a return train ticket to cover the dates in question. There was also CCTV footage of him buying the ticket at Darlington railway station, and that sealed it.'

'My goodness.' Lapslie exhaled as if he'd received a stomach punch as he sat back. 'So now we have a possible family circle connection. No doubt nobody bothered to check whether Dimock got on the train or not?'

'No, sir.' Graves cast her eyes down briefly, as if she'd been personally responsible for that oversight. 'The combination of the alibi and the train ticket offered by his solicitors was seen as enough.'

Bradbury smiled tautly. 'Combined with the fact that at a second interview the eyewitness said that she suddenly "wasn't so sure". That was the last nail in the procedural coffin.'

Lapslie closed his eyes briefly, as if seeking strength. 'So once again we have a high probability, but nothing we can nail firmly to the mast.'

Bradbury left him alone with his own thoughts for a moment, the background clatter of the café suddenly seeming more evident.

'That's not the only thing, sir. The solicitors representing Dimock were a certain Hibbett Rayleigh.'

'Am I meant to know them?'

'Not them directly, sir. But I wanted to check them out more thoroughly – which is why I was held up in the office a bit longer. For trial preparation, Hibbett Rayleigh regularly use three barristers.' Bradbury grimaced. 'And one of those, Toby Sinclair, is very much known to you.'

Lapslie was still in a daze from the information as he walked out of the café.

How best to deal with it? He couldn't possibly haul Tulley back in for questioning as to why he'd provided an alibi for his cousin Gavin Dimock eight years ago – not without it coming to Rouse's attention.

And if he tackled it from the other way by questioning Dimock in Darlington, it would come to the attention of Hibbett Rayleigh, and in turn Toby Sinclair, so would just as quickly end up on Rouse's desk too. Then there was the thorny question of how to sidestep Benedict Allsopp as well. Even if he was deft and crafty enough to keep it all under Rouse's radar, Allsopp was another matter. Allsopp was already suspicious from seeing their little trio, now a quartet, huddled in the corridors or heading out of the office at the same time, so at the first whiff of a new line of investigation with Tulley, he'd notify Rouse and have them shut down in no time.

The other problem was that he had nobody else to share his thoughts with, to bounce options off and get feedback, as they'd all arranged to head off separately. Rebecca Graves had left three minutes beforehand, and said she'd be heading around the back to her car and straight off – so hopefully wouldn't be seen by anyone looking out from the station. And Bradbury said she'd hang on for twenty minutes in the café to finish some notes on another case.

But all of these efforts at secrecy were going to be for nothing if he put a foot wrong in progressing the next stages of the case. How to probe further with Tulley or Dimock, without making either Rouse or Allsopp aware?

At that moment he saw Derek Bain walking swiftly towards him, beaming as he gave a half-wave of acknowledgement. What has he got to smile about? Unless he was rushing out of the station to tell Lapslie he had the ideal solution to his dilemma.

'Think we might have hit gold with Interpol,' Bain announced as he approached, catching at his breath from his brisk walk. 'I was tracking down a boy from two years ago who they thought might have disappeared in Spain.'

Lapslie looked anxiously past Bain. There were still some corner buildings between them and the station; they couldn't be seen. 'And is that where he was finally found?'

'No. He was found about forty miles from where he first disappeared, in Belgium.'

'Belgium,' Lapslie echoed blandly, raising a brow. 'And the significance to our case?'

'First of all, the date matches – mid-May.' Bain's smile had faded, but now took on even graver overtones. 'But also the way in which the boy was killed and one limb removed. His right forearm.'

18

Sandpits Road, Richmond, Surrey

'I think they're getting too close.'

'It does appear so,' Sinclair commented in response to Mandrake's summary of fresh activity on the case. This time Mandrake had got hold of him early evening at home, so he had more time to deliberate and could speak more freely. Still he took the precaution of going into his private study out of earshot of his housekeeper. 'And now there are four of them working the case, you say?'

'Yes. The recent addition is a young DC, Derek Bain.'

'Does his addition to their team pose a specific problem for us?'

'No, he's a lightweight. But he's spent a while with an Interpol liaison division, which is why I think Lapslie chose him. And it was Bain who picked up on the connection with Eric Arles and the Luke Meerbecke case.'

'So not completely useless.' Sinclair sighed. 'When is Lapslie planning to meet Arles?'

'Later in the week, Thursday. Lapslie would have gone over straight away, but Arles was on the last few days of a holiday in Brittany. So that's the earliest it could be arranged.'

'And the connection between Tulley and Dimock. Did this new bright spark dig that up too?'

'No, that was one of the other two: Graves or Bradbury. It looks like Graves does the main donkey work, then Bradbury evaluates and digs deeper where necessary.'

'Regardless, now that they've made that connection, it will have to be dealt with. Time to enact plan B . . . or is it C now? I forget.' Sinclair swirled a freshly poured port in its balloon glass and took an appreciative swig.

There was a moment's silence the other end, then, 'There's another problem,' said Mandrake. 'That digging deeper I mentioned. I think they might have also hit on the connection between you and Dimock's solicitors.'

'*Think?*' Sinclair pressed sharply.

'There . . . there was a lot of background clatter in the café at that point. It . . . it wasn't totally clear.'

'I see.' Sinclair picked up on Mandrake's stammer, no doubt brought on by his insistent tone. Mandrake's only failing amongst his main attributes as a stealthy snooper and ice-cold killer. Sinclair sighed. 'It will have to be dealt with sooner than I planned. Perhaps we should have taken more drastic action earlier to avoid things getting to this stage.'

Chelmsford, Essex

At first, the images were only in Lapslie's mind. A shadowy figure, maybe two of them, moving around downstairs. And a smell and taste somewhere between saltwater and blue-vein cheese. Not wholly unpleasant, but sharp enough to wake him from his dream.

Lapslie rolled over and looked at the digital display on his alarm clock: 4.11 a.m. But then it struck him that the taste was what he normally associated with his personal space or belongings being encroached upon. The question was, had that been triggered by his dream, or was it happening in reality?

Lapslie sat up in bed, staying stock-still, listening out to the sounds of the house: the faint drone of traffic from the bypass half a mile away, the ticking of the grandfather clock in the downstairs hallway. Nothing else that he could discern. Or, if someone *was* snooping around downstairs, could they have heard his movement in the bed as he awakened, and in turn stayed stock-still, not daring to move.

He realized he wouldn't know without investigating. He got up and slipped on his dressing gown, grabbing the long black nightstick from the corner of the bedroom as he went out on to the upstairs hallway.

He didn't have a gun in the house; the nightstick had been a present from a fellow NYPD officer during a trip over seven years ago, and Lapslie had gone to the trouble of actually going to a few combat training exercises to learn how to use it effectively – it was not dissimilar to the Jō stick used in Aikido.

He had quickly learned that at reasonably close quarters a nightstick could be just as lethal as a gun, especially in the dark.

Lapslie made his way down the stairs slowly, stealthily, pausing every few seconds and listening out for any faint movement from downstairs. A faint rustling sound from the lounge as he was two-thirds of the way down, but as he paused again at the bottom, nothing beyond the ticking of the grandfather clock eight feet away.

He consciously held his breath. Could he have been mistaken with that rustling? Perhaps the trees at the side of the house brushing against the fence in the wind. He waited a full ten seconds without any further discernible sounds before moving on towards the lounge. He reached out towards the door handle with his left hand, the nightstick gripped in his right hand ready to swing. But still he observed the procedure of armed officers entering a fresh room – swinging the door open and stepping back from the open space. No gunfire. No discernible movement.

Lapslie crossed the threshold swiftly: there was enough moonlight coming in from a side window for him to see anyone inside the room. No visible figures. He moved around cautiously, at the same time listening out for movement from the adjacent dining room or kitchen; again, nothing.

Lapslie flicked on the light, and started on a fuller check of the room. He then checked the dining room and kitchen – nothing there either, nothing disturbed – before returning to the lounge. Satisfied after a few minutes, he was on his way back out of the lounge when he glanced to one side and noticed the middle drawer of his desk half an inch open.

It wasn't a big thing, but it was something he was particularly fastidious about. Even as a young child, he'd fully close any drawer he found left slightly open. He wouldn't have left the drawer like that. He opened the drawer to see what papers were there.

Mandrake got into his car three blocks away from Lapslie's house, then carefully put the three papers in his hand on the passenger seat – he wanted to avoid folding them, if possible – before starting up and driving off. He was sure that he hadn't been seen approaching the house or leaving. If he could slip into a Taliban camp in the dead of night without being seen, then suburban Essex was a doddle.

He could have waited a couple of days and gone in while Lapslie was in Belgium, but they didn't have the time. And besides, he wanted to stage a dry run: gauge Lapslie's exact position in the house and how he might respond to an intruder. He could have gone in and out without waking Lapslie, but to run his test he'd made just the right amount of noise to wake Lapslie, which could then be mistaken for the surrounding bushes and trees moving in the wind.

So, Lapslie carried a nightstick. If he'd come down the stairs with a .45 or an Uzi, he might have had to revise his thinking.

He knew now exactly what to do upon his return.

Chelmsford Police Headquarters, Essex

The large brown envelope was sitting in the middle of Lapslie's desk when he turned up at the station. On the front was typed simply his name: *Chief Inspector Mark Lapslie*. And in the bottom left-hand corner: *The file of Betty McCauley*.

He opened the envelope to find a foolscap folder full of papers, with a typed note on top:

```
I thought you might be ready for
this now. Before, it might have
seemed like wild ramblings, which
indeed was the thought of many who
first looked at Betty's case.

But now you have another murder in
Belgium of a young teen boy with his
right forearm severed. Now it appears
to be going beyond mere
circumstance.

Meanwhile, be careful who you
share this with internally. There
are those who'd like this case closed
down before it gains momentum. Not
least our good friend Toby Sinclair.
```

> All I can say is you're going the
> right way about it so far.

There was no name or address, no signature. Lapslie leafed through the first dozen pages in the folder and saw a selection of newspaper clippings related to Toby Sinclair and various child disappearances and murders.

He looked up sharply and went out into the general squad office.

'Did anyone see who delivered the large brown envelope now sitting on my desk?'

A few vague, nonplussed looks.

DC Kempsey was the first to answer. 'A messenger by the looks of it. Hot-Runners I think was the logo on his shirt. Local Essex company, if I recall rightly.'

Lapslie nodded and went back into his office, looked up the number for the Hot-Runners office in Chelmsford, and dialled.

After a few options *one*, *two* and *three* and a receptionist who didn't appear to know much, he finally got hold of someone useful.

'Ah, yes. Package 6574942. Delivered at 8.21 a.m. to Chief Inspector Lapslie at Chelmsford Police HQ.'

'Yes, that's the one. I wondered, could you tell me who asked you to deliver that envelope to me?'

'I'm afraid I can't do that, sir.'

'Oh, I think you can. This is Chief Inspector Lapslie himself speaking. And if I don't receive that name, I'll have a court order and warrant on your doorstep in no time.'

'I don't think that would help, sir.'

'Why's that?' A slightly incredulous tone.

'Because the man who gave me the package for delivery was also from the police: Scotland Yard. And he asked specifically that his name not be given.'

Berlare Lake, Belgium

Lapslie peered out across the lake. 'So is this where Luke's body was found?'

Eric Arles nodded solemnly, as if making it clear that Luke being his young nephew had given the case a special significance for him.

'Yes. In the shallow waters there, about seven or eight feet in.'

'And do you think it was their intention that Luke's body be found, or just that they were careless?'

'Neither.' Arles noted the faint surprise in Lapslie's face, and held one hand out. 'Oh, at first the police who found the body weren't sure. The lake's water level was lower than normal due to the prolonged summer heat, and then a young couple seeking cover in the thick reeds one side discovered it. So that's all that appeared in the official report. But I wasn't wholly satisfied with that, so I did a bit more digging on my own . . .'

Arles went on to describe getting hold of a local water-ways and fishing department. There had been a problem five years ago with thick mud at the bottom of Lake Ber-lare in which bacteria had thrived and impaired its fish stock. They therefore started treating the water – and that, combined with two hot summers in the couple of years following, had solidified the base mud.

'. . . and it also made it safer for anglers in the shal-lows, who beforehand could find themselves sinking deep into the soft mud.'

Lapslie nodded. 'So the situation when Luke's body was found would have been different from previous years?'

'Yes. With three feet of soft mud and thick reeds above, I don't think it was the intention that the body ever be found. Following that information, I had some police divers come out a few months later, and they found some ropes nearby. Those could have been from an old boat mooring, but equally they could have been from roped-in weights intended to keep a body down.'

Lapslie was impressed. Obviously the personal involvement had led Eric Arles to go the extra mile to discover what had happened to his young nephew. 'And the ropes get somehow caught up, the weights loosened, and the body floats free.'

'Yes. Exactly.' Arles joined Lapslie in taking in the broader expanse of the lake beyond the shallows for a moment. 'Could have been a fishing line or a small boat propeller. Only boats of a certain size are allowed here.' Arles sighed. 'In fact, a boat prop was one of the first theories put forward to explain young Luke's right forearm being severed and the stomach wound.'

Lapslie looked at Arles. 'But that wasn't in the end found to be the case?'

'No. At autopsy, both appeared to have been done with a scalpel and surgical saw not long before his body was left here.'

'But *after* death?'

'Yes. Strangulation and a broken neck appeared to be the cause of death.'

Lapslie maintained a brief silence after receiving that information, reflecting how Arles' personal involvement must have made the case doubly difficult. Lapslie had read half of the file left on his desk while still in his office, then the rest at the airport waiting to board and in flight. But despite its intriguing and gruesome details being so fresh and vivid in his mind, he didn't think Eric Arles was quite ready to hear that his young nephew's murder might be linked to a 500-year-old clan of cannibals.

So he kept it simply to, 'As you know from our brief phone conversation, we're investigating a few cases with a similar MO. And that's what has brought me out to see you now. To judge the similarities between the cases.'

'And *are* they similar?' Arles asked flatly.

'Yes. In many ways they are. Young teenage boys, each with their right arm forearm severed. And all of the missing boys abducted at a similar time of year.'

'How many boys?'

'Two bodies so far, in addition to this one.' A short silence followed, as if Arles sensed there was more and Lapslie was holding back. But that would then risk getting into Betty McCauley territory. Although there was one element he could reveal without getting into the realms of 500-year-old folklore. 'And we suspect it wasn't the initial intention that these bodies be discovered either.'

Arles was thoughtful for a second, scanning the cold, flat lake where his young nephew's body had been found. 'You know, it's strange. I had a journalist from England come and see me not long after Luke's body was found, and she too was specifically interested in the date of the murder and his right arm being severed. Though, in her case, she had only a very old case in England she was linking to, going all the way back to 1944. And another, in Poland, in the seventies.'

Lapslie felt a twinge of alarm. Arles seemed to be drifting into McCauley territory without any help from him. 'When was this?'

'Early in 2014, if I recall correctly.'

Lapslie nodded. Before the Ben Tovey case. 'And do you recall her name and which newspaper?'

'Some fringe journal. Never heard of them, I'm afraid. But she left me her card.'

19

Coggeshall village, Essex

It was one of the quietest villages in Essex, so not the sort of place where you'd expect a smuggling ring to be operating. But at least it was a smuggling operation more in tune with the village – small and low-key.

Annette Pierce had an extended family who were forever jetting off abroad or nipping across on the ferry to France, none of them smokers – so they'd make sure to stock up on duty-free or local cheap brands, which she'd then sell on to locals at almost half shop prices and still earn 20 per cent on the deal.

One of those who knew her trade and was a regular customer was sixty-two-year-old grandmother Janet Henshaw. A forty-a-day smoker for most of her life, now she'd managed to cut down to twenty a day, so felt she was being 'good'.

But the main reason for her cutting back was that her years of smoking had increasingly taken her energy and breath away – her 'puff', as she termed it. Ten years ago she could easily have made the half-mile to Annette's to pick up her packs of 200 cigarettes, but now she could hardly make it a few hundred yards without getting exhausted. So for the last few years she'd been using her grandson Brad for the task.

She minded him three or four times a week during school holidays while her daughter Samantha was at work. Samantha had always told her not to let Brad go out on his own, but what was going to happen to him in a village like Coggeshall? Besides, he was twelve now.

It was only a twenty-minute return walk, and she always instructed Brad to go straight there and back: 'And don't stop to talk to anyone on the way, particularly strangers.'

Annette would also do her bit by wrapping the cigarettes in gift paper, so if perchance he got stopped by the police on the way he wouldn't get into trouble for transporting 'smuggled tobacco'. If stopped, Janet had told him to say that it was Lego or a present for his grandmother, so he had no idea what was in the package.

As a final precaution, Janet would look out of her

front bay window so that she could watch Brad's progress the first two hundred yards of his journey there and back, before he took the turn into Honeywood Avenue.

Now she reminded young Brad, as she packed him off that morning to Annette's with a twenty-pound note in his hand, 'I'll look out for you from the bay window. Don't forget – go straight there and back, and don't stop to talk to anyone on the way.' She'd finished her last cigarette late the previous night; now, by late morning, she was gasping.

'Will do. Don't worry.'

Brad gave a smile of reassurance as he made his way out of the front door and Grandmother Janet dutifully took up her position by the bay window, watching his progress down the road.

Brussels Airport, Zaventem, Belgium

'He was a good kid. Had a tough time of it too with his mum splitting from his dad. It was a messy divorce, so it was hard on Luke and even harder on his younger brother, Justin. That's where it seemed Luke was heading that day when he was abducted – to get a stamp album for Justin for his birthday.'

'Oh, I didn't know,' Lapslie said, almost apologetically.

'No reason why you should. It wasn't in the official report.' Arles gestured with one hand lifted briefly from the steering wheel. He'd agreed to run Lapslie to the airport at Zaventem, because it would then give them extra time to discuss the case. 'It's been a strong feature of both boys' lives these past few years – missing their father. That was in fact the first theory we pursued when Luke disappeared: that his father might have abducted him and he was down with him in Denia.'

Lapslie nodded. 'Probably the reason the case turned up on the Interpol files.'

'Yes, there is that to it. Happy accident.' Arles grimaced awkwardly. 'We put out these international notices, but when a solution is found close to home, often we forget to notify them.'

'I'm sure by then you had far weightier things on your mind.' Lapslie in turn returned a tight grimace. With all Arles had been through, the last thing he wanted was him worrying unduly about a bureaucratic oversight.

They drove in silence for a moment, then Arles commented, 'And have you had any suspects for these two murders with similar MOs in England?'

'Yes, we charged one with the first murder, but then

he was cleared at trial. And another man was charged with the second murder.'

'And did you secure a conviction against him?'

'Yes, we did. But there were elements about that second case I was never fully satisfied with. Now, on top of that, we have the factor that he couldn't have been responsible for this murder in Belgium, *if* they are connected.' Lapslie sighed. 'I took the trouble of checking before flying out. The second man convicted hasn't left the UK in six years.'

Arles nodded thoughtfully. 'Well, at least you are two suspects ahead of our police here, even if you aren't happy with them.'

'Yes, I suppose that's one way of looking at it.' In going through the case in detail earlier, Arles had revealed that at no time had they identified any possible suspects for Luke's murder: *a handful of eyewitness claims, but none of them amounted to anything.*

Arles took a fresh breath. 'And if your two cases in England – and this one here with Luke – *are* connected, do you have any theories as to motive and who is behind them? As I mentioned to this journalist, when she told me about the historic cases, cross-continental mass murderers are not that common.'

'No, they're not,' Lapslie said.

Obviously, this was a topic Arles had touched on previously with this British journalist, but he doubted she'd said much – either because she herself didn't know or because she was going light on the details in view of Arles' personal involvement – otherwise Arles wouldn't be probing again now. Lapslie didn't want to step into that minefield for much the same reasons. He'd found the details in the Betty McCauley file gory and stomach-churning enough, God knows how it would hit Arles with his personal attachment to Luke. And it was still too early; he'd only been in possession of the information for eight hours, he needed more time to let his thoughts settle and determine how it all might tie in.

Probably safest to throw the question back. 'And what did this journalist have to say on that front? Did she have any possible culprits or hypotheses?'

Arles stared at the road ahead, a wry smile teasing his mouth after a second. 'No, she didn't. She was as cagey as you are on the subject, Chief Inspector.' He lifted one palm from the wheel. 'But then that was before these two murders in England – or any possible suspects for them.'

'I know.' Lapslie sighed. 'And, believe me, we're working those suspects and all possible links as hard and as fast as we can, including the information you've now given me. So hopefully we should have some clearer direction within the week. At which time, you'll be one of the first on my list to notify.'

Arles grimaced his accord, and it was difficult for Lapslie to read whether he was put out by getting a standard interdepartmental response, or accepted that Lapslie was doing his level best and being guarded for a reason. He could almost hear the cogs in Arles' mind turning, perhaps gearing up another question, but at that moment his mobile started ringing in his pocket.

'Excuse me.' He was glad of the interruption – until he heard the sharp edge in Emma Bradbury's voice at the other end.

'There's been a new development, sir. You need to get back here *urgently*.'

'I'm actually on the way to the airport right now, as we speak. Why, what's happened?'

'There's been another one.'

Coggeshall village, Essex

It was late evening, nearly 10 p.m., by the time Lapslie got to the crime scene. Two white tents had been erected at the scene: a small tent surrounding the body itself and a larger tent where Jim Thompson's SOCO team bagged and labelled everything they'd collected, and conferred when necessary. Bright arc lamps lit up the tents and the fields immediately surrounding the area of farmland. Less than half a mile from Coggeshall, it stood out like a bright beacon, and so it was hardly necessary to consult a satnav on the final stretch from the village.

Emma Bradbury watched as the taxi that had run Lapslie from the airport drew up at the side of the field. She approached and greeted him twelve yards from the tents. He was still carrying his shoulder travelbag, having not returned home as yet. She'd already given him a quick breakdown by phone, and now she filled in the gaps as they walked towards Thompson and his team.

'So what was the boy's name again . . . Brad Hensley?'

'Henshaw,' Bradbury corrected. 'Twelve years old, so the same age range as the other two. The right forearm severing looks the same too, and there's a deep stomach wound – though obviously we'll know more when Thompson's finished.'

Lapslie nodded, briefly acknowledging Jim Thompson who gave him a mock half-salute from a few yards away as he was going between the two tents. 'And a local boy, you say?'

'Yes. Lived less than a mile away and was staying close by at the time, with his grandmother. He went out briefly on an errand for his grandma – but didn't return.'

'How long before the grandmother called in to say he was missing?'

'No more than an hour after he was gone.' Feeling Lapslie's eyes on her, searching, obviously expecting more – with previous disappearances the delay had been far longer before any alarm was raised – she elaborated. 'It was a short walk to a friend's house that Brad had done many times before. As soon as he didn't return on time, she sensed something was wrong. When she finally phoned her friend to be told that Brad had never even shown up there, she knew for sure. She phoned the police straight after. The call was logged at 12.53 p.m.'

'And how long before the body was discovered?'

'Just over four hours later.' Bradbury gestured. 'The farmer who owns this field gets the cows grazing here back into his barn at the end of the day. It's quite an open field, as you can see, and there was little or no effort made to conceal the body.'

Lapslie took in the expanse of the field in each direction. With the bright spotlights nearly all of it was visible up to a line of trees on one side and the road on the other, where his taxi had pulled up. 'So it looks like they wanted his body to be discovered, or couldn't be bothered either way.'

'Looks like it, sir.'

Lapslie's gaze drifted back to the line of trees for a moment. Less than a hundred and fifty yards away, even if they'd been in a rush, it would have taken them only an extra two minutes to ensure more effective concealment amongst the trees. For whatever reason they'd wanted this body to be discovered quickly. Speed had also obviously been an issue with the murder itself. Less than four hours between young Brad's disappearance and his body being found; during which time – if his murder followed the pattern of the others – he was strangled and his neck broken, his right forearm severed, an organ removed and his body dumped.

Lapslie shuddered. 'Okay. Let's see him,' he said, grimacing tautly.

They walked towards the small tent. Inside, there was only Jim Thompson and one of his assistants crouching down by the body and inspecting the surrounding area;

the other four in his team were in the larger analysis tent.

With a brief nod at Thompson, Lapslie studied the body. Unlike the previous corpses, Brad's skin tone was fresh, his face almost angelic, as if life hadn't yet ebbed fully from him. Although the gore lower down belied that.

'What estimate for time of death?' he asked Thompson.

'Sometime between two and three this afternoon. We'll know more when we get back to the lab and study organ lividity and stomach content.'

Lapslie did a quick mental calculation: so, only an hour or two after he was reported missing. His eyes shifted to the missing forearm; it looked different from the others, a darker mottled red, almost black in parts.

'Has the forearm been severed in the same way as the two previous victims? It looks different.'

'The main difference is that it has been cauterized; that's what has made it almost maroon in colour, and smoother. The same has been done on the stomach wound too. But where there are gaps in the cauterization, the cut marks look the same – a surgical implement or sharp saw. Again, I'll know more once I get the body back to the lab.'

'*Cauterization?*' Lapslie was reminded of the gruesome details in the Betty McCauley file, with tales of severed limbs being cauterized. 'What, as in being put in an open fire?'

'Yes, that's one way of doing it. But at first examination, this one looks like it's been done with a blowtorch.'

'And internal organs removed?'

'I can actually feel the liver in place, but one kidney appears to be missing – which I'll be able to verify back at the lab.'

Lapslie sighed. 'So the same limb removal and type of cut, but everything else is different. Not a semi-truant boy who could go missing for hours or days without an alarm being raised. And then the tremendous rush to carry out everything.'

Jim Thompson nodded. 'That was possibly the reason for the cauterization. Removing limbs and organs so soon after death would have been a messy affair. A lot of bloodstains on those moving and dumping the body.'

'And the murder date is different too,' Bradbury commented. 'Six to seven weeks beyond the date frame of the other murders.'

Thompson raised a brow. 'Is that significant?'

'Could be,' Lapslie said. He looked towards Thompson's assistant who was straightening up after lifting a strand of something a yard from Brad's body and bagging it. 'Many fibres found?'

'A half-dozen or so,' Thompson said. 'We won't know how important they are until we've matched them against those taken from the boy's clothing and the farmer's, which will be done back—'

'I know, in the lab,' Lapslie cut in. He smiled tightly. 'We're in something of a rush too on this one. So what time can we convene there?'

Thompson studied the boy's body for a second, then looked back in the direction of the larger tent, as if reminding himself what was still to be done there. 'Late tomorrow afternoon, four to four thirty. I should have 90 per cent of it wrapped up by then.'

'Okay – 4.15 at the lab.' Lapslie nodded and made his way out, Bradbury just behind him. As soon as he was clear of the tent, he crouched down and reached inside his bag, taking out the large folder inside. He handed it to Bradbury. 'We're going to have a busy morning with this murder now, full steam until the end of the afternoon with Jim Thompson. So leave an hour early tomorrow morning, and have this lot copied at a bureau on the way in. Four copies – one each for me, you, Graves and Bain. I want all of your thoughts on this by early afternoon, along with this current murder and how it all might tie in. So we'll grab an hour or so at 2 p.m. at the Old Windmill.'

Bradbury was thoughtful for a second. 'Are you thinking this murder might *not* be connected, because of all its differences?'

'Either that, or it's a complete ruse to throw us off the scent – because now we've got too close to successfully linking the other murders.'

20

Chelmsford Police Headquarters, Essex

Lapslie got into the station ten minutes early. Rebecca Graves was already in and confirmed that Bradbury had texted her late the night before about a meeting at 2 p.m. at 'Place 1', the Old Windmill. Derek Bain wasn't in, nor Emma Bradbury – no doubt still photocopying the voluminous Betty McCauley file.

No fresh messages, emails on his computer or notes on his desk about the Brad Henshaw murder, but then it was only the start of the day.

He was just sifting through general emails which had arrived while he was in Belgium when his office door opened and someone he wasn't used to seeing in that setting stood there – Chief Superintendent Rouse.

'I'd like to see you in my office . . . *now!*'

He was slow in getting up from his desk, following a good six paces behind Rouse – still somewhat in shock from the surprise visit. Rouse hardly ever visited his office, would normally phone down or send a messenger. But in this case he could see Rouse's messenger, Benedict Allsopp, hovering just behind Rouse's shoulder as his office door had opened, and now dutifully following a step behind Rouse.

Rouse headed straight to his desk and took his seat while Allsopp acted as doorman, holding it open with a prim smile for Lapslie to enter ahead of him.

Lapslie took the seat directly in front of Rouse's desk while, unsettlingly, Allsopp took the only spare seat slightly to one side and behind Lapslie. Unsettling, because Lapslie couldn't see Allsopp or gauge his reactions without craning his head.

Rouse held one hand out. 'What's all this I hear about you being away in Belgium when this latest murder took place?'

'Yes, that's true, sir. But I was following a lead connected to the past two young-teen cases, and so possibly this one too.'

'*Connected?* In what earthly way? Those last two murder cases were cut and dried, the book shut, with the conviction of Harvey Reid.'

'That might have seemed the case, on the face of it.

But this boy in Belgium was killed in almost exactly the same way, with his right forearm surgically severed. And the date-period matches too.'

'The *date-period* matches?' Rouse's patience, already paper-thin, appeared to be wearing even thinner.

'Yes, sir. Early to late May. The first boy murdered in Essex was in the same period. And the second within a related time frame.'

'Ever thought that it might be just a coincidence?' The exasperation was clear in Rouse's voice.

'Perhaps with two, yes – but with this third one in Belgium, that *coincidence* starts to be stretched too far.'

'Except with this one now – which you should have been here for, rather than on a wild goose chase in Belgium – is a completely different date. Somewhat destroys your theory.'

Lapslie fell silent for a second, then suddenly found he was voicing the thought he'd promised himself to hold back until he'd deliberated more. 'But we believe this current murder is purely a ruse to throw us off track now that we're getting too close.'

'A ruse to throw you off track?' Rouse echoed incredulously. 'Then why not the murder in Belgium a possible ruse? Because certainly that appears to have been successful in making sure you were off the scene while another boy was murdered.'

'Except that the murderer we convicted, Harvey Reid, is now languishing in prison – so it couldn't have been him.'

'Yes,' Rouse said impatiently, as if Lapslie were missing the obvious. 'Which leaves us with a possible copycat murder, or the likelihood that Reid had an accomplice in the last two murders, which we didn't uncover first time around.'

Accomplice? They were getting into the area that Toby Sinclair had suggested at Reid's trial – the existence of a third-party evidence-planter. And a key factor in Lapslie weighing up Reid's innocence had been that Reid might be unable to engineer an elaborate and sophisticated frame-up of Tulley – which factor could also be answered by an accomplice. He shook the thought quickly away; it went against everything he'd discovered since, including the Betty McCauley file.

'I'm afraid there's too much now that stands against that, sir. It appears that Toby Sinclair might have been at the centre of orchestrating much of this.'

'*What?* Harvey Reid's barrister? But he defended Reid robustly, if I remember rightly.'

'Yes, he did. But I believe Sinclair expected Reid to go down for it, which would then clear his main client, Alistair Tulley.' Lapslie leaned forward and held a hand out, sensing Rouse's patience waning again. 'And we now discover that Sinclair would have been the likely defending barrister in a child disappearance case from 2008 – the main suspect in which was none other than Alistair Tulley's cousin.'

Rouse blinked slowly as he let the information settle, then started shaking his head. '*Likely* defending barrister . . . child *disappearance* rather than murder. You don't seem to appreciate, even from your own vocabulary used, how tenuous this all sounds.'

'And then there's the file that arrived just the other day.' Lapslie gestured with the same hand, pushing the point. 'Which puts Sinclair at the centre of a number of other possible cases.'

'*File?*' Rouse quizzed sharply.

'Yes.' Lapslie eased back, suddenly realizing that in his haste to build his case he'd crossed another line he'd cautioned himself not to; and also ignored the warning to take care who he shared the file with internally. Rouse's disbelief was already teetering on the edge. God knows what Rouse would think if he hinted at an international child murder ring linked to a 500-year-old cannibal clan. He kept the focus on Sinclair: 'The involvement of Sinclair with these past cases is now impossible to ignore, and takes it beyond mere coincidence.'

Rouse nodded sombrely. 'And who, may I ask, sent you this file?'

'Uh . . . it was sent by someone at Scotland Yard.'

'Did you get a name?'

'No, I didn't,' Lapslie said on the back of a deflated sigh. 'I enquired of the messenger service who sent the file, but apparently the Scotland Yard man who gave it to them asked specifically that his name not be given.'

'Did he now?' Rouse smiled patiently. 'I suppose now you're getting a better understanding of how a ruse actually works. Sometimes these object lessons come late in life.'

Lapslie felt like reaching across and throttling Rouse, some chlorine vapours stinging his sinuses and trickling down the back of his throat. The taste of powerlessness and how it felt to be trapped, probably stemming from when he'd almost drowned as a child in the swimming baths.

'I too received a call from Scotland Yard,' Rouse

continued. 'Telling me in no uncertain terms that you were off on a wild-goose chase with some Interpol enquiry, while meanwhile ignoring duties on your home patch. And they *did* give me a name – though I'm not about to share it with you.'

Lapslie looked around and glared at Allsopp – the first time he'd looked his way since entering Rouse's office.

But Allsopp held his hands out with a contrite, 'What, *moi*?' expression.

Lapslie looked back at Rouse. 'But don't you see, sir. This is one of Sinclair's cronies, calling to bury my line of enquiry before we get too close.'

'That's as may be. But if I were a barrister of Toby Sinclair's standing and reputation, I too might be concerned about someone digging around making wild, unsubstantiated claims – and make a few calls.' Rouse let out a tired breath. 'Look, Mark. It all ends here, *now*. No more digging into sideline cases with Sinclair. You pursue this current murder case of this young boy in Coggeshall, but nothing outside of that. If it ends up pointing at Sinclair, then fine, I'll back you up with it. If, as I suspect, it doesn't – fine, also. Clear?'

'Yes, sir. *Clear.*' Lapslie stormed out of Rouse's office.

But that was only his wishful thinking; in reality, it was more of a subdued slinking out with his tail between his legs.

Hackney, north-east London

Mandrake was quite happy sitting silently watching somebody. He could sit for hours, motionless, with hardly a blink or a muscle twitching. He'd sat for four hours one night watching a Taliban camp before deciding on the best time to strike; aware that the slightest movement might alert them to his presence and likely lead to his death. On the other two killing missions, both involving night-time sorties, he'd only had to wait an hour or two. But for most people that would feel like a lifetime, staying stock-still and keeping even your breath and heartbeat subdued for fear of death; for most people that thought alone would increase their heartbeat and breathing.

But he noticed that his silent-watching routine would also have a similar effect on those he was watching.

The calligrapher they'd brought in was originally from Cambodia, but apparently they'd found him in the back-streets of Bangkok, three blocks from the floating market.

The first few versions, each one discarded after only ten minutes, he'd done with a steady hand. Now on his seventh version, the hand was still steady, but beads of sweat had broken out on the old man's forehead . . . and in the silence Mandrake was sure he could hear the fall of the old man's laboured breath.

But the old man didn't say anything – hardly surprising, because he had little or no English – so all that had passed between them had been grunts, nods and finger-pointing – he simply raised his eyes from the papers before him to stare back steadily at Mandrake. A look that said: *if you want me to finish quickly and not spend another two hours on discarded copies, then you'd better stop staring at me.*

'More tea?' Mandrake enquired.

Only a grunt returned, so Mandrake pointed to the old man's cup from his last green tea an hour ago.

'More?'

The old man nodded, and Mandrake went into the kitchen.

The Old Windmill public house, Essex

Lapslie looked at the scrap of paper on which he'd written the name and number from his meeting with Arles: *Josie Dallyn, TNT publications.*

It had been too late the night before to make the phone call, and the meeting with Rouse meant he hadn't had the chance earlier in the day, as he'd originally intended. Then, after the meeting, he'd become nervous about making the call from the office, so he'd delayed until his planned meeting at the Old Windmill, getting there fifteen minutes early and punching in the number on his mobile while scanning the pub car park.

A woman's voice answered and he went through the preambles of announcing himself and asking for Josie Dallyn.

'I'm afraid she doesn't work here any more. But let me put you through to our editor, Dennis Ashby. He'll possibly have more information.'

A full minute's pause, in which time the receptionist had obviously explained the enquiry, because Ashby came on the line and repeated that Josie Dallyn no longer worked there, 'She only does the occasional freelance article for us.'

'How long since she left to go freelance?'

'Oh, a good eighteen months now.' Ashby was being purposely cautious. After Josie's problems and Barton's death, her 'only occasionally freelancing' was the standard line for any caller. Then, if the call related to an article she was working on, a number would be taken and Josie would later make contact. 'Is there a specific story you were interested in?'

'Yes. It relates to a story she was working on about the disappearance of a number of young teens, many of them historic cases. I was given this number by Inspector Arles in Belgium.'

A pause.

Then, 'Before my time, I'm afraid. That would probably have been from when Tom Barton was editor. But give me your number. I'll ask Josie to phone you.'

'That fucking Rouse and his errand-boy, Allsopp. They're up each other's arses so hard they make long-term porridge boyfriends look like choirboys.'

Lapslie was still fuming, hours after his meeting with Rouse in which Allsopp had ridden shotgun, and Emma Bradbury was shocked. She'd rarely heard her boss swear, so two expletives in a single sentence was something of a record. Though Derek Bain seemed to take it easily in his laddish stride; suddenly Lapslie was more like 'one of the boys'.

'I think choirboys would go down a treat with long-termers,' Bain retorted with a sly smile.

The banter went over Rebecca Graves' head, she appeared to focus solely on the underlying intent. 'Does that mean we simply do as Rouse has instructed and drop everything we've been pursuing? Seems a shame when we—'

'No, we don't,' Lapslie cut in, sighing. 'But it does mean that we'll have to be more cautious. So fewer meetings like this, and watching our backs more. We can't afford to slip up and get caught.'

Graves and Bain both nodded a tame accord, but Bradbury appeared more circumspect. 'That's all very well, sir. But all that's going to make the process longer ... and how long do we keep our little game running in secret? Because we won't be able to pursue anything against Sinclair, let alone involve the CPS, without Rouse's backing.'

'I appreciate that. But right now we only have two or three possible links. We need to find more, and try to shift the possibles to probables or definites. We'll know when the time is right.' Lapslie looked from one to the other for a moment. 'On which front, how did you all get on with the enquiries I gave you earlier?'

Early morning, and without any mention of the meeting he'd just come out of with Rouse, he'd given them each separate assignments. Emma Bradbury was first to speak. They'd caught the tail-end of the lunchtime trade, so the Old Windmill was busier than normal. Although they'd tucked themselves away in their usual alcove, she had to raise her voice slightly to be heard above the background clatter.

'Nothing on Gavin Dimock or Alistair Tulley possibly being in the Coggeshall area at the time of Brad Henshaw's murder. In fact, Tulley was on holiday on the Costa Brava at the time.'

'When did he fly out?'

'Just two days beforehand.'

Lapslie pursed his mouth. 'Seems a tad convenient. Flies out just two days beforehand. And Dimock?'

'No record of him leaving Darlington in the past few days. Though of course national rail and coach journeys are harder to check.'

'Yes, of course. But try to get CCTV checks on the main rail and coach stations the past few days – in fact, go back a full week, just in case.' Lapslie looked towards Bain. 'And Belgium on the key days?'

'Nothing for Tulley or Dimock there either, checking flights and the ferry terminals. But I did hit gold on another front.' A wry smile teased Bain's lips. 'Our good friend Toby Sinclair booked a flight to Antwerp just a week after Luke Meerbecke's body was found.'

Lapslie nodded. This was the prime time when it might have hit Sinclair that he and his associates could be facing a possible case, time to start shoring up defences. 'Okay. If you can, find out which law firm Sinclair was visiting there, if any. Sinclair can't present a case in Belgium, so he'd have needed someone else.' He took a fresh breath. 'But there was something else interesting that came up in my trip to Belgium.' Lapslie went on to explain about Arles being visited by journalist Josie Dallyn early in 2014. 'But when I phoned her journal, *TNT*, it appears she's left now and only works there occasionally as a freelancer.'

Emma Bradbury was lost in thought for a second. 'I recall there being a big upset at *TNT* when its past editor, Tom Barton, committed suicide. Took them quite a few months to get back on their feet again. That would have been about the same time.'

Lapslie picked up on the inference. 'And was there anything suspicious recorded about his suicide?'

'Not that I recall.' Bradbury shrugged. 'And if she was pursuing this story, I don't remember anything appearing in print about it, either.'

Lapslie sighed. 'Probably in the end simply didn't get enough. But it does go to show that there have been others digging into some of these past cases. On which front . . .' He turned to Rebecca Graves. 'How did things go your end?'

'So-so.' She leafed through the folder in her lap. 'Betty McCauley's list of murders and disappearances check out – some of the more recent ones I'd already covered. And the Gdansk boy in 1977, apart from the body being discovered far sooner, is almost on all fours with the Luke Meerbecke case. Reminds us that these cases are spread over a number of countries.'

Graves flicked back two pages in the file. 'But there might be more to the 1962 disappearance of paperboy Martin Berry in Somerset than Betty realized. Some of Berry's blood was found in a Taunton warehouse, and the warehouse owner was originally charged, then released. It was always suspected that young Martin met a gruesome end there, but with the date matching – 9th May disappearance – the blood-spots could as easily have been from his forearm being severed or an organ removed.'

Lapslie nodded. 'Good work. Though it might be seen as circumstantial, especially with the resistance we now face from Rouse. So we need more of that, plus a few hard-and-fast facts. And pretty soon we'll have stitched together a patchwork quilt to smother Rouse's doubt.'

Bain grimaced. 'And do you think it was Balls-Up who ratted on you?'

'Yes, I do. I think he wound Rouse up, had a mate call from Scotland Yard, then just sat in the background gloating as Rouse did his bit.'

Bradbury looked uncomfortable about something. 'Sir, you mentioned earlier that this current murder might simply be a ruse, a diversion. If that's the case – and Sinclair's behind it – then no doubt he has a specific garden path in mind to lead us up.'

'Yes, fair point,' Lapslie agreed. 'Whatever's behind it, it's going to take up a fair bit of our time over the coming weeks.'

'And likely lead us further away from our current

direction,' Bradbury finished the thought. 'If that's what Sinclair has in mind.'

'No doubt it is.' Lapslie sighed. 'But in rushing everything this time, hopefully they'll have made a mistake. Shown us their Achilles heel and given us the final missing key.' Lapslie looked keenly at his dedicated team of three, pressing the message home. But he could sense doubt setting in again; probably them questioning whether the likes of Sinclair *ever* made mistakes. He took a fresh breath, patting his copy of the Betty McCauley file. 'So while we're all complaining about possible obstacles and delays, here we have someone who has spent many more years than us trying to nail Toby Sinclair. Apart from its gruesome nature and, at times, wild ramblings – what general thoughts on Betty's file?'

'Wild ramblings, yes,' Bradbury agreed, 'and no doubt some wild imaginings too – but a lot of it is spot-on with our findings to date. Or, at least, makes some coincidences too significant to ignore.'

Bain grinned. 'On the imaginings and folklore side, it's easy to see why your phantom sender advised you not to share this with Rouse or any of the hierarchy.'

'A real labour of love,' Graves commented, 'and an impressive piece of research, too, tying all this together.' Her mood quickly became sombre. 'Couldn't have been easy, either. Losing your only child, then devoting all those years to compiling this.'

They were silent for a moment, the surrounding clatter of the pub imposing briefly.

'I think that's all part of it,' Bradbury offered. 'While she's working on this, a part of her still feels *with* him. The role of many a mother – doing something on behalf of her child. Only this time she's trying to find his murderer. Find justice.'

21

Within two hours of getting the call from *TNT* editor Dennis Ashby to say that Inspector Lapslie had phoned, Josie got hold of Scobe to ask his advice.

'Should I phone him back, what do you think? What should I say?'

'What made him call you at this juncture, do you think?'

'Dennis mentioned something about him getting my name from Inspector Arles in Belgium.'

'Oh, right. Lapslie's recently picked up on that link too. He's just come back from a trip over there, so that ties in. Makes sense.' Scobe took a fresh breath. 'But I'm not sure what added value your contact would have at this stage. Your information is mostly two years old, which Lapslie would have already got first-hand from Arles. Your other cases are far more historic, and he's had a ton of those dumped on his desk just the other day with the Betty McCauley file.'

'So are you saying don't make contact?'

'Not exactly. We might well decide that you should make contact later, just that now's not the best time. Lapslie's got an awful lot on his plate right now, not only delving through the Betty McCauley file, but the fact that there's been another murder on his patch.'

'Yes. I saw the news about that. But the date doesn't tie in.'

'No, it doesn't.' Scobe sighed. 'And this is strictly off-file and off-the-record – because nothing so far has been officially recorded or mentioned in the press – but the boy's right forearm was severed.'

'Oh, jeez. Where does that leave us?'

'Exactly. And I think that's been the intention. To throw a curve ball in to destroy the date link, point to a murderer operating only in Essex.'

'But what about Luke and Arles in Belgium? And the boy in Gdansk I discovered from the seventies?'

'I made sure the Gdansk case and the Plymouth boy at the end of the war were included in the Betty McCauley file for Lapslie, under the heading: *Other cases related to Betty McCauley in the course of her enquiries.*'

'I see.'

With the moment's awkward silence that followed, Scobe added, 'Sorry for taking that decision without consulting you – but I thought it was important that Lapslie's team had those cases as well. And I didn't want to risk putting your name directly under a police spotlight, given your past problems.'

Josie eased her breath after a moment. 'No, you're right . . . you're right. It was the best move.'

'But no doubt, with these recent Essex cases now, they'll claim that the MOs on these other murders were just coincidence. Especially when spread over such a long period.'

'Are you saying that Sinclair and his mob will get away with it in the end – after all we've done? All our efforts, all those years devoted by Betty.'

Scobe could hear the exasperation in Josie's voice, and he wished there was something more positive he could say to salve her concern. 'We would hope not. But Lapslie and his team are under a lot of pressure right now. Not only this fresh murder, but also straight after returning from seeing Arles, Lapslie was called in to his superior's office. They're trying to shut his side investigations down.'

'Oh, for God's sake. Then we'll be completely adrift again.'

'And we should also remind ourselves that when you started digging deeper into cases two years ago, before you even met Arles, they latched on to you pretty quickly and set you up with Swan-Tattoo.' As Scobe said it, something nagged at the back of his mind about that detail.

Josie eased out a slow, deflated breath. 'So, no contact for now?'

'No, not now. Let's see how the dust settles on all of this, then pick our time to do battle again.'

Chelmsford, Essex

Lapslie was exhausted. The night before he hadn't slept that well; images of the dark lake with Luke Meerbecke's submerged body and Brad Henshaw's body in the field with its dark maroon, cauterized arm mixed with the bloodied cadavers from the Bennane Caves depicted in Betty McCauley's file.

He'd awoken abruptly with the starkness of the images. Sometimes when that happened some previously overlooked element of a case would be sparked in his mind, and he'd hastily write it down on a notepad he kept by his bedside. But there had been nothing the night before, only the stark, gruesome images, and tonight he had the notepad at his lounge desk as he made a few final notes about the day's activity while he sipped at a cup of tea.

Jim Thompson had found only two suspect fibres amongst the half-dozen bagged at the scene. The other four appeared to match Brad Henshaw's clothing.

'Probably caused as he was dumped or dragged into position in the field.'

'And the others?'

'We have to first of all eliminate the farmer's clothing. Then we can only hope they're from some reasonably rare brands of clothing. If they're from something sold by the bucketload by Primark or M&S, we won't get far with it.' Thompson sighed, then looked up hopefully. 'Unless of course you already have a suspect in mind and we can go through his wardrobe.'

Lapslie didn't. Nothing significant either from foot-prints near the body. Or from the cauterization which might indicate the type of blowtorch used. The hopeful looks quickly died, for both of them.

The only remaining hope was any useful sightings from neighbours in Honeywood Avenue, where they suspected Brad had been abducted. Nothing so far, but they had callbacks to five houses where nobody had been in when his team had done a house-to-house today.

But so far it didn't look as if the haste of Brad Henshaw's abduction and murder had led to any mistakes, as he'd first hoped.

After seeing Thompson in the lab, he'd gone straight on with Emma Bradbury to visit Brad's grandmother, Janet Henshaw, the last to see the boy alive. Bradbury had explained on the way that Brad's mother, Samantha, had never been married, so they both carried the same surname. Brad had been the result of a seven-month live-in boyfriend, now long departed.

Lapslie had hoped to be able to see both the grandmother and mother together, but Samantha Henshaw was still under heavy sedation from shock and couldn't be interviewed until the following day at the earliest. Also, Bradbury had related that there appeared to be some friction between the two of them, with Samantha blaming her mother for letting Brad out of her sight. So possibly best to interview them separately, in any case.

But in their interview, grandmother Janet Henshaw seemed to be blaming herself enough for young Brad's abduction and murder. She kept repeating like a mantra, 'Should never let him go out on his own . . . never should have.' And Lapslie noticed her hands clasping nervously together.

'Did he go regularly to this friend of yours nearby? To Annette's?' Lapslie had asked.

'Fairly regularly.'

'One a week . . . twice?'

'Well, normally only once a week . . . but sometimes he'd miss a week.'

'And what, may I ask, was the purpose of those visits to your friend?'

'Uh . . . I . . .' Janet Henshaw appeared instantly hesitant and tongue-tied, her hands clasping more anxiously.

Emma Bradbury looked at Lapslie before intervening. 'It's okay. We know from the local station that your friend, Annette Pierce, supplies cut-price cigarettes to some locals. But as long as it's kept just to small numbers in the village, it isn't the sort of thing we'll be following up.'

Janet nodded, looking down for a second. 'But for goodness' sake don't tell my daughter about the cigarettes – she'd *never* forgive me if that was what I sent little Brad out for.'

Lapslie and Bradbury had exchanged another glance, not sure how they'd work their way around that one.

Lapslie took a fresh breath. 'So you're a regular smoker, and it was a fresh carton of cigarettes you sent Brad out for that day?'

'Yes, it was ... but not anymore.' Janet Henshaw shook her head resolutely. 'Haven't had a single one since Brad's disappearance.'

So Janet Henshaw was punishing herself by going cold turkey, and that explained the shaky hands too; but Lapslie wondered how long that abstinence would last.

Nothing extra of any value was gleaned from the interview beyond what they already knew.

He looked back over his notes now, focusing for a moment on where he'd written *Purpose? Direction? Possible alternative theories?*

Could Rouse's suggestion that it might simply be a copycat murder hold water? He weighed up the pros and cons for a moment before deciding against it. If that had been the case, they'd have waited longer before dumping the body so that it matched the less hurried time-scale of the earlier murders, and they wouldn't have used a blowtorch for cauterization. While Lapslie had kept details of the boys' forearm removal out of the initial police reports, the finer points had come out at trial.

Lapslie studied his notes a moment longer, but nothing immediately leapt out at him. Hopefully the next few days might change that.

He swilled back the last of his tea and went to bed.

It seemed only an hour later that he was wide awake again, but as he glanced at his bedside clock – 2.47 a.m. – he could see that almost three hours had passed.

He'd fallen asleep straight away, not long after his head hit the pillow. No dreams and no sudden flashes of inspiration on cases, which might normally waken him. So what was it?

He sat up sharply, suddenly realizing it was the same noise which had awoken him three nights ago, but its position now was slightly different. Where *was* the noise coming from?

He honed his hearing sharply, hearing the faint click-clack of the grandfather clock downstairs, but nothing beyond it.

And the taste was there too, saltwater and blue-vein cheese, so he was sure he wasn't mistaken.

He leapt out of bed, reaching for his dressing gown. And he'd only half got it on, with his right hand already reaching for the nightstick in the corner, when he felt the arm wrap around his shoulders and neck and grip him from behind.

A powerful, body-bracing stranglehold, he could hardly move – let alone reach the remaining two feet for his nightstick.

Lapslie was confused. Where had the man come from? Surely he'd have heard or sensed him so close in his room?

The grip tightened, constricting his breath, the last of it smothered by the cloth clamped across his nose and mouth. Sharp ammonia vapours hit his sinuses – only this time it was real.

Lapslie sank into darkness.

The sound of Emma Bradbury's mobile ringing woke her from a deep slumber. She rolled over groggily and glanced at her bedside clock: 3.36 a.m.

She sat up, mumbling under her breath, 'What the hell?' The only person who ever phoned her at this time was her boss Mark Lapslie, and only then if it was a dire emergency – so she was more than a little peeved to find Derek Bain at the other end.

'What is this . . . some bet with your squad mates to call me in the middle of the night?'

'No. Chief Inspector Lapslie's been taken,' Bain said flatly. 'They've got him right now.'

'How do you know this?'

Bain sighed. 'Long story, which we don't have time for now. We need your help, so we're on our way round to you right now.'

'They . . . *we*? What's going on?'

'Another long story. See you in six minutes.'

The line went dead.

Dom was now sitting upright in bed beside her. 'What was all that about?'

'Someone's grabbed Mark Lapslie.' She leapt out of bed, started dressing. 'Gotta go.'

She could see Dom's eyes fixed on her steadily. What was that in his expression? Doubt, because he still feared she was seeing someone else, or reluctant acceptance? If she were seeing Peter, she'd have made sure he didn't call so clumsily in the dead of night. In fact, the only two times she'd seen him in the past eight months had been afternoon or early-evening rendezvous and covered by her work roster, so that no suspicions were aroused.

But perhaps she felt some of that residual guilt now as she offered, 'I think it's to do with these child abductions and murders I mentioned.' She reminded herself that Dom appeared more settled when he was somehow involved in the investigative process with her and Lapslie, not shut out of their circle.

'What? The barrister who represents nonces?'

'The same.'

Dom's expression was deadpan at first, gave nothing away. Then a slow smile creased his face. 'Good hunting! And give him one in the bollocks from me.'

'Will do.'

'Oh, one other thing.' Dom reached over to the bedside drawer. 'Take this with you. You might need it.'

22

Harbour dockyard, Clacton-on-Sea, Essex

The surrounding shadows were heavy, or perhaps it was the last of the ammonia haze lifting.

As Lapslie's focus came back, he could see two figures ahead and was aware of another man at an angle behind him, just out of his line of vision. He appeared to be strapped to a chair and so could only half-turn. A single light bulb hung on a cable from a beam almost directly above, and from the next beam along a heavy rope was suspended.

It was George's boat hangar and workshop. Obviously they'd planned this while George was away on a long weekend with his friends in Portsmouth. But how had they known that?

'So, you're back with us, Chief Inspector Lapslie?'

Lapslie recognized the voice before the figure stepped

into the arc of light from the single bulb – Toby Sinclair!

The man a yard to his side also moved forward at that stage, becoming clearer: he was no taller than Sinclair but twenty years younger, and stockier and well-built, his muscle-tone clear in his tight white T-shirt.

He had an elongated tattoo which seemed to spread out from his left shoulder and down that arm, which at first Lapslie thought was a snake; then, as he focused more keenly, he realized that it was a swan's neck snaking down.

'My assistant, Mandrake,' Sinclair said with a smile. 'He boasted that he could have brought you here alone – which I'm sure he could have – but with your dead weight from being unconscious, I didn't want to take any chances, so made sure he had a helper.' Sinclair gestured to the man just out of Lapslie's line of vision.

'My pleasure,' Lapslie said dryly, looking down for the first time at what was holding him to the chair.

'Good to see you still have a sense of humour under these circumstances,' Sinclair said equally dryly. 'Oh, and sorry about the pink fluffy handcuffs. It's important that your body is not marked when it's found. Except for the obvious mark around your neck, that is.'

Lapslie looked up past Sinclair; now that his eyes had adjusted to the dim light, he could see that the rope on the beam behind Sinclair was tied in a noose, a chair directly beneath it.

Lapslie swallowed imperceptibly, but still managed a challenging leer. 'Except you've forgotten one thing. Right now I've got no reason to take my own life, and there's no suicide note. Also, I'm slap-bang in the middle of a chain of child murders in which your name is centre stage. You'll be prime suspect.'

'Oh dear, Chief Inspector Lapslie.' Sinclair started pacing. 'On your two courtroom confrontations with me, have you learned nothing? Surely from those alone, you'll have realized that I cover every possible detail. Every eventuality.'

Sinclair nodded, and Mandrake stepped forward and held a letter eighteen inches from Lapslie's face. He instantly recognized the handwriting as his own, but he'd never seen the text before:

Dear Charlotte,

I'm so, so sorry to leave you like this. I don't think anyone appreciated how debilitating my illness had become, how it tolled on my nerves these past years. The constant smells and tastes, the medication, and people forever fussing around me, making allowances for me. And there was pain too, which I was also good at keeping quiet about. Especially to you. After all, why should I burden you? You've got your whole life ahead of you, and that's all I've felt at times – a burden to you and everyone else with this kaleidoscope of smells and tastes constantly assaulting me.

This child murder case now was the last straw. Not only are we no further ahead, with the murders still happening, but I'm sure too in Harvey Reid we've imprisoned the wrong man. I'm responsible for that and it weighs heavier on me with each passing day. And just when I finally thought I was seeing a glimmer of light, Rouse shut down any further pursuit in that direction. No hope for Reid any more, nor for me now it feels. Unless I was happy just muddling through, doing Rouse's bidding and following paths my heart's no longer in. That's no life, and I feel tired . . . oh, so tired.

Once again, I'm so sorry to leave you like this, but I'm sure you understand.

Much love, as always – and promise me you'll have one last day out on the boat with me, this time scattering my ashes over the side. You and George are probably the only ones to know my favourite spots!

Mark

X X X X

Lapslie found that his eyes were watering as he came to the last lines. Not due to his own emotions, but imagining Charlotte's reaction as she read the note in five or six hours' time, combined with his own sense of powerlessness at how to stop that happening, how to halt his own demise.

'That's just a copy,' Sinclair commented. 'The original is now sitting on your desk at home.'

'You seem to have worked everything out.'

'Oh, yes, I certainly have. It took a skilled calligrapher a full seven hours to get that right, copying your handwriting from some recent notes and letters, and also to get the style and tone right.' Sinclair held a palm out.

'Which indeed I helped with, because the calligrapher doesn't actually speak English.'

Lapslie nodded. So that explained someone going through his desk drawers a few nights back; that's what had been taken. Though one element immediately hit him. 'Except it won't work. Emma Bradbury and others know that I don't feel defeated at all by Rouse clipping my wings. Put out and pissed off, yes – but far from suicidal. They won't buy the letter.'

Sinclair shrugged. 'Certainly, there'll be a few initial voices of contention, but they'll soon fade away. It won't take them long to recall how defeated you were after a similar setback when you lost the Tulley case. Going AWOL for weeks and shuffling from your house to the local pub in your carpet slippers like the walking dead.'

Lapslie glared at Sinclair. There was little use reminding Sinclair that he had been in a totally different frame of mind then. The point made was that this phase would be remembered by some. Lapslie shook his head. 'But I don't understand. If Rouse has shut down my line of pursuit, why are you bothering with this now? You've won anyway.'

'Ah, but I know you well, Chief Inspector Lapslie. You're like a dog with a rabbit – you won't give up.'

'Yes, of course. You know *everything*,' Lapslie said with hollow sarcasm.

Sinclair smiled. 'Well, maybe on this occasion my intuition did get a helping hand.'

Sinclair took a small hand recorder out of his pocket and pressed play:

'Does that mean we simply do as Rouse has instructed and drop everything we've been pursuing? Seems a shame when we—'

'No, we don't. But it does mean that we'll have to be more cautious. So fewer meetings like this, and watching our backs more. We can't afford to slip up and get caught.'

'That's all very well, sir. But all that's going to make the process longer . . . and how long do we keep our little game running in secret? Because we won't be able to pursue anything against Sinclair, let alone involve the CPS, without Rouse's backing.'

'I appreciate that. But right now we only have two or three possible links. We need to find more, and try to shift the possibles to probables or definites. We'll know when the time is right.'

Sinclair stopped the recorder and held up what Lapslie instantly recognized as his own mobile phone in his other hand. 'Nifty little device slipped into your mobile phone. We've been tracking you and monitoring your conversations for weeks now.'

Lapslie suddenly recalled that moment in the pub after the Reid conviction, hearing his mobile ringing on the bar counter, but he couldn't remember leaving it there. Then next thing Benedict Allsopp was coming up to talk to him! So not only had Allsopp been the main plant internally, he'd also pulled a few tricks for Sinclair on the side.

Sinclair grimaced. 'We'll slip the device out before putting the mobile back in your pocket, and nobody will be any the wiser.'

Lapslie felt empty inside. They'd never had a chance from the start trying to nail Sinclair. He'd been watching them all along, just waiting for the best time to strike and stop their little game. He closed his eyes for a second, shuddering. 'And this little boy killed the other day, Brad Henshaw. That was purely to shut me down and cause a diversion?'

Sinclair feigned a hurt expression. 'You say *purely*, as if making light of the tremendous forethought that went into it. Not just the fabulous timing while you were away in Belgium so that you looked negligent, but also the different date and another local murder. That then kills any speculation about May-period murders on a wider national and international front.'

'But part of that might now come back and bite you, because it casts doubt on Reid's conviction. And if it wasn't him, focus might swing around again to Tulley, or indeed his cousin.'

'Which is why I ensured that both Tulley and Dimock were nowhere near the area at the time. But think in terms of the other element you were never satisfied with regarding Reid: his mental capacity probably not making him capable of framing Tulley so elaborately. But an accomplice?'

Sinclair let the thought settle for a moment with Lapslie before continuing. 'Over the coming days – although you won't be around to witness it – there'll be a phone tip-off regarding a white van seen in Honeywood Avenue around the time of Brad Henshaw's disappearance. That van belongs to none other than Chris Logan, one of Harvey Reid's asphalting crew. We chose Logan because he has some past form for theft and a pub brawl, plus he was in the area and has no alibi for the time in question.' Sinclair took a fresh breath. 'When the police search Logan's van, they'll find some of Brad Henshaw's blood spots there, plus more smeared on a rag. Logan will then be seen as Reid's likely accomplice in James Lewis's murder too, which should then neatly complete the circle.'

Lapslie nodded slowly, an icy chill running through him at Sinclair's cold, methodical planning.

But Sinclair seemed to relish it, smiling challengingly as he finished. 'Given all of that, I think it could safely be said that this little boy now died for a perfectly good reason, wouldn't you say?'

'You fucking shit.' Lapslie strained hard against his hand and ankle cuffs. If he could have got a hand free, he was sure he'd have floored Sinclair. Having put up with Sinclair's smarmy, arrogant deliberations through two court cases, now hearing him coolly justify young Brad Henshaw's murder pushed him over the edge. 'I've met some slimy, cold-hearted bastards in my time, but you take the biscuit.'

But Sinclair seemed more concerned about Lapslie's sudden movements than the rebuke. 'If you're going to move around and possibly leave marks on your wrists and ankles, then we'll yank you up right now and put the noose around your neck! But I'm sure you might like to know first why all this is happening.'

Lapslie shrugged. 'I think I pretty well know already. After all, if you've been monitoring me, you'll know that I've already seen the Betty McCauley file.'

'Ah, yes. "Mad Betty" they call her at Scotland Yard.

They're only half-listening to her now, won't take long before they stop listening completely. And you'll be complicit in that.'

Lapslie's brow creased. 'In what way?'

'Betty has already latched on to these local Essex murders. With this final one, she'll be steered into the same dead end as you: three local murders, all linked. People will stop listening to all her wild theories about May disappearances and murders on a wider scale.'

'So is that what all this has been about? Some ancestral link to a five-hundred-year-old cult of cannibals? All the brutality, all the ruined lives since?'

'*Brutality?* Have you ever considered what was done to our ancestors? Limbs cauterized, then the men's other limbs removed. Left to bleed to death while the women and children looked on to consider their own fate. Then all of them thrown on to an open fire in front of a baying mob, including infants and babies. *Horrific!*' Sinclair stared the message home, his steely-blue eyes for a moment reflecting the fire that had consumed his ancestors; it was the first time Lapslie had seen him expressing rage. 'What we do to our victims is humane in comparison. They're rendered unconscious and then their necks are snapped cleanly – they don't feel a thing.

We take no glory in their pain or their deaths. Our only interest is in their flesh, which we gather to partake in annually, between Easter and the summer solstice – the date our ancestors were massacred and a small group escaped. No more than a slice each, in homage to our fallen ancestors and their tradition.'

So that explained the varying dates, Lapslie considered: Easter was a moveable feast, while the summer solstice was a set date. But with the explanation, Sinclair appeared the same as so many murderers and villains he'd encountered: they always had a justification and rationale for their actions. It was always someone else's fault, or what they'd done wasn't so terrible; they were invariably adroit at finding some comparison which painted their actions in a better light.

He shook his head. 'Do you really feel something like that – a taste for human flesh – is passed down through the generations?'

'Oh, Chief Inspector Lapslie. How little you know about DNA, and how human traits are inherited from our ancestors. Take today's trend: people getting sexually stimulated by flagellation. Do you know where that stems from?'

Lapslie shrugged. 'From people reading *Fifty Shades of Grey*?' Despite his dire situation, he couldn't resist the jibe.

Sinclair waved one hand, as if swatting the comment away. 'It dates back to the pilgrimages of the thirteenth century in Britain. On those long treks, pilgrims would read the Bible, and any unwanted sexual thoughts were driven away by them whipping their own shoulders and backs, self-flagellating. But at some stage the sexual thoughts and the flagellation became merged in their minds to the extent that they actually started to enjoy the whipping. And that trait exists still today with the current generation. So these things *do* pass down through the ages.'

Sinclair had obviously been doing a lot of research on the subject, which no doubt came with the territory, Lapslie considered; he had an awful lot to try to justify, make sense of.

'So if neither Tulley nor Dimock killed Brad Henshaw the other day, who did?'

Sinclair gestured towards Mandrake. 'My assistant here. He's ex-British Army, so is used to killing on instruction. This particular killing had no wider clan significance, he just copied the past killings.'

Lapslie nodded. 'Probably why he made a couple of mistakes.'

'Such as?' Sinclair's brow knitted.

'Such as the unidentified fibres left by Brad Henshaw's body. I've already instructed my unit that I suspected a break-in at my house three days ago, and asked forensics to go through it with a fine-tooth comb. How long do you think it will take them to get a fibre match?'

It was a lie, but he could see that Sinclair's power derived largely from being in control, covering every possible base. The thought that something might have been missed unsettled Sinclair. Lapslie himself would be dead soon, but at least he'd go with the satisfaction that Sinclair would be rattled for days to come.

Sinclair glared at Mandrake. 'I thought you said that you were careful.'

'I was. Went through the place cleanly and I was as silent as a lamb.'

'Not *that* careful,' Lapslie said. 'You left a drawer partly open, which was how I knew that—'

Lapslie broke off as two sharp bangs sounded at the back of the boat hangar, as if someone had hit the corrugated iron with a hammer.

'Go and see what that is,' Sinclair instructed the man behind Lapslie.

But at that moment Lapslie's heart sank as he saw another figure emerge from the shadows straight ahead – Benedict Allsopp! Obviously he'd turned up to catch the last bit of glory and personally watch Lapslie's demise. Lapslie watched the gun levelled in Allsopp's hand, and it also struck him then that he was the only one to have noticed Allsopp. Sinclair and Mandrake's eyes were still fixed on their colleague who was checking the banging at the back.

There was also another figure two yards behind Allsopp, still indistinct amongst the shadows. Then Allsopp did a strange thing: he held one finger to his lips as he looked directly at Lapslie, as if silencing him.

Then everything happened quickly. Mandrake appeared to be the first to notice Allsopp and reacted instantly, raising his own gun. Three or four shots sounded in rapid succession, and he saw Allsopp fall to one knee, struggling to rise again. He heard the sound of a window shattering, and some scuffling and a flurry of footsteps from somewhere behind him. Then two more shots – though Lapslie couldn't tell whether they'd come from the figure behind Allsopp or from another direction.

Three minutes earlier . . .

They cut the engine of the Audi S3 at the top of the ramp leading down to the boatyard units and coasted silently the remaining distance.

Benedict Allsopp was driving, with Derek Bain in the passenger seat and Emma Bradbury in the back. As they came to a halt, Allsopp put on the handbrake. He took the Browning 9mm out of his jacket pocket and slid the cartridge open to check that it was full.

'Are you sure you know how to use that thing?' Bain questioned.

'Yes, thanks. And none of your usual quips tonight. I don't have any spare bullets for you.' Allsopp smiled wryly. 'You're just jealous because you only have a base-ball bat and a taser. You ready, Emma?' Allsopp glanced towards the back.

'Yes, fine,' she said, not used to the new familiarity.

'Don't forget, only use it if you have to. I'll take the main flak.'

'Understood.' She had a taser as well, and had shown Allsopp the loaded Smith & Wesson .38 Dom had given her. Dom had assured her that it was licensed, but nevertheless using a non-commissioned police gun in an operation would involve a ton of paperwork and an official explanation after the event.

'Okay . . . let's go.'

They eased out of the car silently without even fully closing the doors, and walked the final twenty yards to the boathouse unit. No sounds that might alert anyone, Allsopp had instructed. As expected, Allsopp saw that the front of the unit wasn't locked, the latch simply pushed to. He directed Bain towards the back without speaking, and from then on they timed everything digitally on their mobiles.

He silently turned the latch ten seconds before Bain was due to hit the back with his baseball bat. Glimpsing through the gap, he could see two figures turned away from him and facing Lapslie, who was strapped to a chair. But he was sure he was still in heavy shadow at that point, so he ventured in the first few paces, beckoning for Bradbury to follow.

The two bangs from the back came then, causing the two men closest to Allsopp to turn sharply towards the noise. One of the men, he could see clearly, was Toby Sinclair; he was directing another man in the shadows at the back to investigate.

But as Allsopp took a step closer, he could tell that he was now visible to Lapslie, and held one finger to his lips in warning.

Then Mandrake, looking back, also noticed him – he couldn't delay any longer! And they were right about Mandrake, he was surprisingly fast – his own first shot came almost in unison with Mandrake's return fire, even though Mandrake had started to raise his gun later. But seeing his adversary's gun, he'd already started moving to make himself a more difficult target, and the shot caught him on his right shoulder.

He dropped instantly to one knee – partly from the shock of the hit, but also to make himself a smaller target – and fired off two more quick shots at Mandrake, who was still standing. Mandrake jolted back and seemed to teeter before he fell, and Allsopp only realized then that a second shot fired in answer from Mandrake had hit him in the thigh. If it had hit the femoral artery, he'd bleed to death within half an hour.

The sound of shattering glass came from the back, and he saw Bain swinging his baseball bat at the lumbering muscleman moving in on him. Then, seeing that the muscleman was still advancing, Bain lost patience and tasered him.

Suddenly, in horror, Allsopp watched Mandrake half-rise and try to fire at him again. His own gun hand, though, was suddenly numb, the shot he'd taken to the shoulder obviously taking its toll on his nerve pathways. He was helpless in the face of a cold-blooded killer.

As Mandrake's gun rose the last inch, targeting Allsopp at point-blank range, two shots came from behind, sending the killer and his gun sprawling.

Emma Bradbury emerged from the shadows.

As she approached, Toby Sinclair raised his hands. 'Let's not be hasty – I don't want any trouble.'

'*Hasty?*' Emma Bradbury moved in and pressed her gun into the soft flesh of Sinclair's neck. 'I'm sure that in the courtroom – or when you've spilled someone's beer brushing past them in the pub and are worried they might start a fight – such lines might work well. But in this situation, they just make you a master-asshole of understatement.' Bradbury stepped back and kneed Sinclair heavily in the groin.

With a guttural groan, he went down like a sack of potatoes.

'What was that for?' Lapslie asked. Although from his tone and gentle leer, it was clear he was pleasantly surprised rather than reproachful.

'Something I promised a friend I'd do.'

EPILOGUE

23

Camden Market, London
July 2015

Benedict Allsopp met up with Lapslie and Bradbury six days later at Bar Cuba in Camden Town.

The thigh shot had thankfully missed his femoral artery, but the wound did require surgery and strapping. The shoulder wound was more serious, having damaged a tendon, and required more delicate surgery and a further two days in hospital for recovery.

He therefore had only given them brief snippets of information, straight after the boat hangar assault, and now started filling in the rest of the details once their drinks had been put down on the table. Lapslie noticed that Allsopp's right shoulder was still strapped and that he lifted his drink with his left hand.

As Lapslie chewed over the main bones of what had happened, he commented, 'So you appearing as Rouse's lackey at Chelmsford HQ was just an act?'

'Yes, I couldn't make it seem as if I was there just to help you or do your bidding – and especially not on the Betty McCauley case and the undue attention paid to Toby Sinclair – otherwise I'd have been shut down in no time.' He gestured with his drink in hand. 'Look what happened when they got wind of you chasing down the Luke Meerbecke case in Belgium. Someone from Scotland Yard phoned Rouse to make sure you were instantly roped and tied. The same would have happened with me if I'd shown my hand earlier.'

'And do you know who that was at Scotland Yard?'

'Yes, I do.' Allsopp sighed. 'I had a couple of suspicions beforehand, but now I'm sure. Turns out he was just a go-between, though. Something didn't add up – it was nagging away at the back of my mind – until I pieced it all together. I realized their main plant must be within Interpol. That's how and why they latched on to you after your trip to Belgium. The same thing happened to a British journalist, Josie Dallyn, after she unearthed a case in Gdansk, in Poland, almost two years ago. She was abducted by our friend Mandrake and was lucky to get away with her life.'

Lapslie's brow knitted. 'Arles mentioned her visit. I tried to contact her.'

'I know,' Allsopp said. 'But for obvious reasons, she's been keen to keep a low profile. Not least because she suspects the death of her old editor, Tom Barton, wasn't suicide.'

Lapslie exchanged a look briefly with Bradbury, commenting, 'Another to add to Sinclair's long list.'

'Very possibly.' Taking a fresh breath, and wincing at the pain in his shoulder, Allsopp went on to relate that Sinclair had been eager to make a deal for a lesser sentence, offering a list of names of all those involved and also the names and dates of victims going back over the years. 'Cheeky bastard was after a mere five-year sentence, claims he never killed anyone personally, just defended those who had. The prosecution agreed to a deal at ten, but between you and me I think the judge at the last minute is going to go freelance and add on five or ten on top of that.' Allsopp smiled. 'The CPS will shrug and tell Sinclair, "We told him only ten, but what can we do if the old fool decides to do his own thing? Some of these judges are a law unto themselves."'

'So you think the intention is to stitch Sinclair up?'

'Yes, no doubt about it.'

Bradbury raised her glass. 'Couldn't happen to a nicer person.'

'I think he's still walking lopsided from that knee you gave him to the cobblers,' Allsopp said with a sly smile. 'Even if they get a tame judge willing to go light on him, there'll be an appeal. It will be raised that it's "not in the public interest" that he gets such a light sentence, and a fresh judge will add five or ten on to the tariff, maybe even more.' Allsopp took a deep breath. 'But it was worthwhile doing a deal with Sinclair. A lot of big names on the list. A couple of prominent MPs, another high up in the military.'

'Do you think the big fish will ever be prosecuted?' Lapslie asked. 'From my experience, the CPS tends to drag its heels with the really big ones.'

'Yes, that's true.' Allsopp grimaced. 'We can only hope they are prosecuted before they die.'

Lapslie gave a wan smile in agreement, sipping at his mojito. The music appeared to get turned up a notch as 'Mas Que Nada' came on the sound system. Lapslie in turn raised his voice as he asked, 'Favourite place of yours? Is that why you wanted to meet here?'

'Not particularly. But it has become the firm favourite of someone I know. Someone who I think you should meet . . . Betty McCauley. Josie Dallyn will also be with her. Josie has been a big help to both myself and Betty along the way, and in fact was responsible for a few of the cases in Betty's file.'

Lapslie was pleasantly surprised that they'd actually be meeting them – particularly Betty. After all, she'd devoted many more years than the rest of them to trying to track down and nail Sinclair's clan; it seemed only fitting and right that she was there when they raised a glass to their final demise.

Allsopp confirmed that the two women would be with them shortly, and Lapslie, still tying up all the loose ends in his mind, commented, 'So it was you who had the Betty McCauley file sent to me that morning?'

'Yes.'

'One thing that struck me after it arrived was why wasn't it sent earlier?'

'Again, I had to be cautious – make sure the time was right. Only when I saw you latch on to the Luke Meerbecke case – another child with a limb and internal organ removed, which took it into an international arena rather than just Essex murders – did I think you were ready for it. Before that, you might have thought all these national and international cases were just mad ramblings from Betty. Which was, to their shame, how half my department viewed Betty's file initially.'

Lapslie sank into thought again, remembering that night in the pub after Reid's conviction. 'So it wasn't you who planted a bug in my mobile phone?'

'No. Not guilty. Though I did see what happened, and in fact it was that which ended up saving your life.' Allsopp went on to explain that he'd seen a man lift Lapslie's mobile from his pocket and head out of the pub that night, then head back in with it ten minutes later and leave it on the bar counter close by. 'I suspected what had happened, so got hold of some contacts at GCHQ in Cheltenham. They tuned into the same frequency as the device secreted in your mobile, so I was able to hear everything Sinclair's crew were getting, plus monitor your movements too. That's how I knew they'd grabbed you that night and was able to act on it so quickly.'

'And did you get Derek Bain along to teach him a lesson for ribbing you?'

'No. That was simply because I wasn't convinced Emma and I could handle the situation on our own. We needed some backup muscle, and Bain was the only one

I—' Allsopp broke off as he saw Betty and Josie walking in. 'Excuse me.'

He dutifully got up to greet them. Having asked what they'd like to drink, he called out the order to the waiter at the bar, then ushered them over to the table. 'Betty . . . Josie. May I introduce you both to Chief Inspector Lapslie and DC Bradbury? The two people I mentioned who kept a light burning on the Sinclair case and refused to give up.'

There were handshakes and greetings all round, with Betty adding as she took her seat, 'Scobe has told me a lot about you, Chief Inspector Lapslie. I'm sorry that the case got you into such hot water in the end.'

' "Scotland-Yard-Benedict",' Allsopp offered in explanation of the nickname. 'Initially I seemed to be the only one doing any digging and searching on Betty's behalf.'

'Yes, well, it beats "Balls-Up",' Lapslie said with a smile, then to Betty, 'No worries. I've been in hotter water before.'

'But probably never looked quite so fetching,' Emma Bradbury jibed. 'You know, I think those pink fluffy handcuffs suited you. You should take a pair back for Charlotte as a memento of that night.'

'Sorry, but not my bag. I don't have thirteenth-century pilgrim ancestors.' He could see that most of it was going over Betty's head, but she seemed to be enjoying the banter nevertheless.

Josie was smiling more openly, and after nodding her thanks to the waiter who'd just put down her San Miguel, she looked at Lapslie. 'Sorry I didn't call you back, Chief Inspector. I was under orders.'

Allsopp held one hand up. 'Yes, my fault. I felt you had a lot on your plate at that point. Though it turned out to be far more than I could have imagined.'

'I understand you had a close call with Mandrake as well,' Lapslie commented to Josie. 'And I'm sorry to hear that your old editor might have been a victim too.'

'We'll probably never know now one way or the other.' Josie shrugged, then smiled tautly. 'Although it appears we have more than enough to nail Sinclair on other fronts. But talking of victims, what's happening with Harvey Reid?'

Emma Bradbury answered, as Lapslie had been in hospital and convalescing for much of the time. 'He's been let out on remand pending a hearing for a dismissal of the original trial verdict based on fresh evidence. He's a free man and likely to continue to be so.'

Allsopp nodded, and raised his glass. 'Plus he'll be in line for a hefty compensation claim. Already he's got big-name solicitors knocking on his door.'

Lapslie smiled softly. 'So a fair few trials and tribulations along the way, but we got there in the end.' He turned towards Betty McCauley. 'I'm only sorry, Betty, that it took us so long. And that you didn't have anyone to believe your story before Benedict came along – let alone fight your corner.' Lapslie realized after he'd said it that he'd used 'us', as if apologizing for the police force at large.

'That's okay,' Betty said. 'All's well that ends well.'

Lapslie grimaced understandingly, then had to look away so that Betty McCauley didn't notice his eyes welling up. *All's well that ends well.* It was so typical of that generation to make light of everything. Losing your only son and, only a few years later, your husband to drink, then embarking on a forty-year crusade of research and countless calls and letters to the police – with hardly anyone listening or paying attention. As Rebecca Graves had commented the other day, it couldn't have been easy.

'I'm just thankful I finally got to know what happened to my David,' Betty said.

Allsopp forced a strained smile. 'I told Betty the other day that David's name was on Sinclair's list.'

He'd asked her initially whether she was sure she wanted to know, and she'd replied: *I've spent so many years now expecting the worst that actually hearing it isn't going to harm any. In fact, in many ways, it will be a welcome release.*

'Hopefully now he's in a better place,' Betty said to the three of them.

'Yes,' Lapslie said emptily, too choked with emotion for a moment to add anything worthwhile. Betty's comment was no doubt partly inspired by her own tough life meanwhile; she had not only been lonely and missing her loved ones, but had lived on the streets for so many years. Then Emma Bradbury did something which touched him profoundly, finding the words he was unable to articulate.

'I think you've been very brave, Betty,' she said. 'And although it might sound strange, I think wherever David is now, he somehow knows and appreciates what you've done for him.' Emma reached across the table and clasped Betty's hand. 'You've given the ultimate gift any mother could give to her son – you've found him justice.'